DISNEY PRINCESS

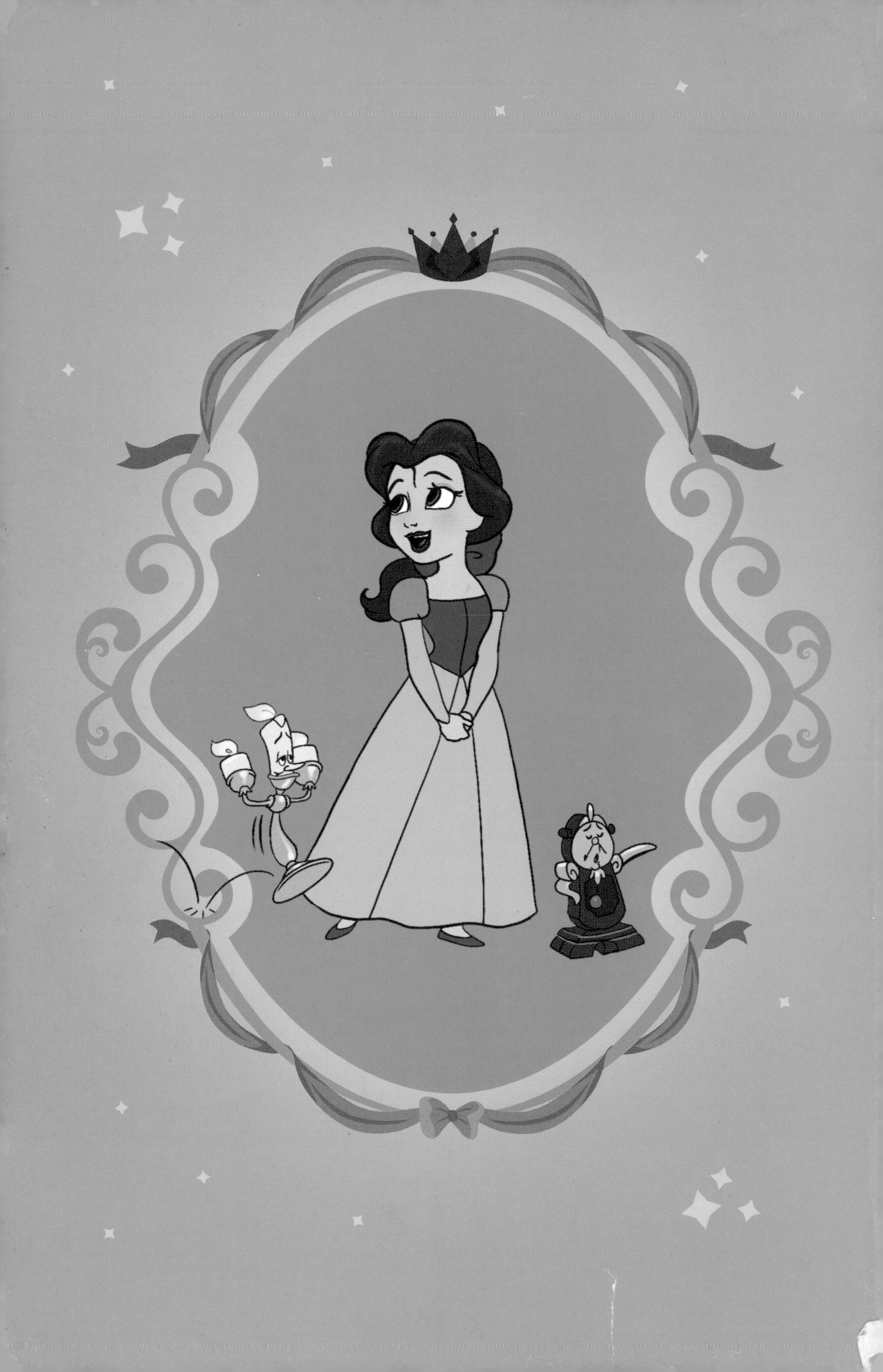

DISNEY PRINCESS

Beyond the Extraordinary

Script by
Amy Mebberson
Georgia Ball
Paul Benjamin
Steffie Davis
Geoffrey Golden
Emma Hambly
Deanna McFaden
Patrick Storck

Illustration by
Amy Mebberson

Lettering by
AndWorld Design

Cover Art by
Amy Mebberson

Dark Horse Books

Before we jump into stories with the Disney Princesses, let's take a moment to learn about some of their favorite pastimes with these fascinating *infographics*!

Here to share their knowledge are Rapunzel, Moana, and Belle . . .

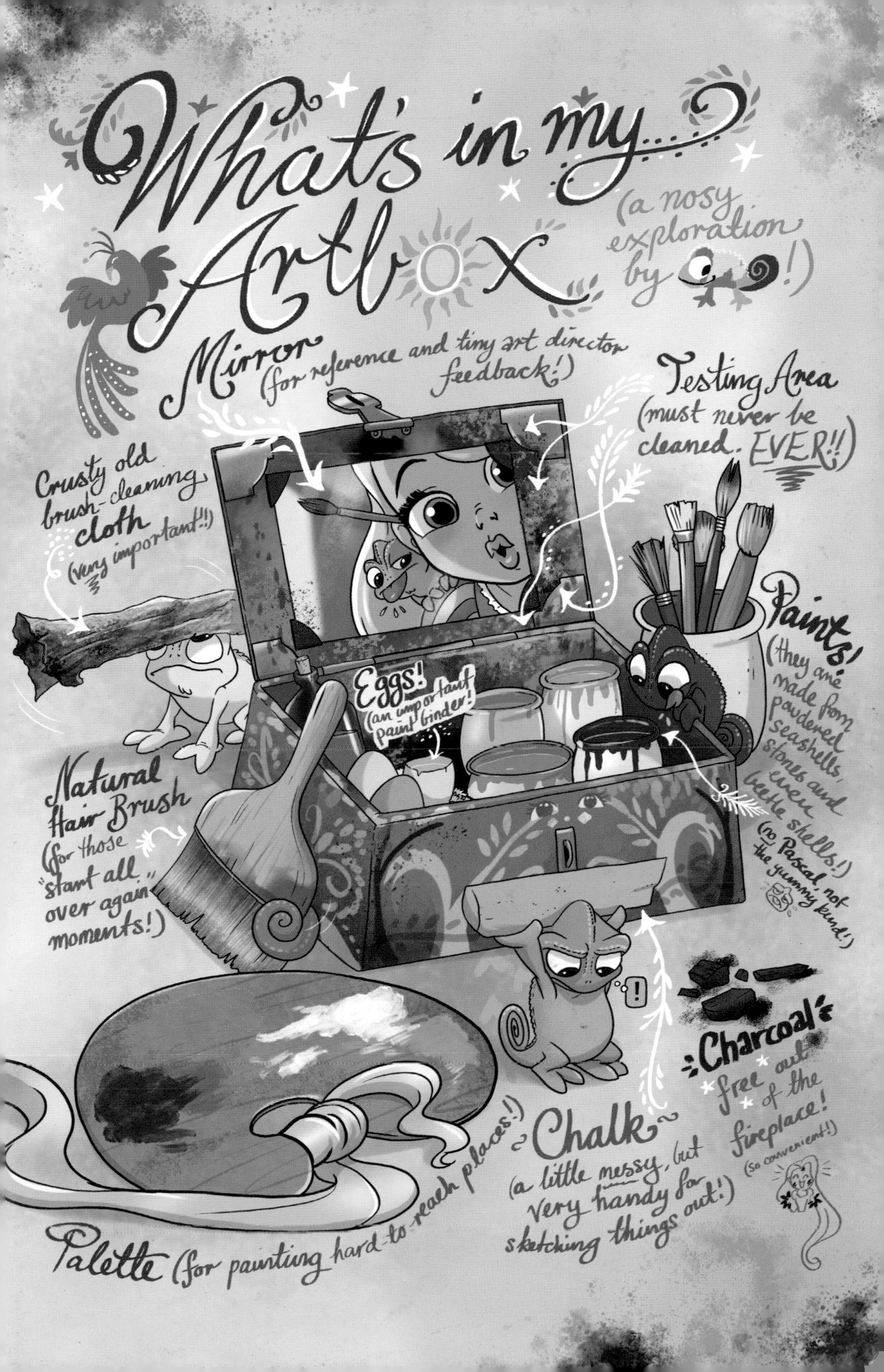

What's in my... Artbox
(a nosy exploration by [Pascal]!)
Mirror (for reference and tiny art director feedback!)
Testing Area (must never be cleaned. EVER!!)
Crusty old brush-cleaning cloth (very important!!)
Eggs! (an important paint binder!)
Paints! (they are made from powdered seashells, stones and even beetle shells!) (no Pascal, not the yummy kind!)
Natural Hair Brush (for those "start all over again" moments!)
Charcoal free out of the fireplace! (so convenient!)
Chalk (a little messy, but very handy for sketching things out!)
Palette (for painting hard-to-reach places!)

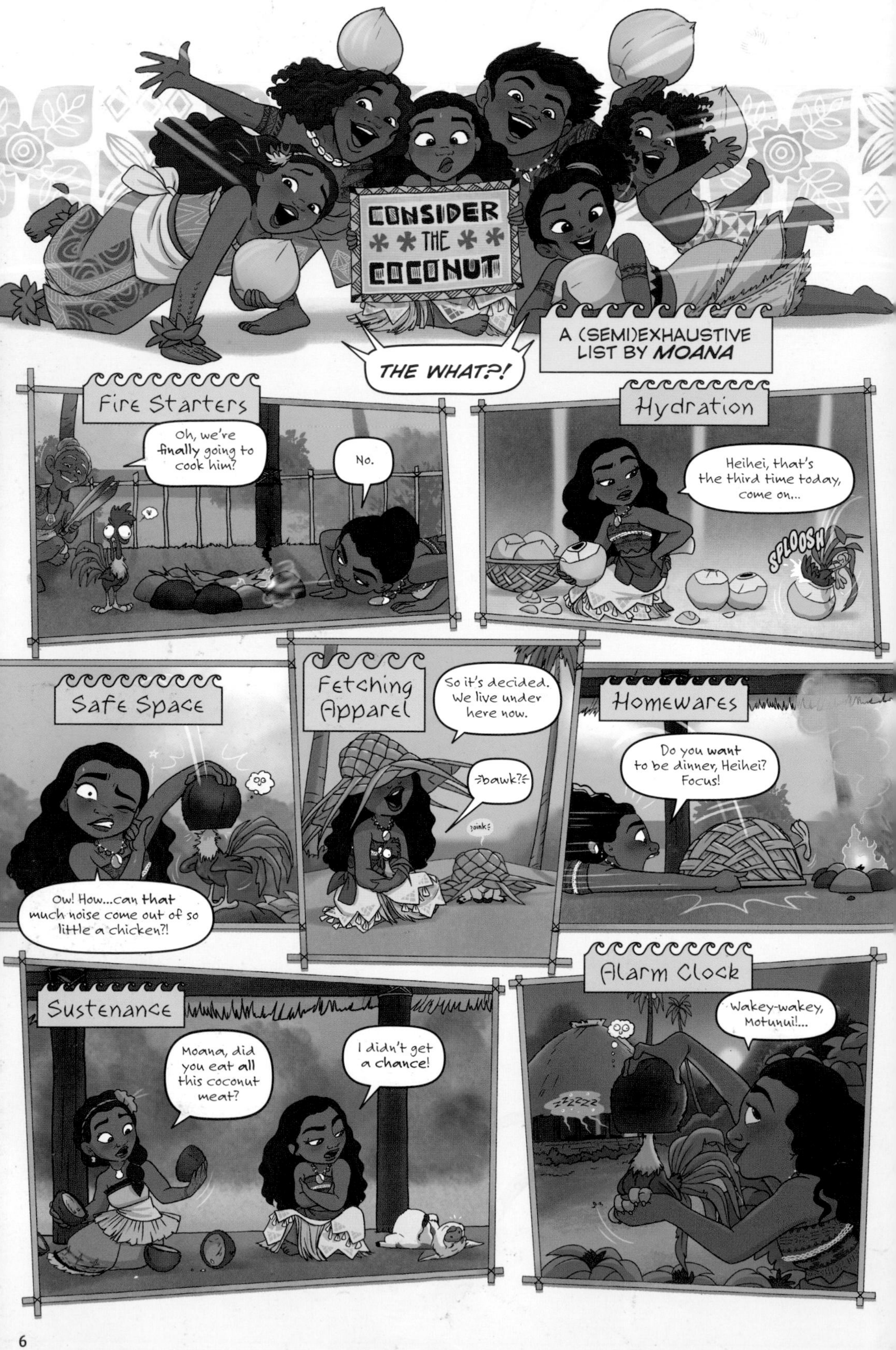
CONSIDER THE COCONUT
A (SEMI)EXHAUSTIVE LIST BY MOANA
THE WHAT?!
Fire Starters
Oh, we're finally going to cook him?
No.
Hydration
Heihei, that's the third time today, come on...
SPLOOSH
Safe Space
Ow! How...can that much noise come out of so little a chicken?!
Fetching Apparel
So it's decided. We live under here now.
bawk?
oink
Homewares
Do you want to be dinner, Heihei? Focus!
Sustenance
Moana, did you eat all this coconut meat?
I didn't get a chance!
Alarm Clock
Wakey-wakey, Motunui!...
ZZZZZZ

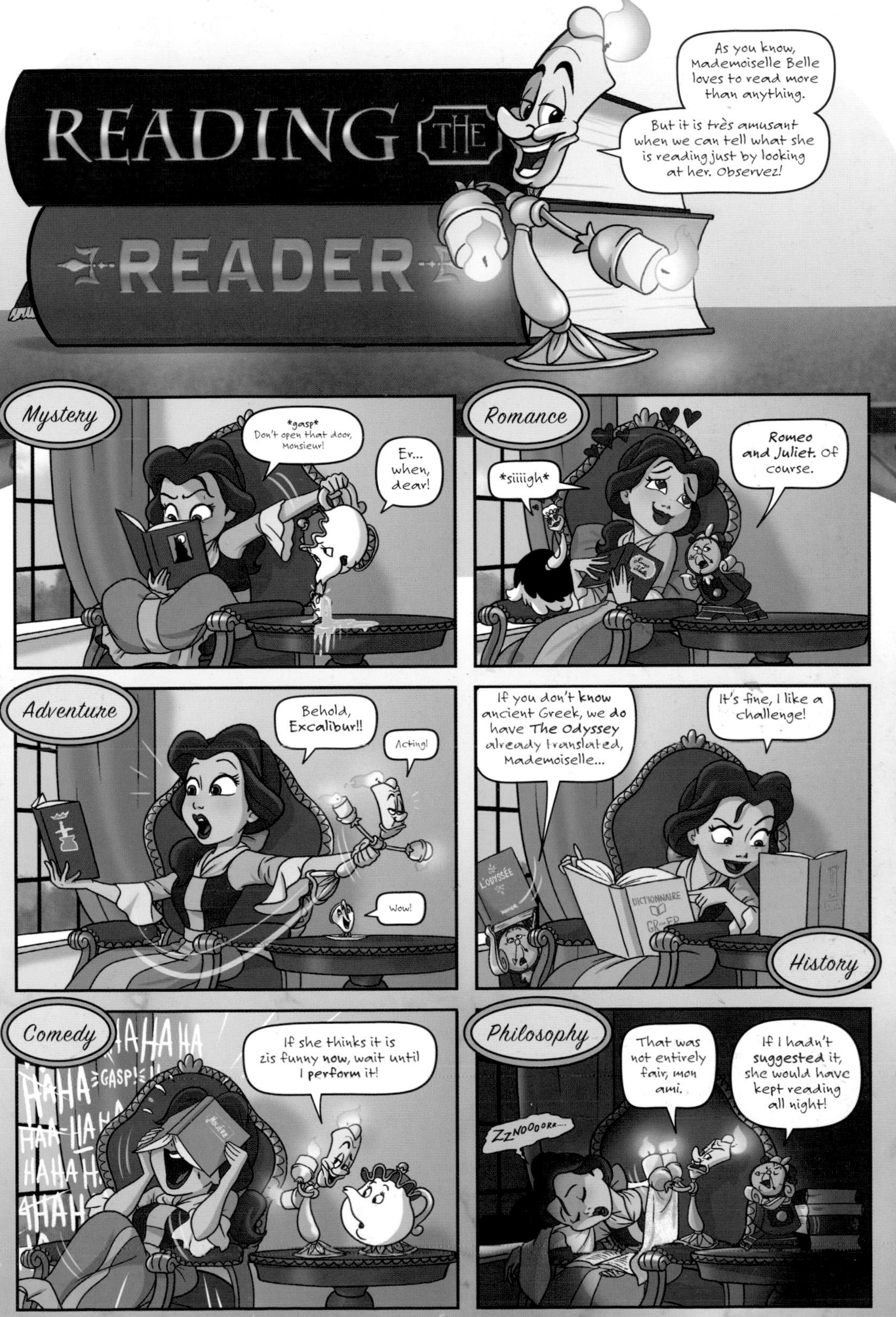

READING THE READER
As you know, Mademoiselle Belle loves to read more than anything.
But it is très amusant when we can tell what she is reading just by looking at her. Observez!
Mystery
gasp Don't open that door, Monsieur!
Er... when, dear!
Romance
siiiigh
Romeo and Juliet. Of course.
Adventure
Behold, Excalibur!!
Acting!
Wow!
If you don't know ancient Greek, we do have The Odyssey already translated, Mademoiselle...
It's fine, I like a challenge!
L'ODYSSÉE
DICTIONNAIRE
History
Comedy
HAHAHA
GASP!
If she thinks it is zis funny now, wait until I perform it!
MOLIÈRE
Philosophy
That was not entirely fair, mon ami.
If I hadn't suggested it, she would have kept reading all night!
ZZNOOOORR...

"SUNKEN TREASURE"

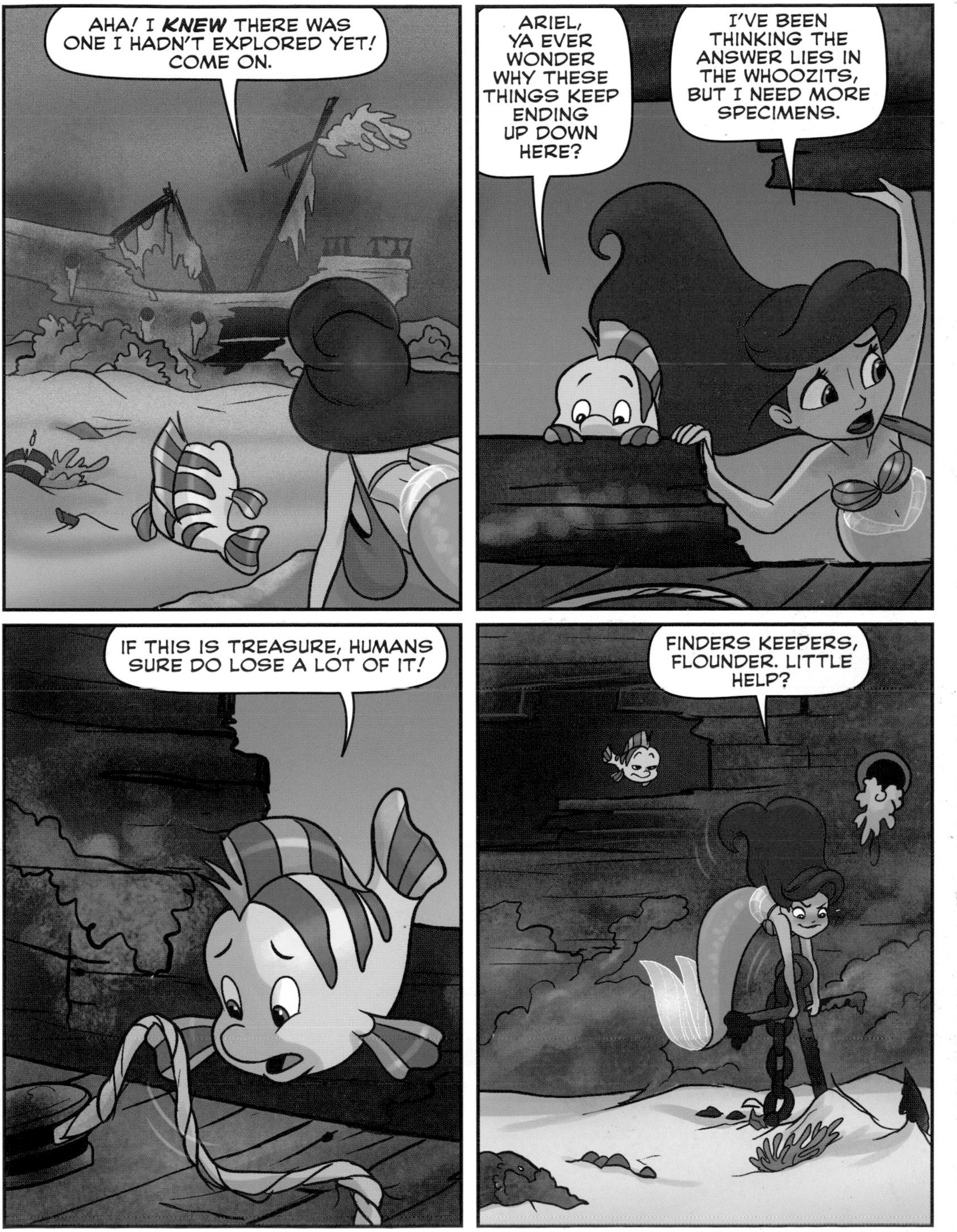
AHA! I KNEW THERE WAS ONE I HADN'T EXPLORED YET! COME ON.
ARIEL, YA EVER WONDER WHY THESE THINGS KEEP ENDING UP DOWN HERE?
I'VE BEEN THINKING THE ANSWER LIES IN THE WHOOZITS, BUT I NEED MORE SPECIMENS.
IF THIS IS TREASURE, HUMANS SURE DO LOSE A LOT OF IT!
FINDERS KEEPERS, FLOUNDER. LITTLE HELP?

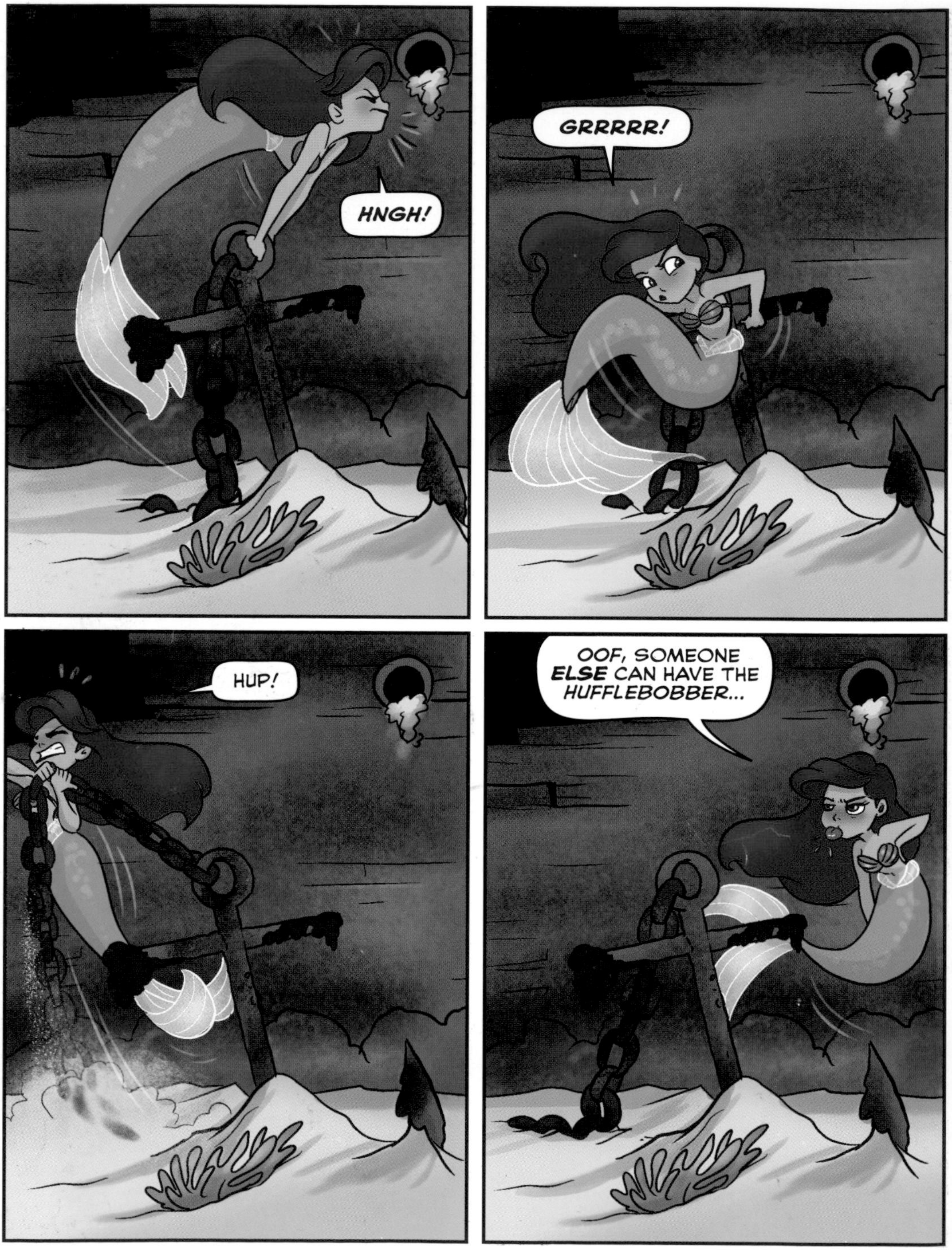
HNGH!
GRRRRR!
HUP!
OOF, SOMEONE ELSE CAN HAVE THE HUFFLEBOBBER...

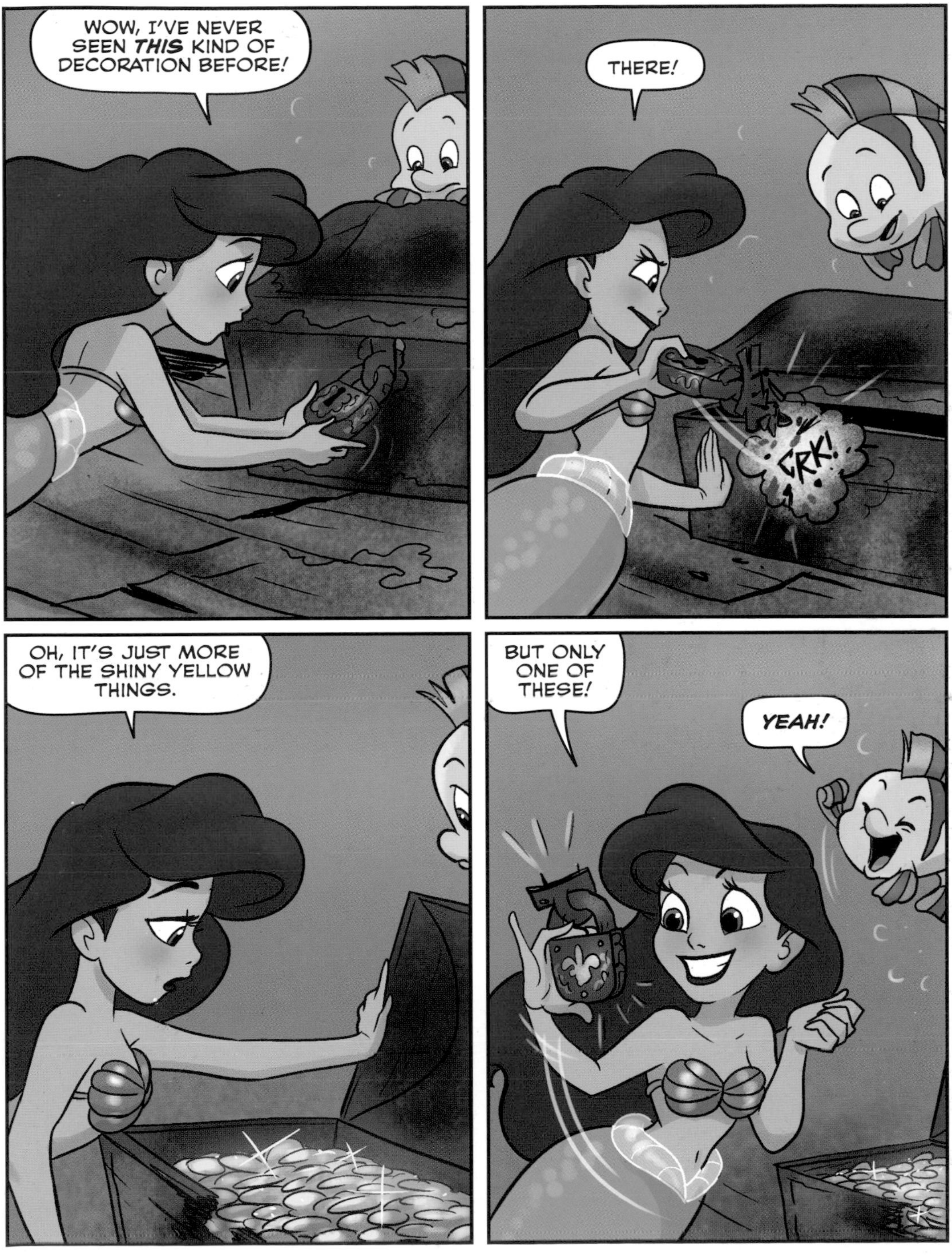
WOW, I'VE NEVER SEEN *THIS* KIND OF DECORATION BEFORE!
THERE!
CRK!
OH, IT'S JUST MORE OF THE SHINY YELLOW THINGS.
BUT ONLY ONE OF THESE!
YEAH!

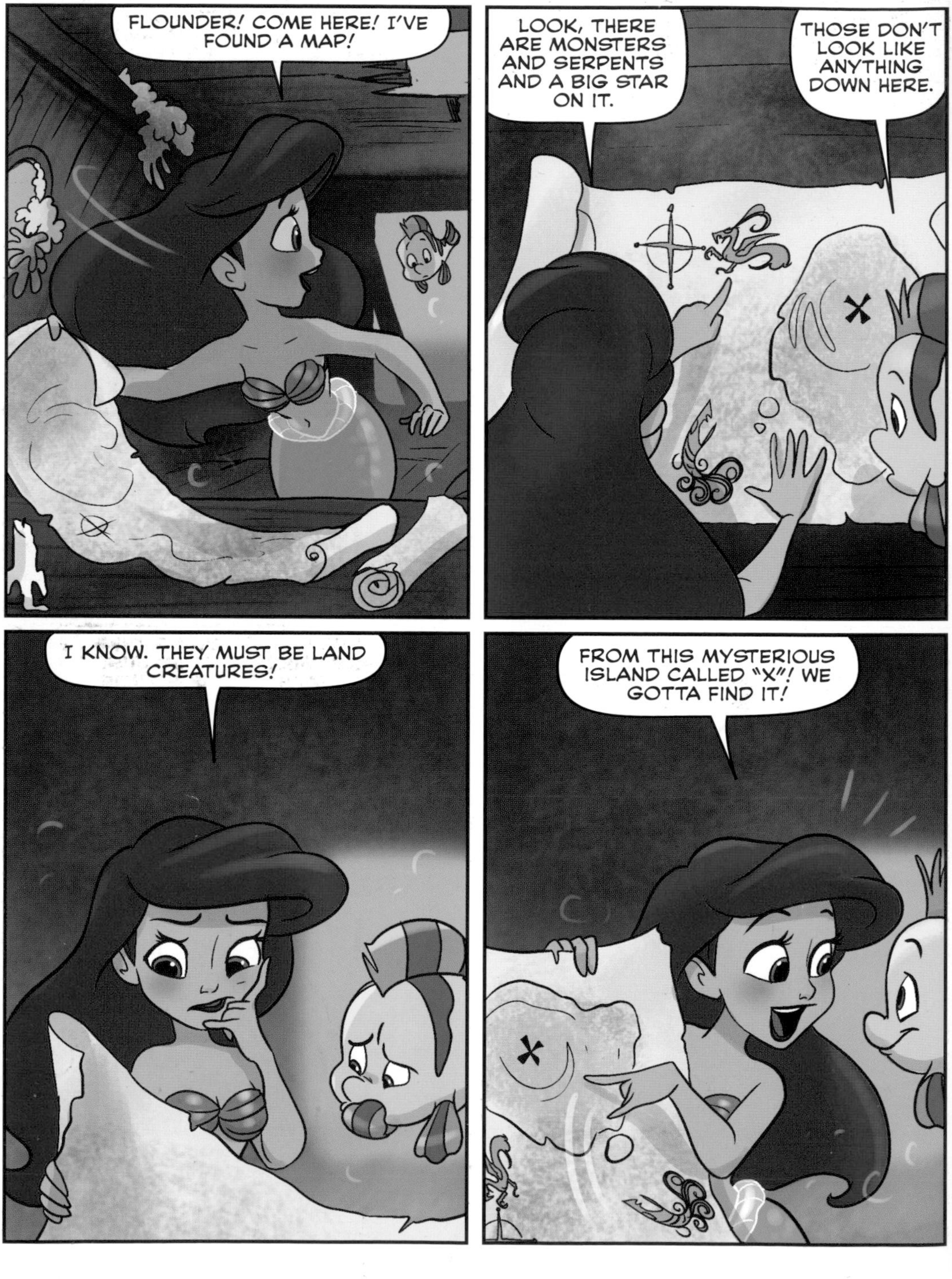
FLOUNDER! COME HERE! I'VE FOUND A MAP!
LOOK, THERE ARE MONSTERS AND SERPENTS AND A BIG STAR ON IT.
THOSE DON'T LOOK LIKE ANYTHING DOWN HERE.
I KNOW. THEY MUST BE LAND CREATURES!
FROM THIS MYSTERIOUS ISLAND CALLED "X"! WE GOTTA FIND IT!

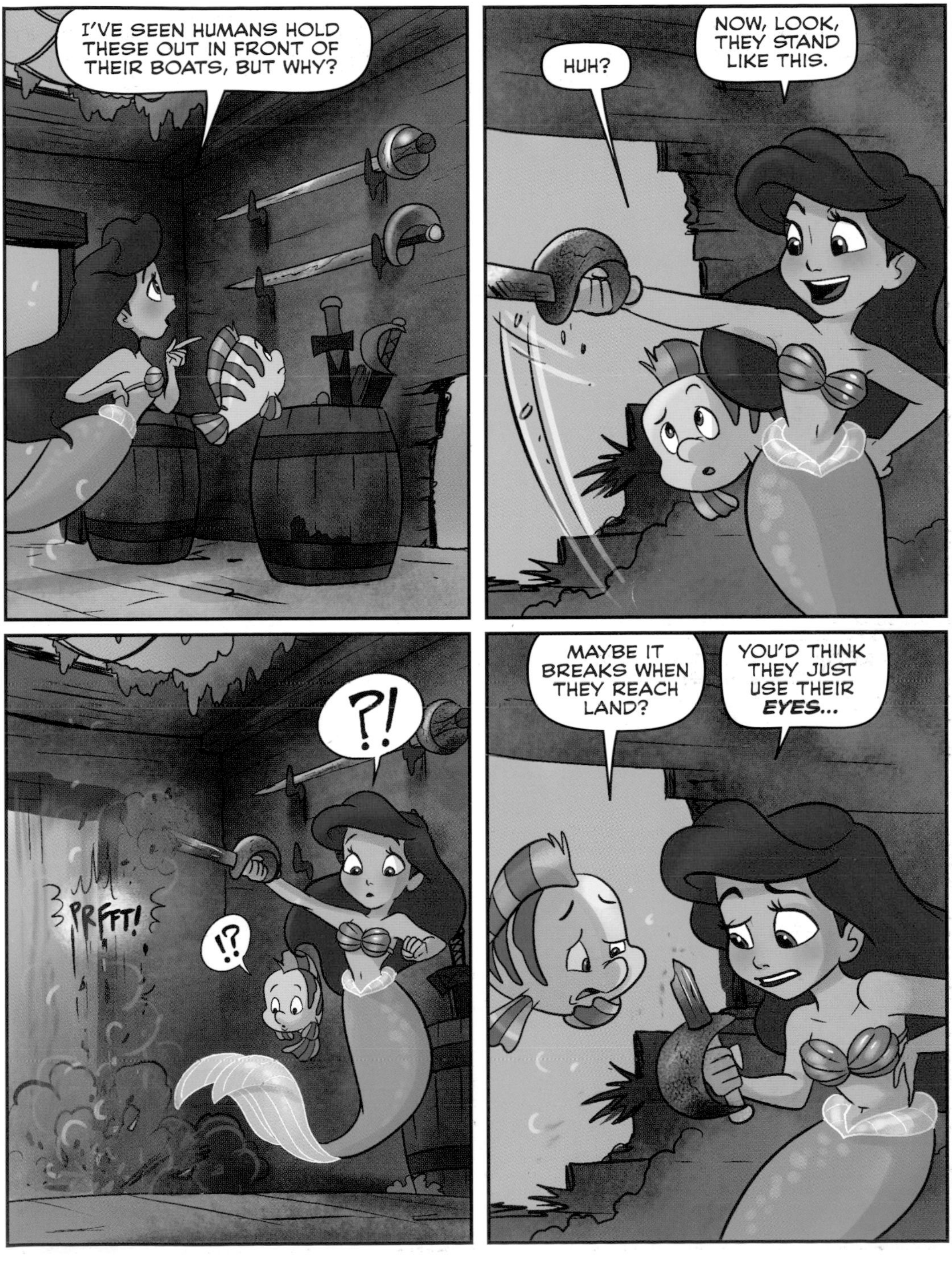

I'VE SEEN HUMANS HOLD THESE OUT IN FRONT OF THEIR BOATS, BUT WHY?
HUH?
NOW, LOOK, THEY STAND LIKE THIS.
?!
PRFFT!
!?
MAYBE IT BREAKS WHEN THEY REACH LAND?
YOU'D THINK THEY JUST USE THEIR *EYES*...

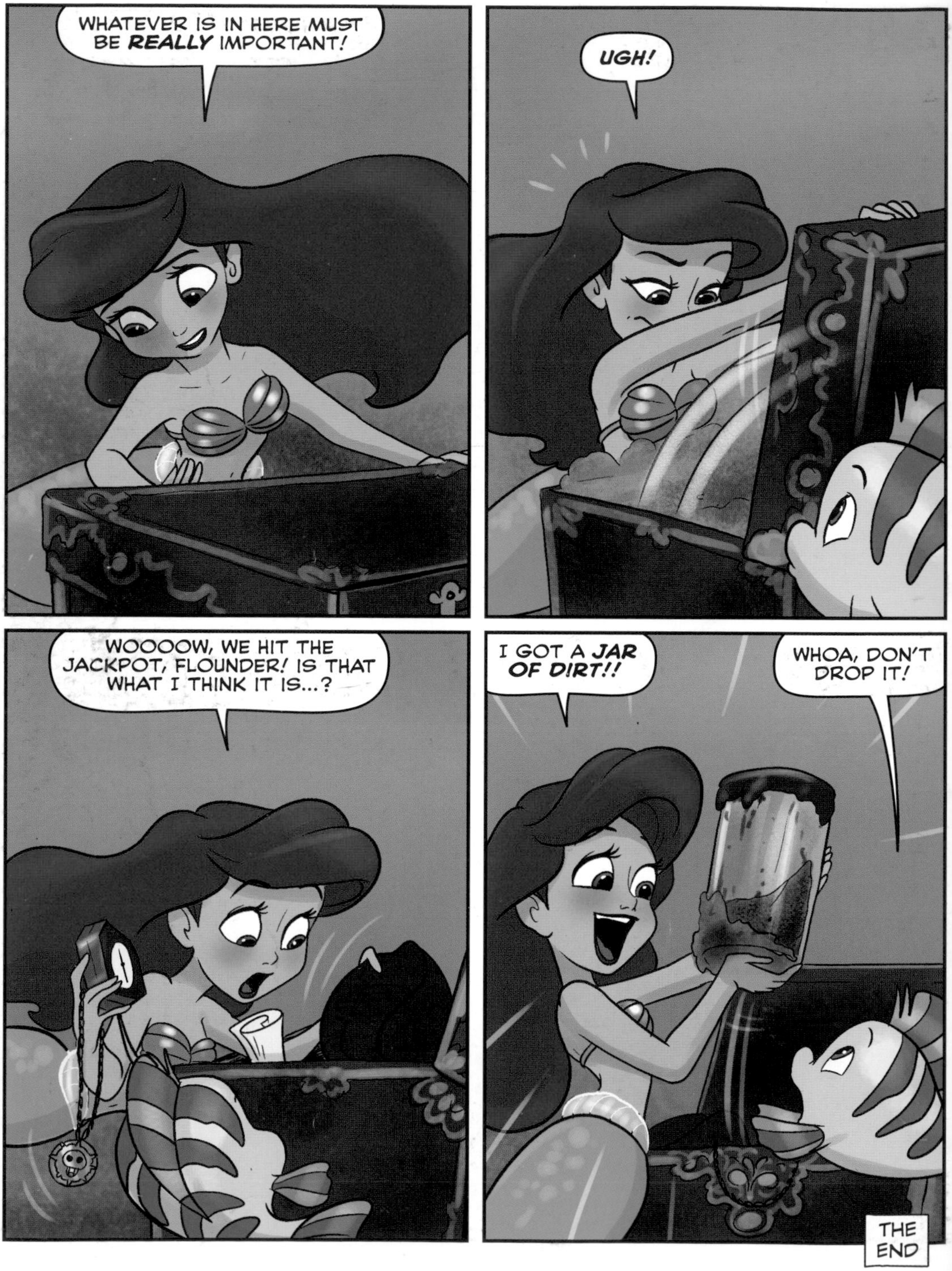
WHATEVER IS IN HERE MUST BE REALLY IMPORTANT!
UGH!
WOOOOW, WE HIT THE JACKPOT, FLOUNDER! IS THAT WHAT I THINK IT IS...?
I GOT A JAR OF DIRT!!
WHOA, DON'T DROP IT!
THE END

"TRADITIONS"

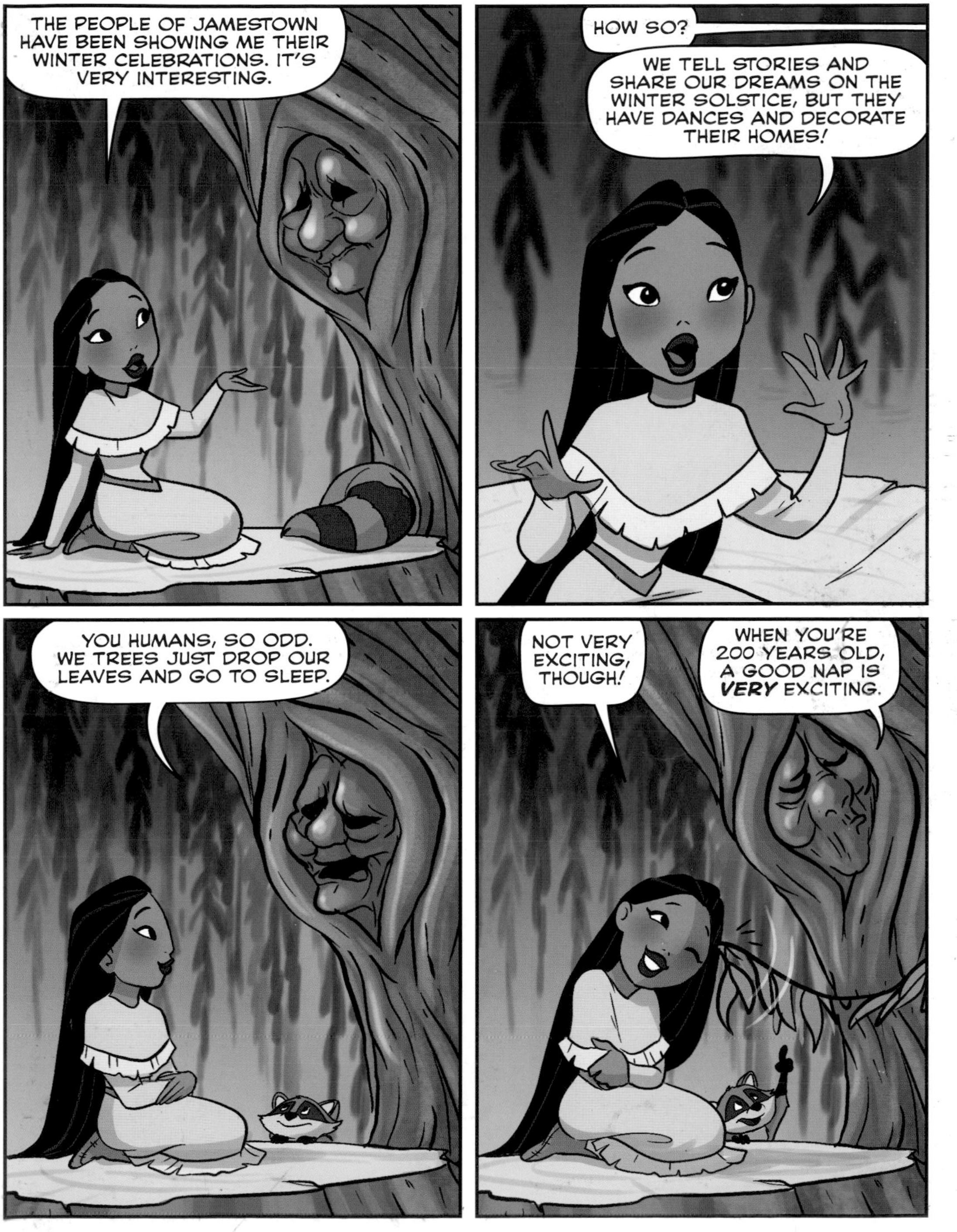

THE PEOPLE OF JAMESTOWN HAVE BEEN SHOWING ME THEIR WINTER CELEBRATIONS. IT'S VERY INTERESTING.
HOW SO?
WE TELL STORIES AND SHARE OUR DREAMS ON THE WINTER SOLSTICE, BUT THEY HAVE DANCES AND DECORATE THEIR HOMES!
YOU HUMANS, SO ODD. WE TREES JUST DROP OUR LEAVES AND GO TO SLEEP.
NOT VERY EXCITING, THOUGH!
WHEN YOU'RE 200 YEARS OLD, A GOOD NAP IS ***VERY*** EXCITING.

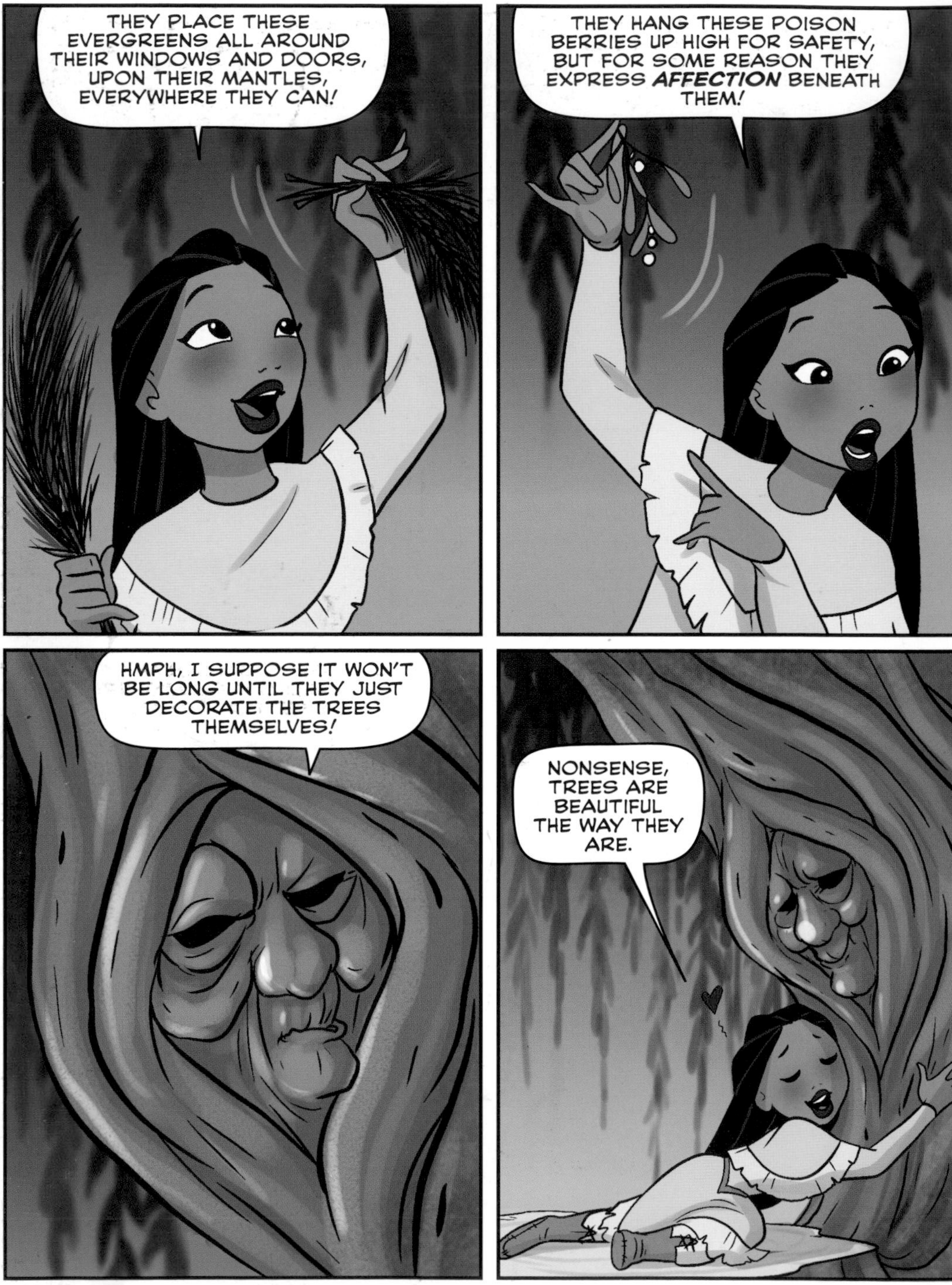
THEY PLACE THESE EVERGREENS ALL AROUND THEIR WINDOWS AND DOORS, UPON THEIR MANTLES, EVERYWHERE THEY CAN!
THEY HANG THESE POISON BERRIES UP HIGH FOR SAFETY, BUT FOR SOME REASON THEY EXPRESS *AFFECTION* BENEATH THEM!
HMPH, I SUPPOSE IT WON'T BE LONG UNTIL THEY JUST DECORATE THE TREES THEMSELVES!
NONSENSE, TREES ARE BEAUTIFUL THE WAY THEY ARE.

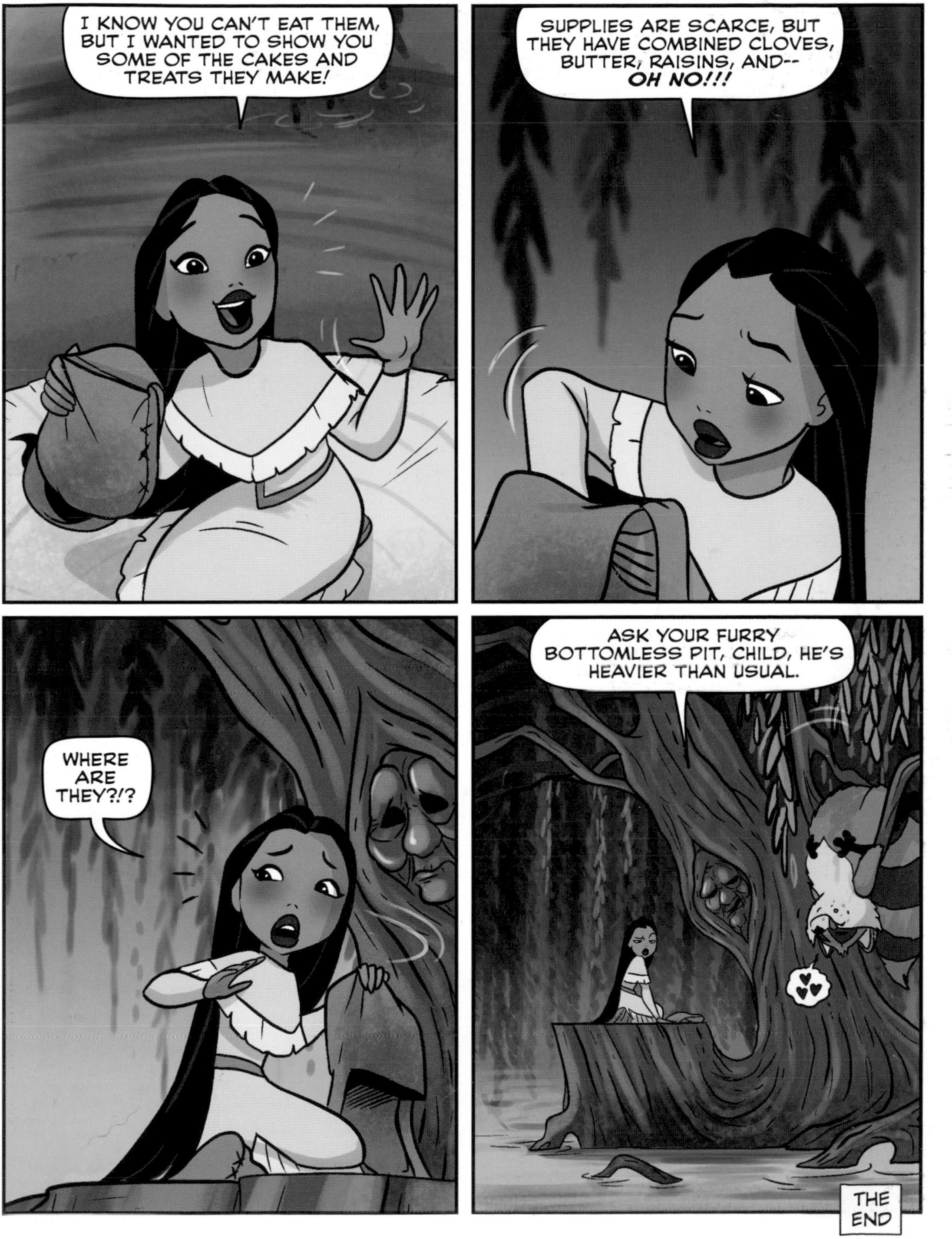
I KNOW YOU CAN'T EAT THEM, BUT I WANTED TO SHOW YOU SOME OF THE CAKES AND TREATS THEY MAKE!
SUPPLIES ARE SCARCE, BUT THEY HAVE COMBINED CLOVES, BUTTER, RAISINS, AND-- ***OH NO!!!***
WHERE ARE THEY?!?
ASK YOUR FURRY BOTTOMLESS PIT, CHILD, HE'S HEAVIER THAN USUAL.
THE END

"DEFEAT THE PUNS"

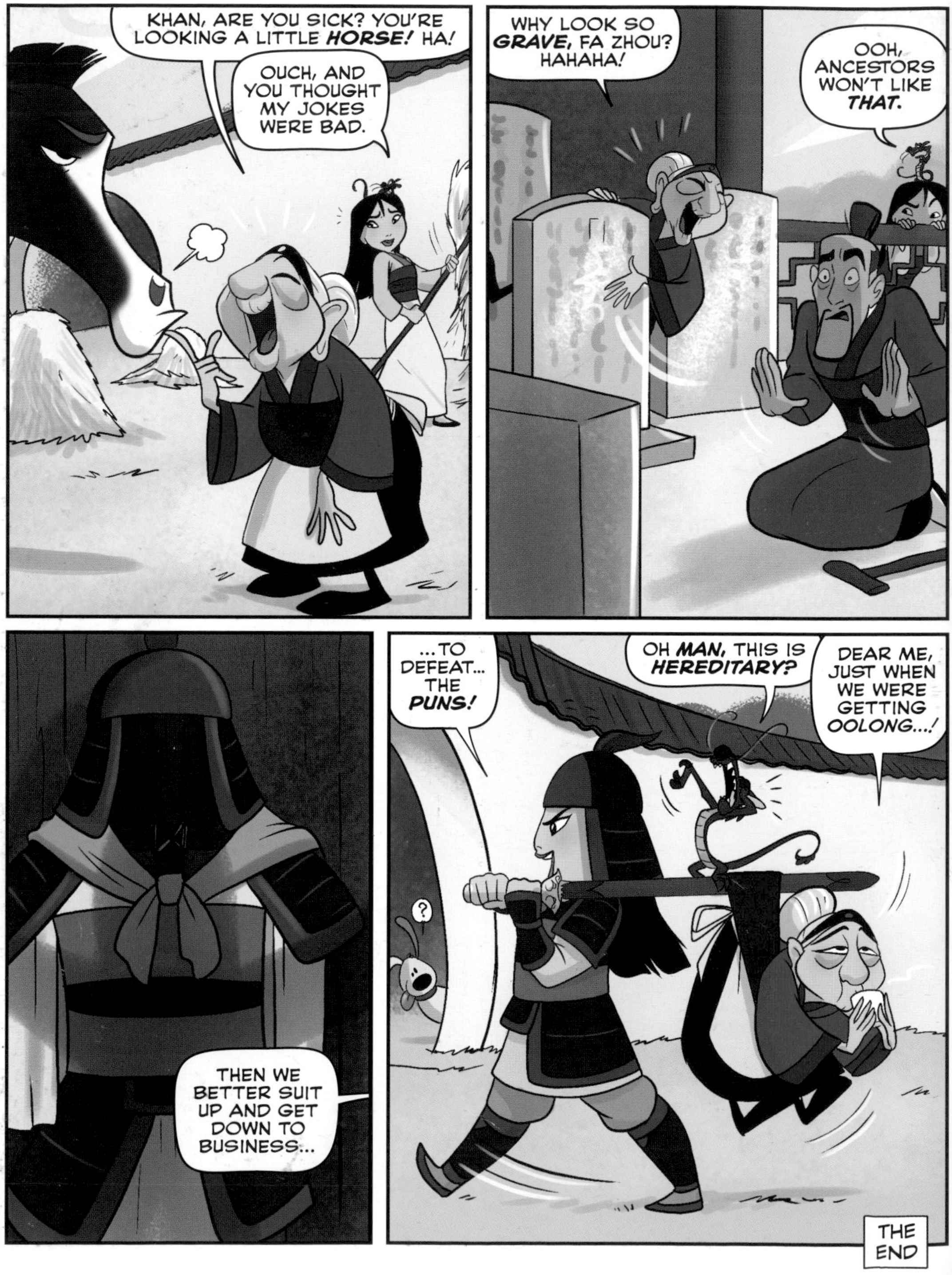
KHAN, ARE YOU SICK? YOU'RE LOOKING A LITTLE **HORSE!** HA!
OUCH, AND YOU THOUGHT MY JOKES WERE BAD.
WHY LOOK SO **GRAVE,** FA ZHOU? HAHAHA!
OOH, ANCESTORS WON'T LIKE **THAT.**
THEN WE BETTER SUIT UP AND GET DOWN TO BUSINESS...
...TO DEFEAT... THE **PUNS!**
OH **MAN,** THIS IS **HEREDITARY?**
DEAR ME, JUST WHEN WE WERE GETTING **OOLONG...!**
?
THE END

"HIDE AND SEEK"

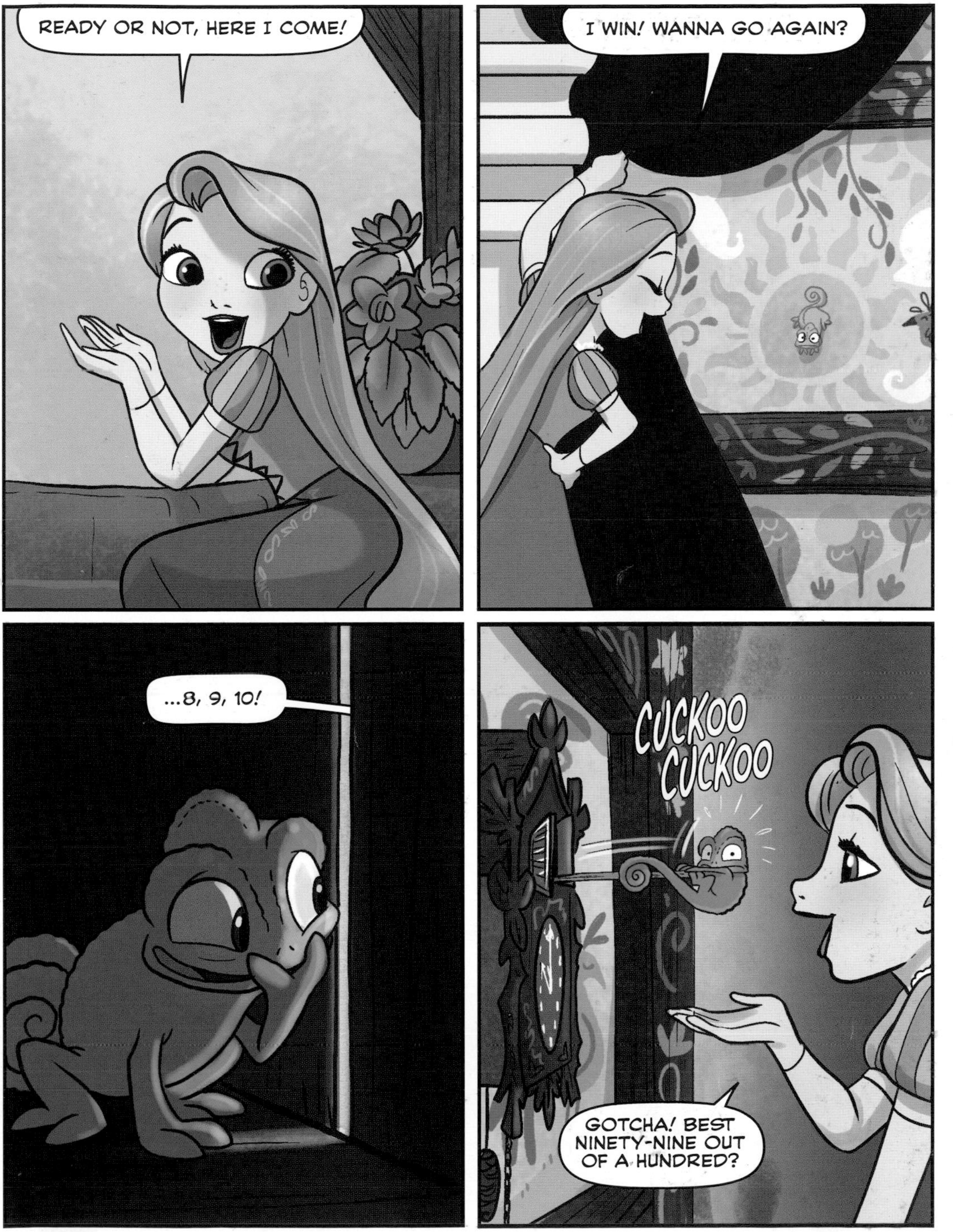
READY OR NOT, HERE I COME!
I WIN! WANNA GO AGAIN?
...8, 9, 10!
CUCKOO
CUCKOO
GOTCHA! BEST NINETY-NINE OUT OF A HUNDRED?

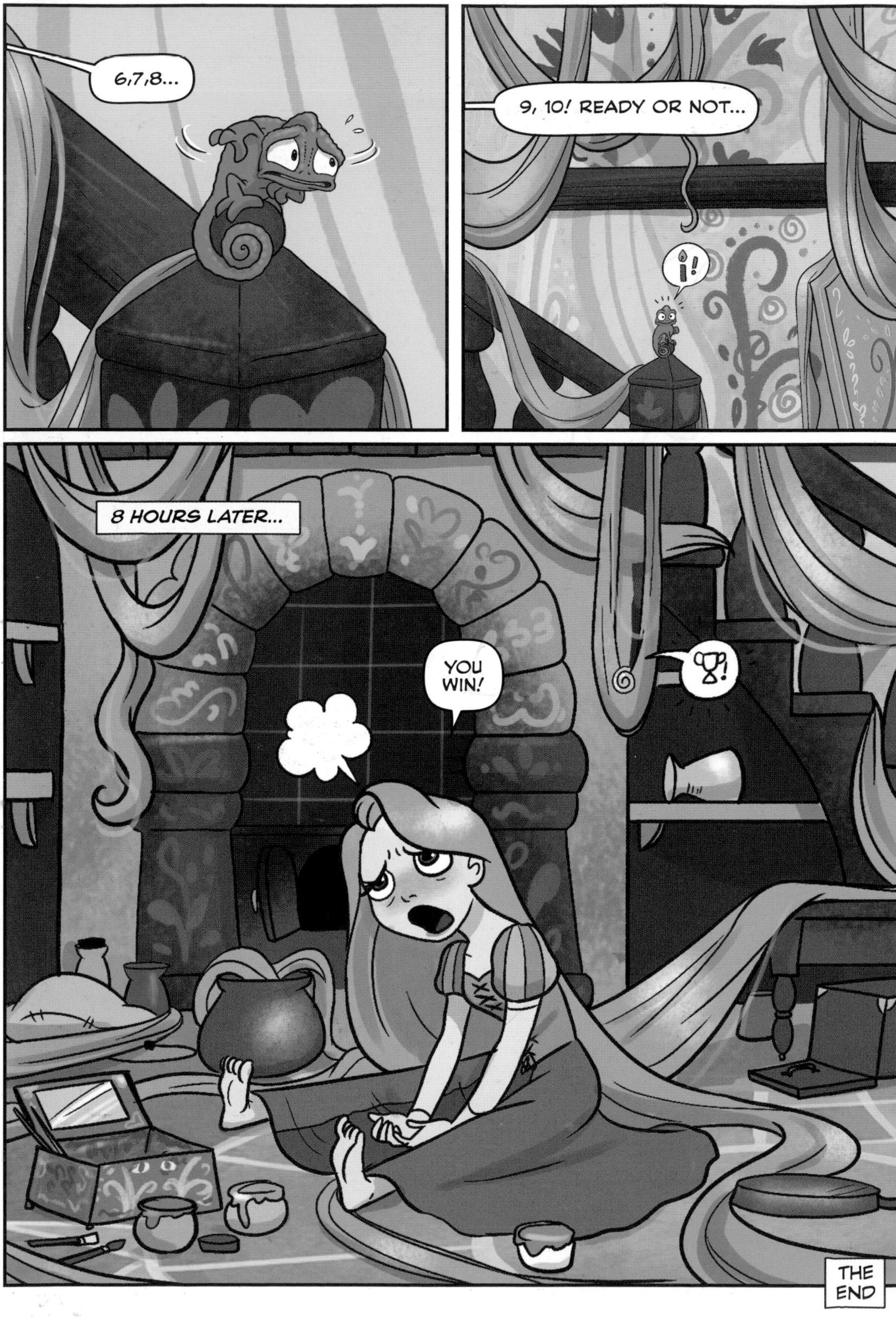
6,7,8...
9, 10! READY OR NOT...
¡!
8 HOURS LATER...
YOU WIN!
!
THE END

"FAIR PLAY"

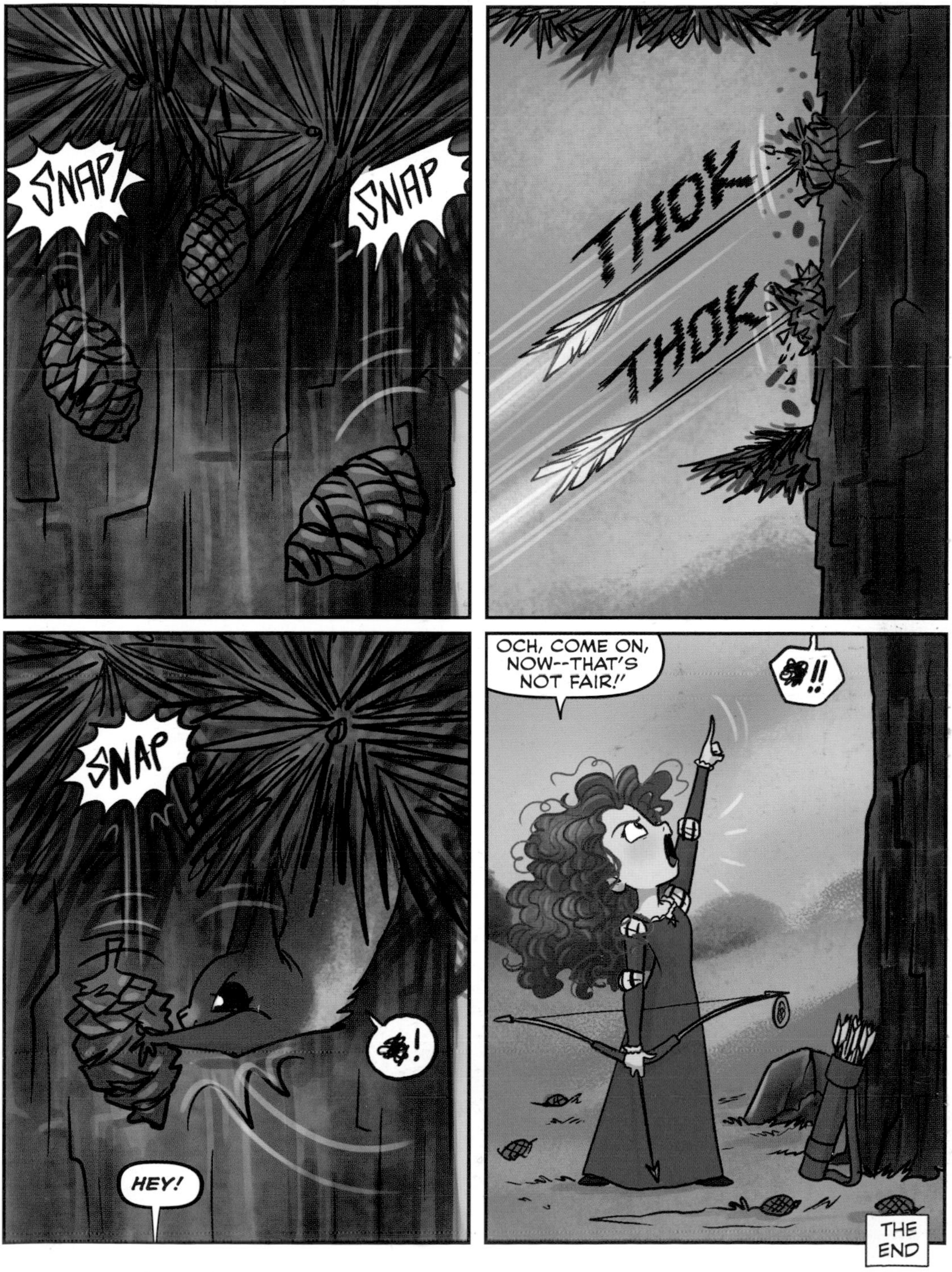
SNAP!
SNAP
THOK
THOK
SNAP
HEY!
OCH, COME ON, NOW--THAT'S NOT FAIR!
THE END

"RIBBON DUSTING"

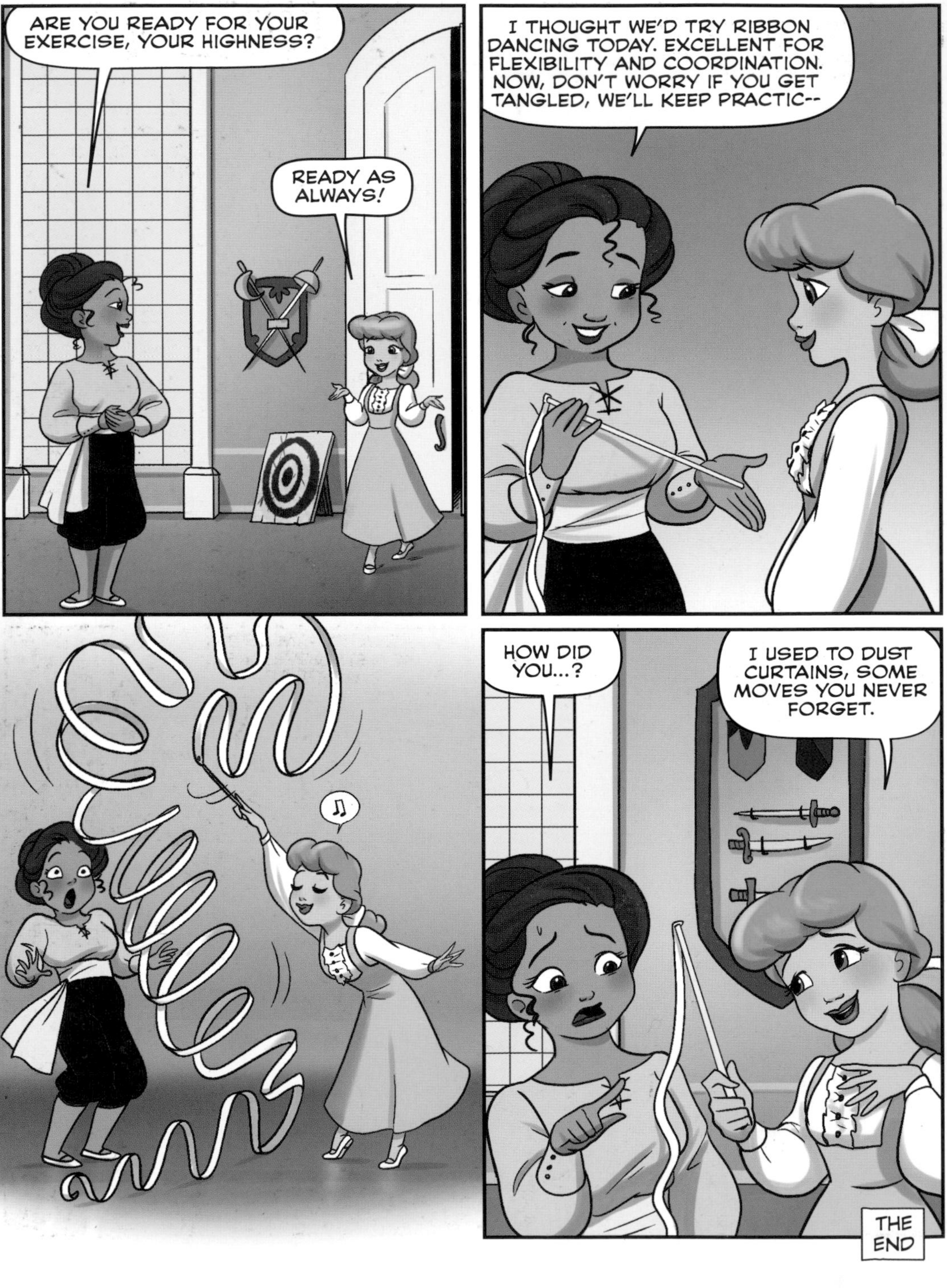

ARE YOU READY FOR YOUR EXERCISE, YOUR HIGHNESS?
READY AS ALWAYS!
I THOUGHT WE'D TRY RIBBON DANCING TODAY. EXCELLENT FOR FLEXIBILITY AND COORDINATION. NOW, DON'T WORRY IF YOU GET TANGLED, WE'LL KEEP PRACTIC--
♫
HOW DID YOU...?
I USED TO DUST CURTAINS, SOME MOVES YOU NEVER FORGET.
THE END

"IN WITH THE NEW"

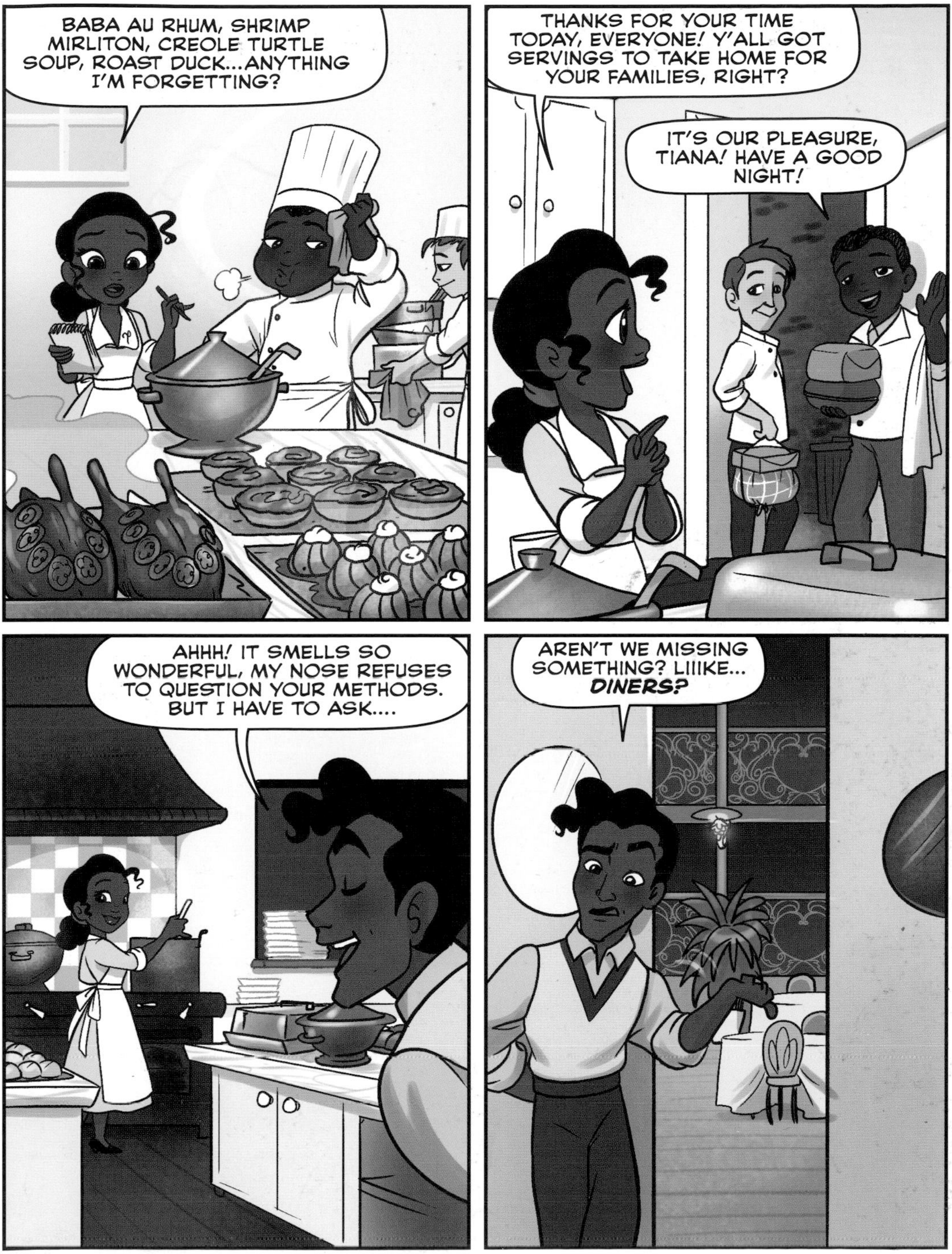

BABA AU RHUM, SHRIMP MIRLITON, CREOLE TURTLE SOUP, ROAST DUCK...ANYTHING I'M FORGETTING?
THANKS FOR YOUR TIME TODAY, EVERYONE! Y'ALL GOT SERVINGS TO TAKE HOME FOR YOUR FAMILIES, RIGHT?
IT'S OUR PLEASURE, TIANA! HAVE A GOOD NIGHT!
AHHH! IT SMELLS SO WONDERFUL, MY NOSE REFUSES TO QUESTION YOUR METHODS. BUT I HAVE TO ASK....
AREN'T WE MISSING SOMETHING? LIIIKE... ***DINERS?***

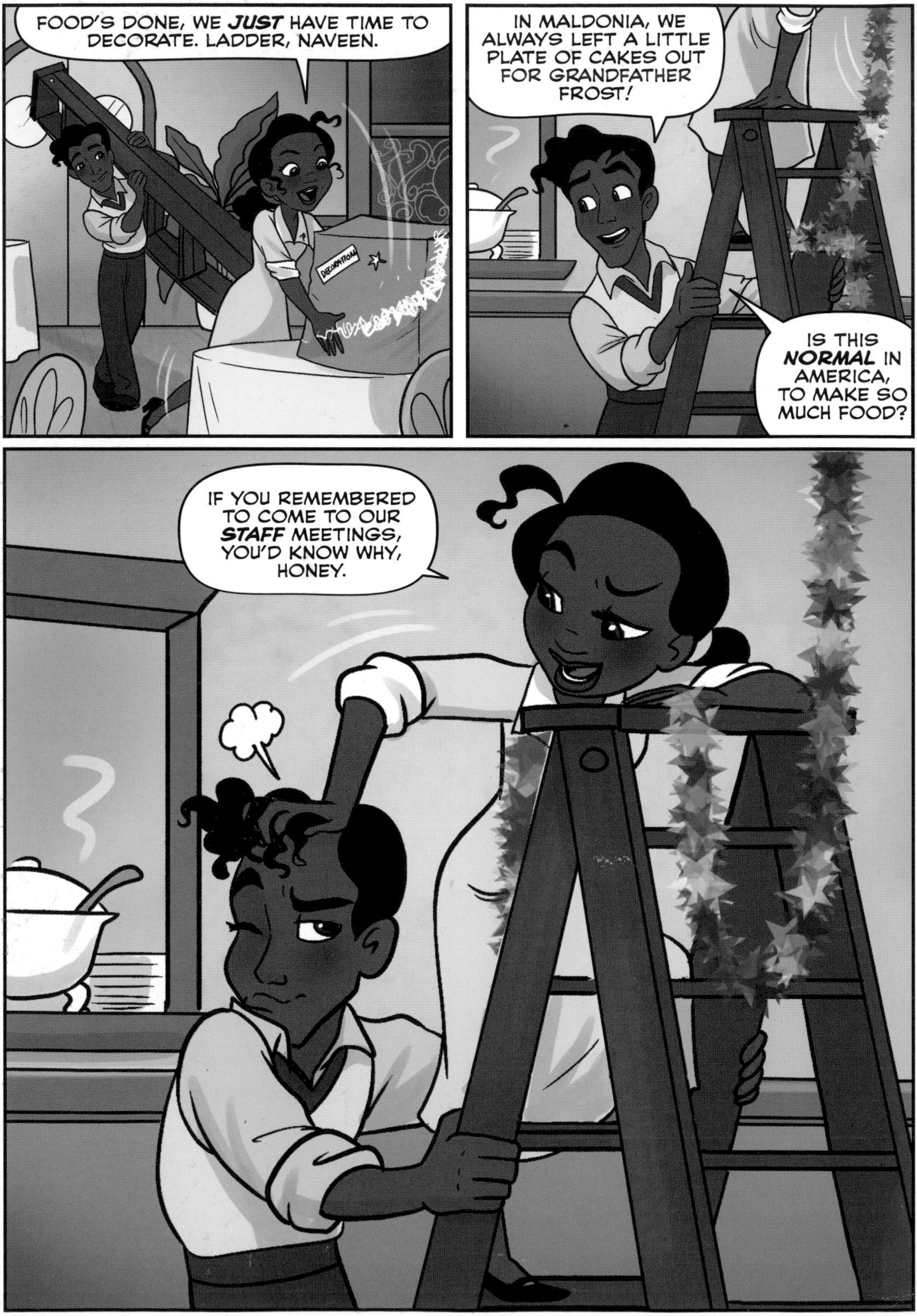
FOOD'S DONE, WE JUST HAVE TIME TO DECORATE. LADDER, NAVEEN.
DECORATIONS
IN MALDONIA, WE ALWAYS LEFT A LITTLE PLATE OF CAKES OUT FOR GRANDFATHER FROST!
IS THIS NORMAL IN AMERICA, TO MAKE SO MUCH FOOD?
IF YOU REMEMBERED TO COME TO OUR STAFF MEETINGS, YOU'D KNOW WHY, HONEY.

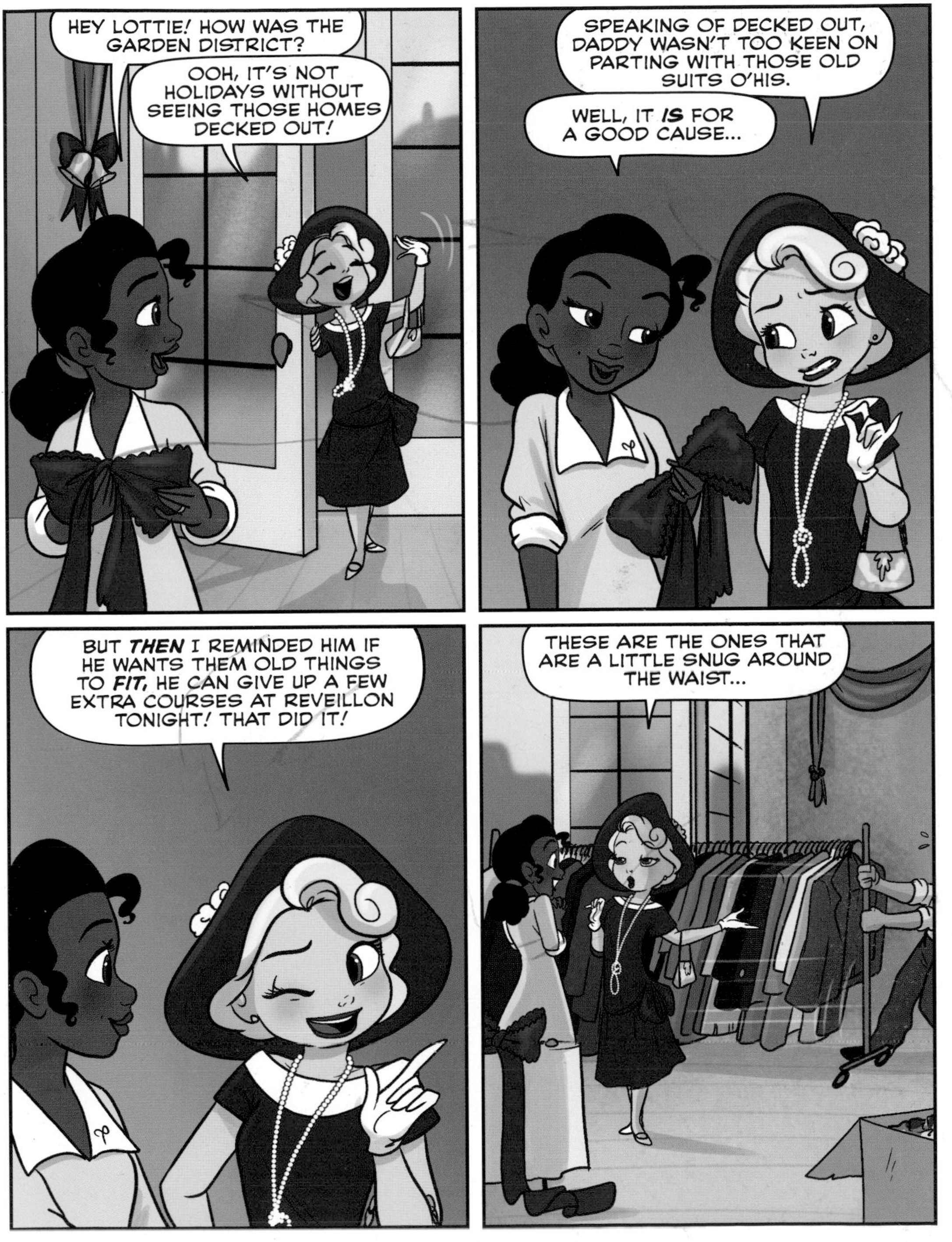
HEY LOTTIE! HOW WAS THE GARDEN DISTRICT?
OOH, IT'S NOT HOLIDAYS WITHOUT SEEING THOSE HOMES DECKED OUT!
SPEAKING OF DECKED OUT, DADDY WASN'T TOO KEEN ON PARTING WITH THOSE OLD SUITS O'HIS.
WELL, IT ***IS*** FOR A GOOD CAUSE...
BUT ***THEN*** I REMINDED HIM IF HE WANTS THEM OLD THINGS TO ***FIT,*** HE CAN GIVE UP A FEW EXTRA COURSES AT REVEILLON TONIGHT! THAT DID IT!
THESE ARE THE ONES THAT ARE A LITTLE SNUG AROUND THE WAIST...

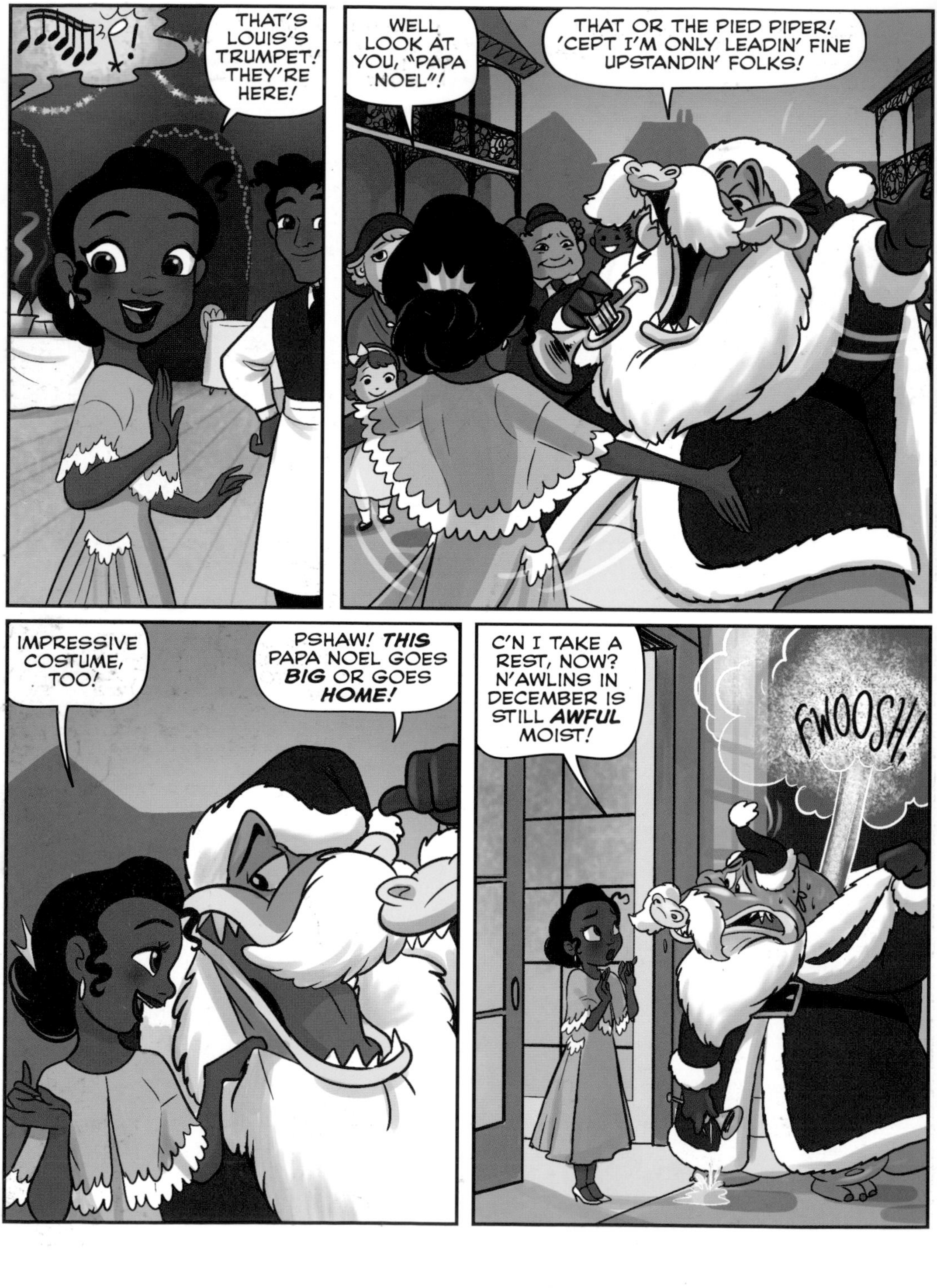
THAT'S LOUIS'S TRUMPET! THEY'RE HERE!
WELL LOOK AT YOU, "PAPA NOEL"!
THAT OR THE PIED PIPER! 'CEPT I'M ONLY LEADIN' FINE UPSTANDIN' FOLKS!
IMPRESSIVE COSTUME, TOO!
PSHAW! ***THIS*** PAPA NOEL GOES ***BIG*** OR GOES ***HOME!***
C'N I TAKE A REST, NOW? N'AWLINS IN DECEMBER IS STILL ***AWFUL*** MOIST!
FWOOSH!

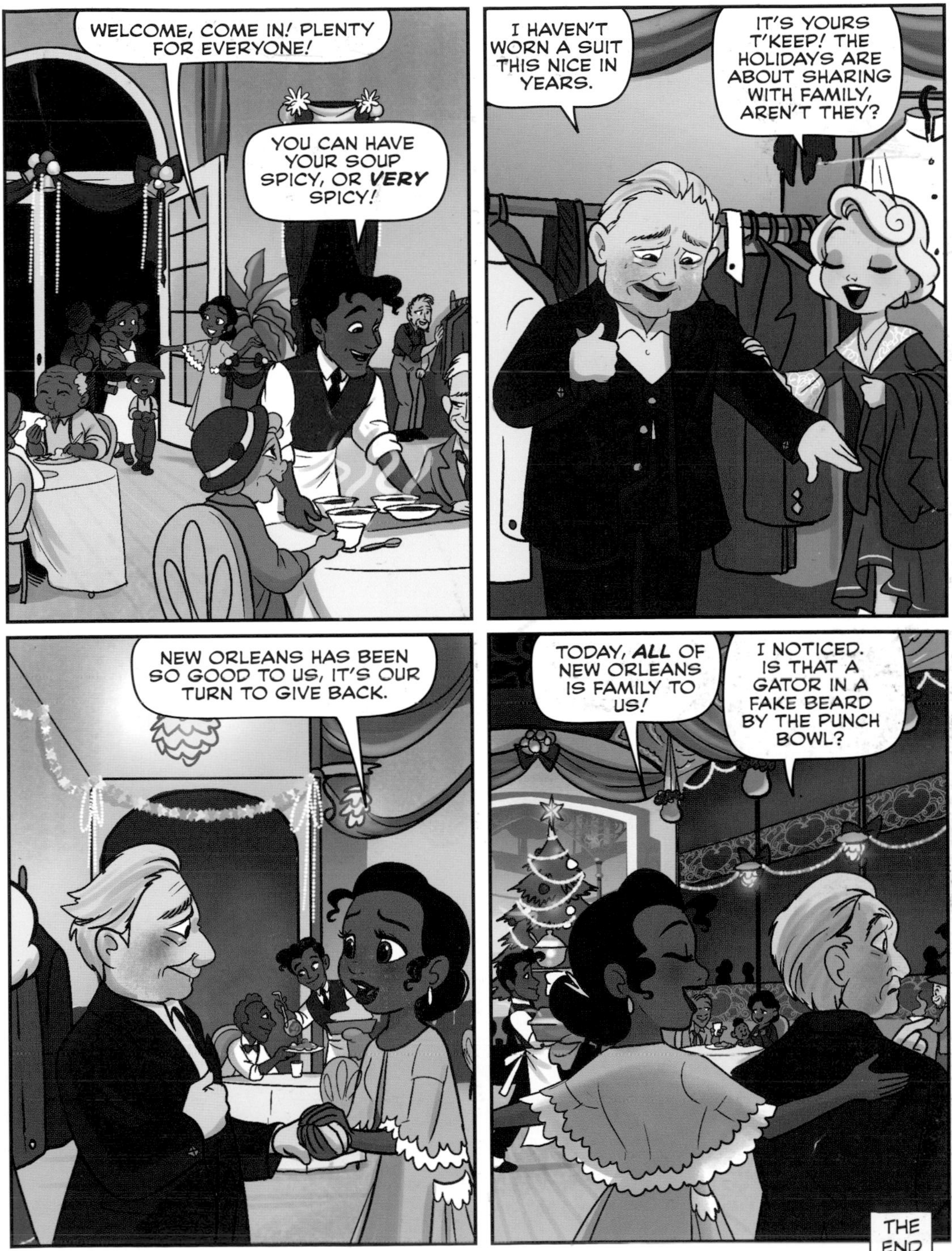
WELCOME, COME IN! PLENTY FOR EVERYONE!
YOU CAN HAVE YOUR SOUP SPICY, OR *VERY* SPICY!
I HAVEN'T WORN A SUIT THIS NICE IN YEARS.
IT'S YOURS T'KEEP! THE HOLIDAYS ARE ABOUT SHARING WITH FAMILY, AREN'T THEY?
NEW ORLEANS HAS BEEN SO GOOD TO US, IT'S OUR TURN TO GIVE BACK.
TODAY, *ALL* OF NEW ORLEANS IS FAMILY TO US!
I NOTICED. IS THAT A GATOR IN A FAKE BEARD BY THE PUNCH BOWL?
THE END

"VIEW FROM THE TOP"

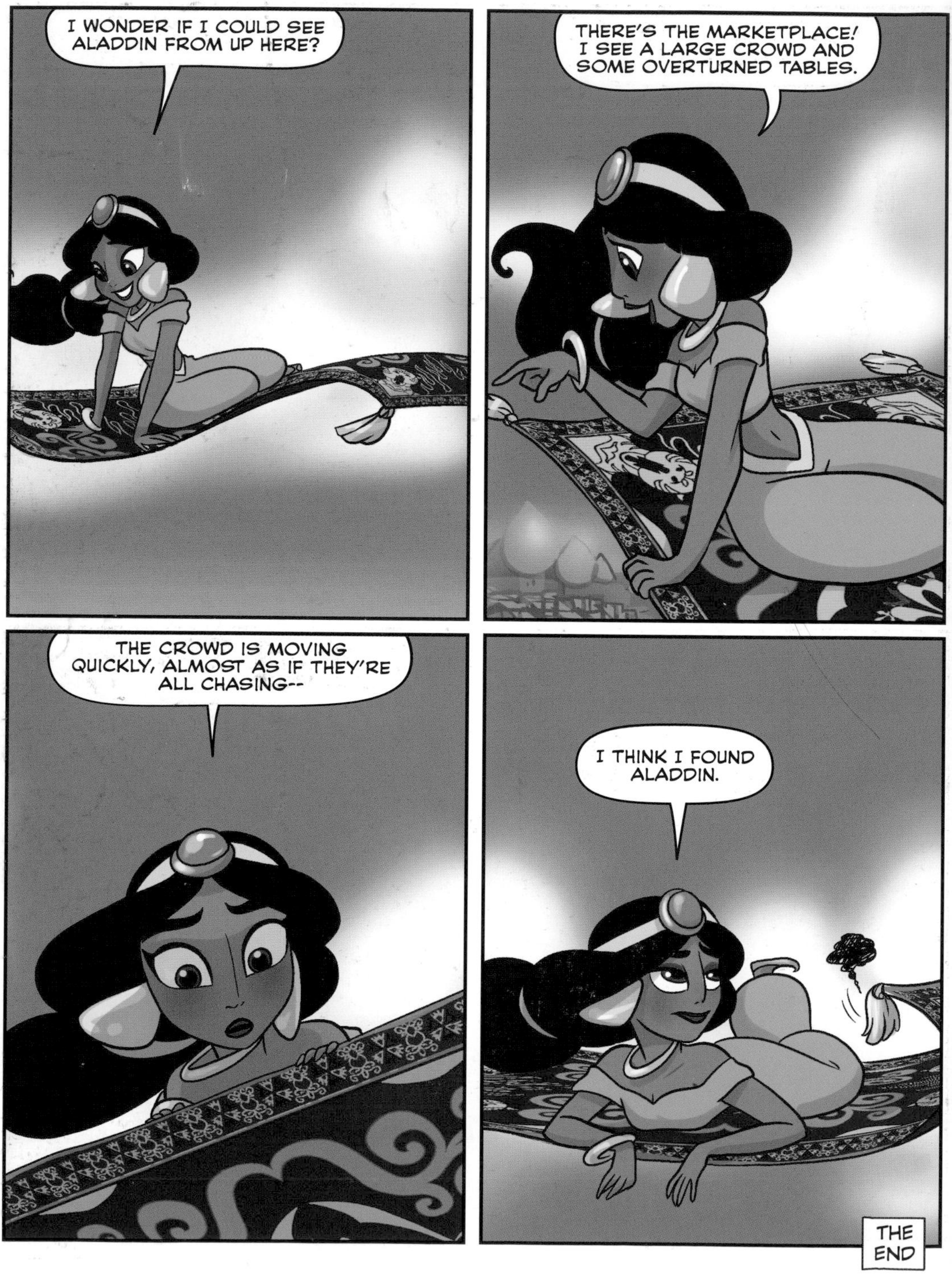
I WONDER IF I COULD SEE ALADDIN FROM UP HERE?
THERE'S THE MARKETPLACE! I SEE A LARGE CROWD AND SOME OVERTURNED TABLES.
THE CROWD IS MOVING QUICKLY, ALMOST AS IF THEY'RE ALL CHASING--
I THINK I FOUND ALADDIN.
THE END

"WHISKS"

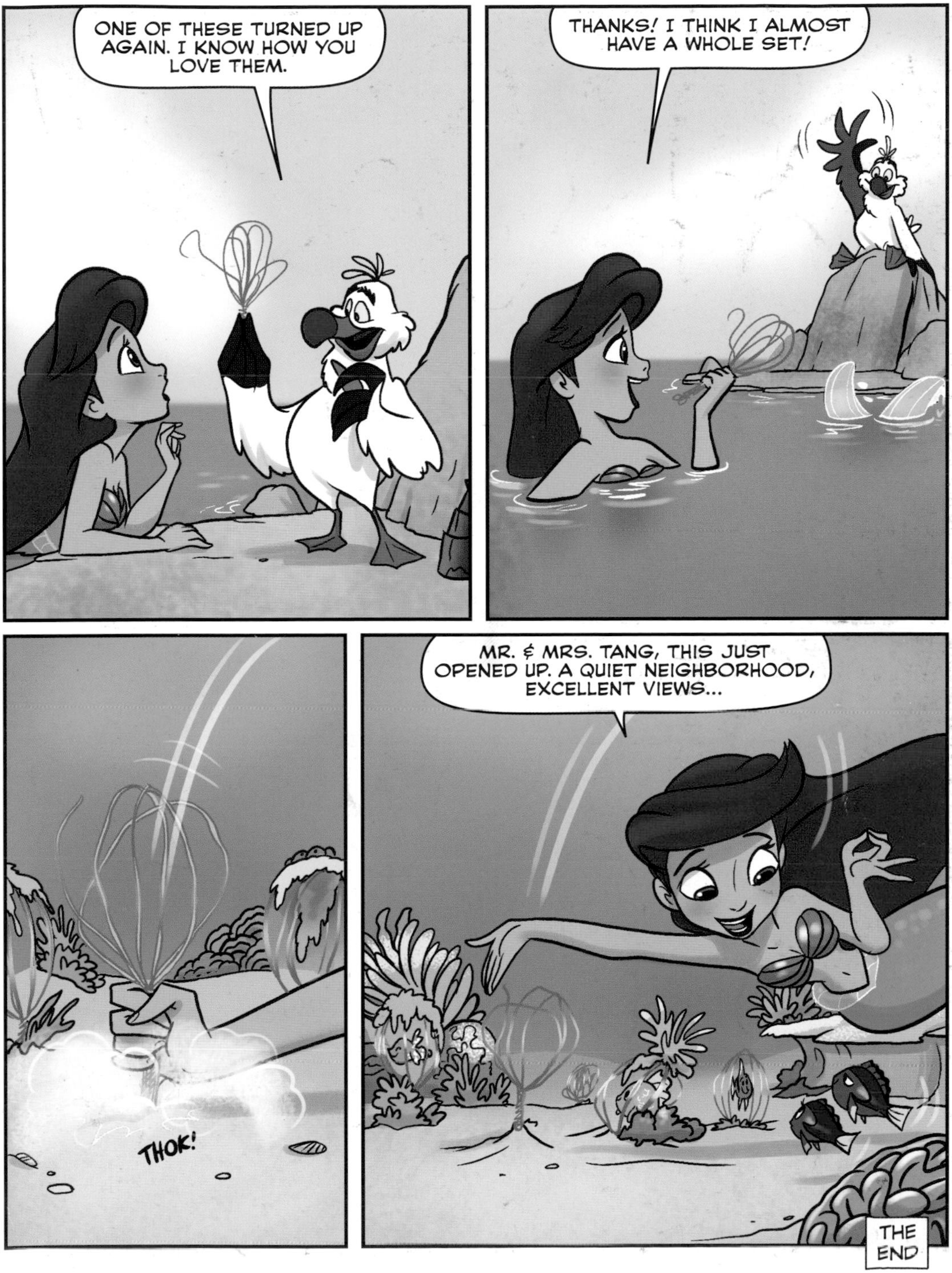

ONE OF THESE TURNED UP AGAIN. I KNOW HOW YOU LOVE THEM.
THANKS! I THINK I ALMOST HAVE A WHOLE SET!
THOK!
MR. & MRS. TANG, THIS JUST OPENED UP. A QUIET NEIGHBORHOOD, EXCELLENT VIEWS...
THE END

"NICKNAMES"

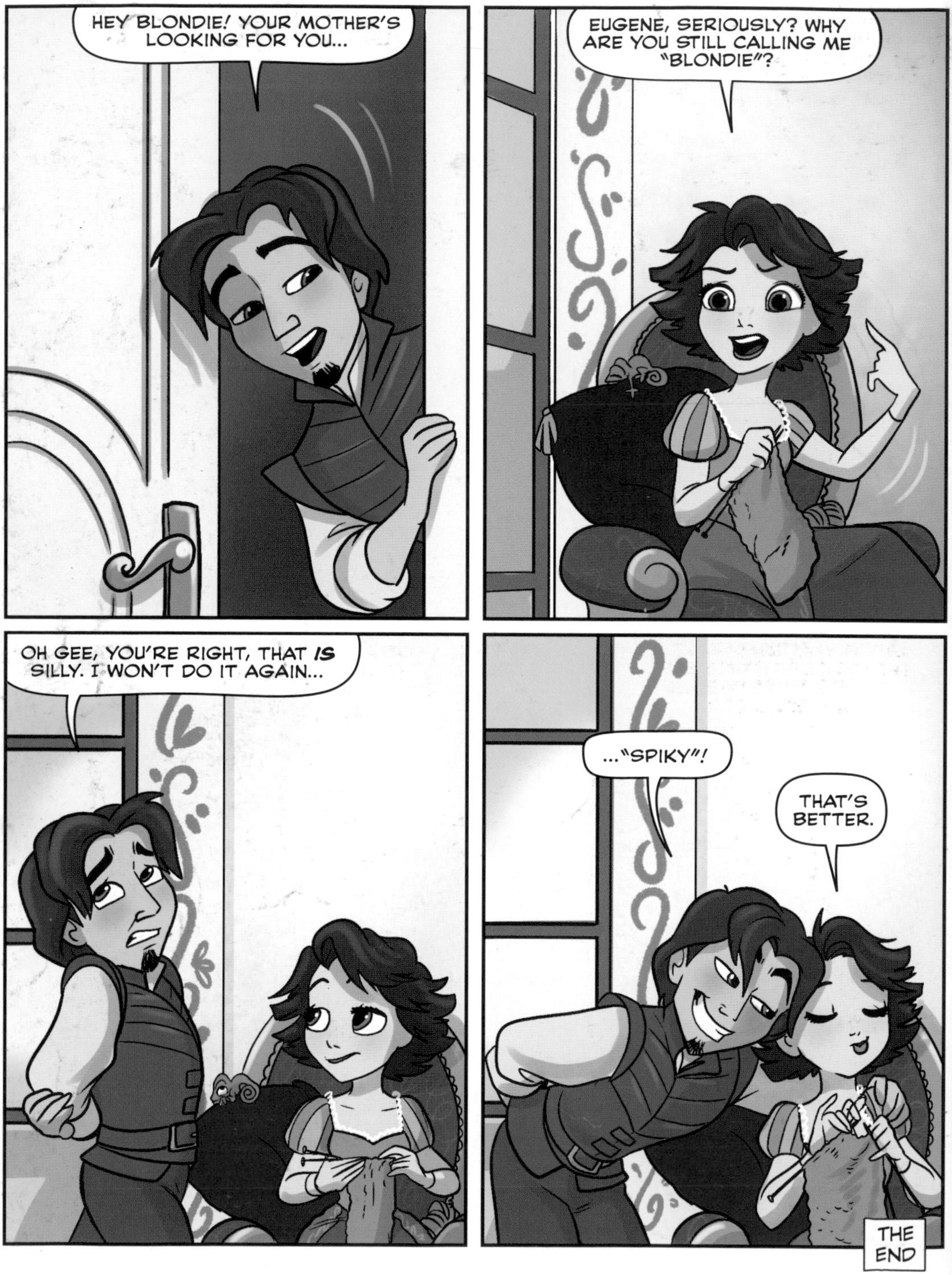

HEY BLONDIE! YOUR MOTHER'S LOOKING FOR YOU...
EUGENE, SERIOUSLY? WHY ARE YOU STILL CALLING ME "BLONDIE"?
OH GEE, YOU'RE RIGHT, THAT *IS* SILLY. I WON'T DO IT AGAIN...
..."SPIKY"!
THAT'S BETTER.
THE END

"HOGMANAY"

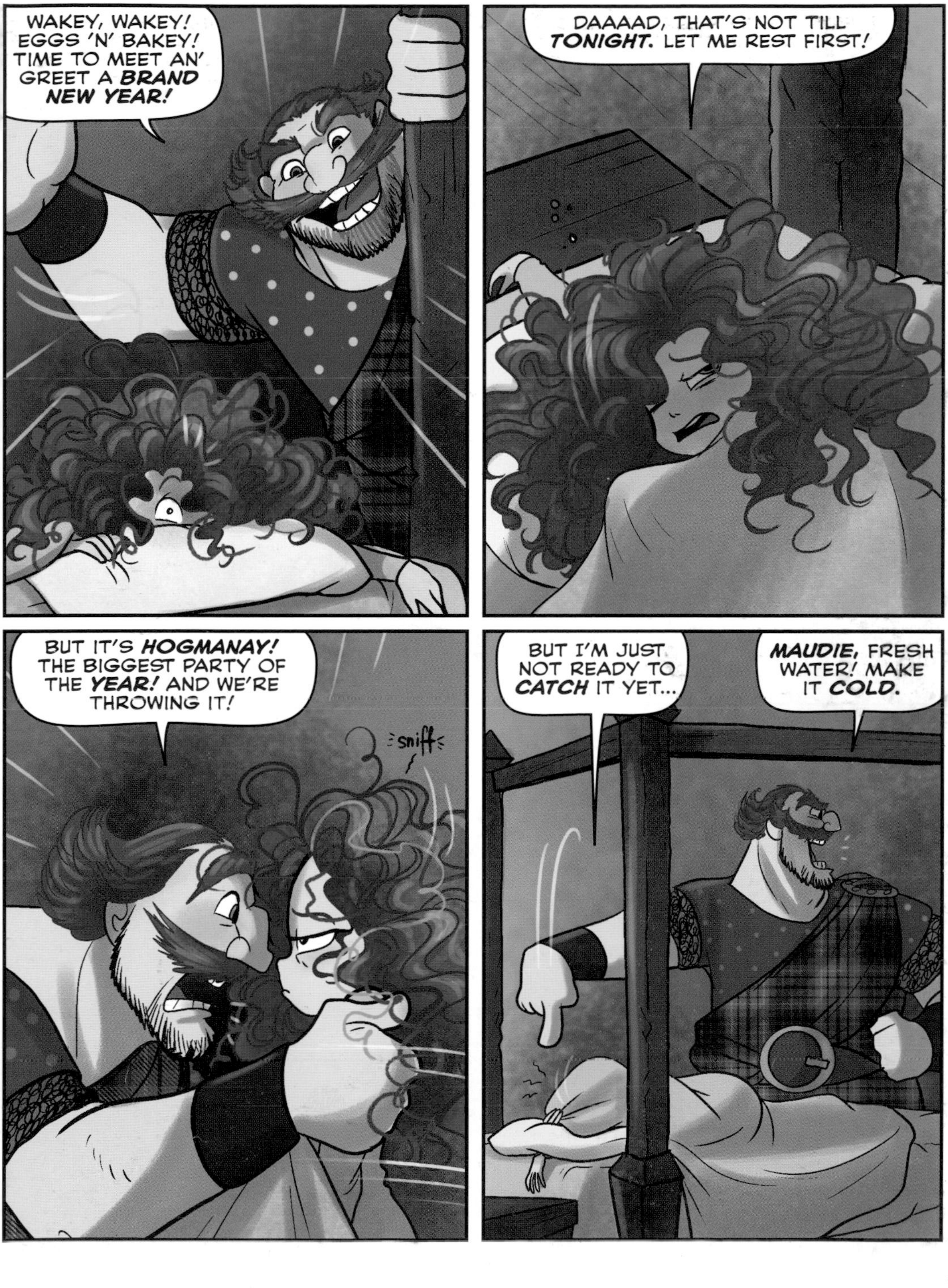
WAKEY, WAKEY! EGGS 'N' BAKEY! TIME TO MEET AN' GREET A **BRAND NEW YEAR!**
DAAAAD, THAT'S NOT TILL **TONIGHT**. LET ME REST FIRST!
BUT IT'S **HOGMANAY!** THE BIGGEST PARTY OF THE **YEAR!** AND WE'RE THROWING IT!
sniff
BUT I'M JUST NOT READY TO **CATCH** IT YET...
MAUDIE, FRESH WATER! MAKE IT **COLD.**

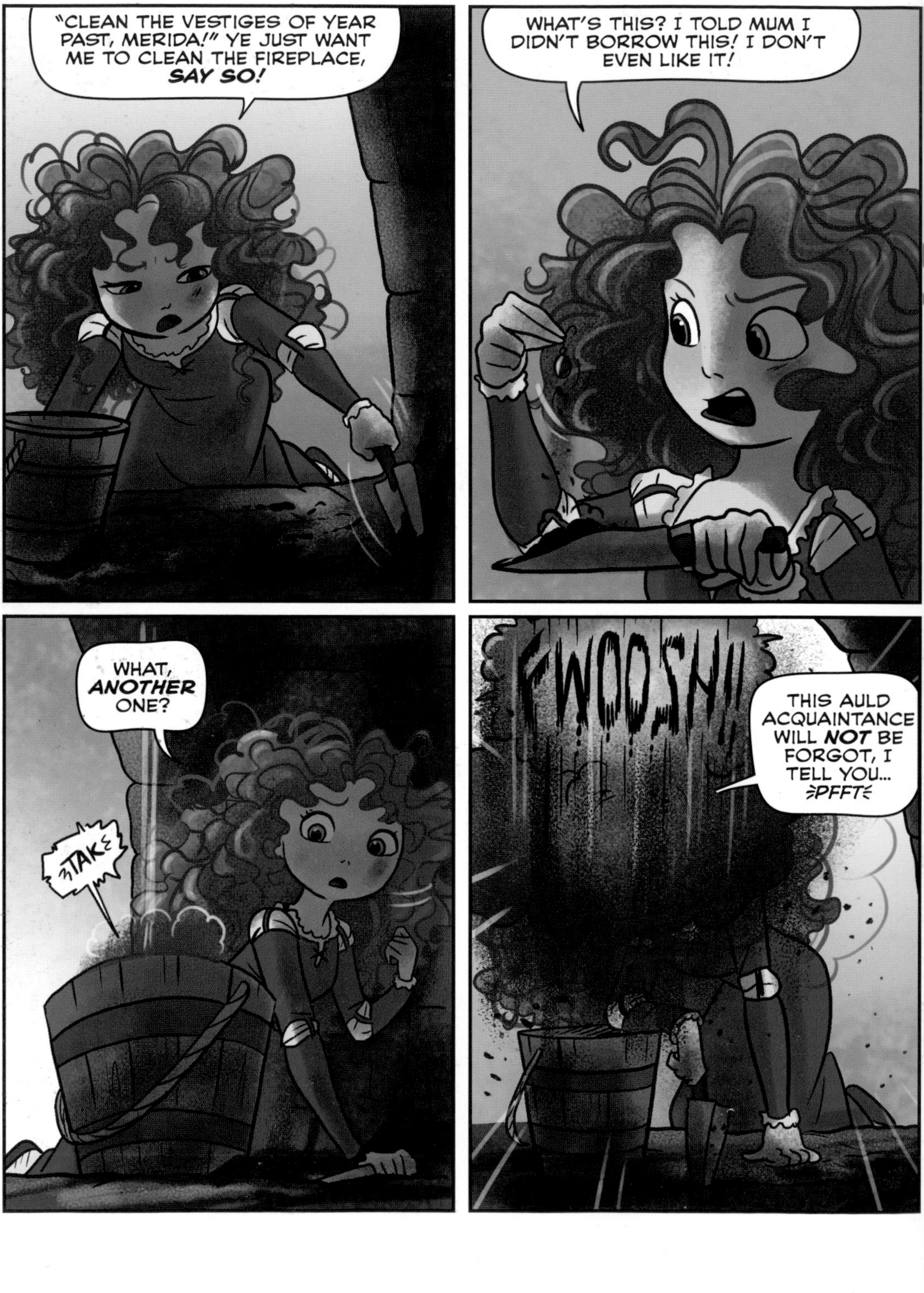
"CLEAN THE VESTIGES OF YEAR PAST, MERIDA!" YE JUST WANT ME TO CLEAN THE FIREPLACE, SAY SO!
WHAT'S THIS? I TOLD MUM I DIDN'T BORROW THIS! I DON'T EVEN LIKE IT!
WHAT, ANOTHER ONE?
TAK
FWOOSH!!
THIS AULD ACQUAINTANCE WILL NOT BE FORGOT, I TELL YOU... PFFT

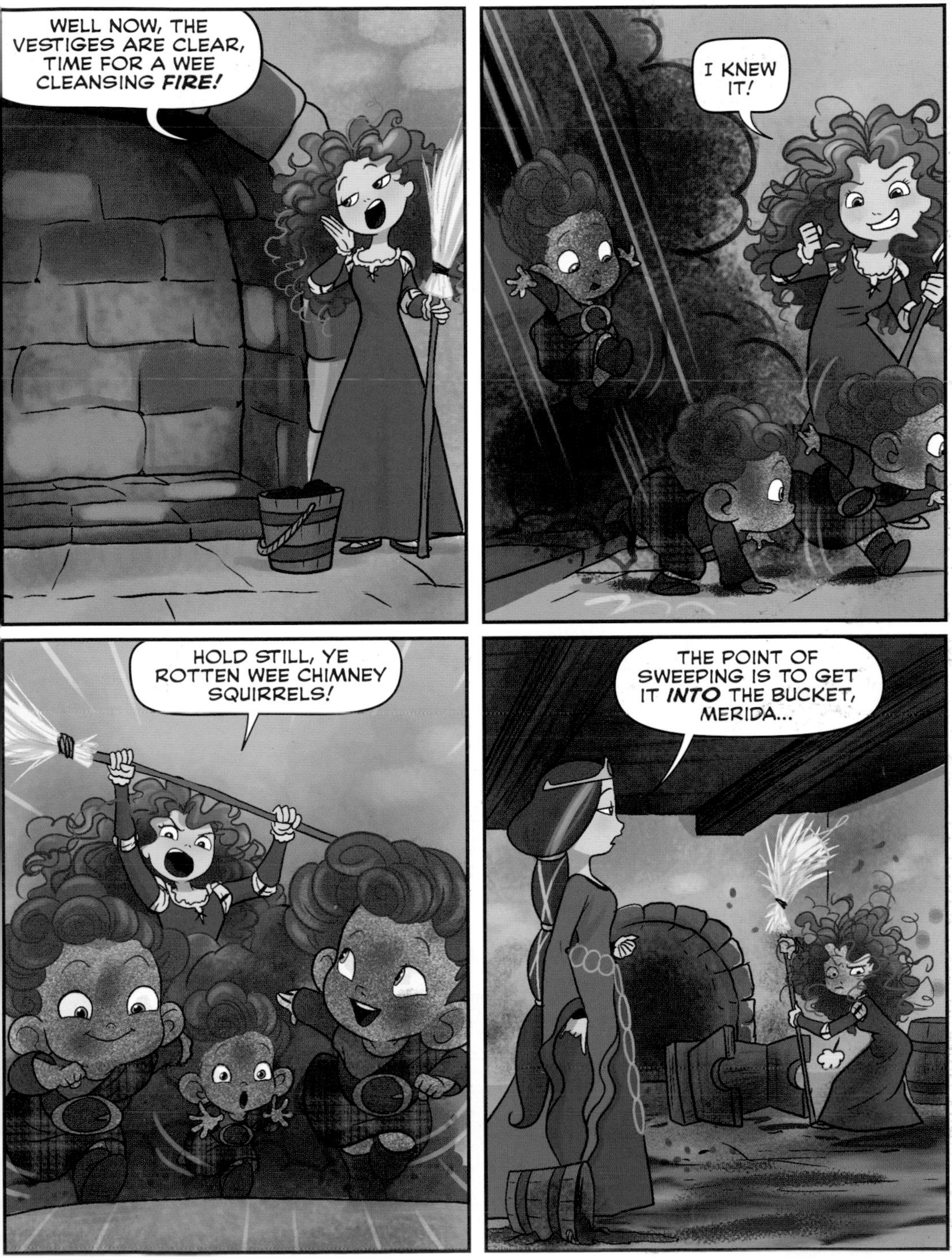
WELL NOW, THE VESTIGES ARE CLEAR, TIME FOR A WEE CLEANSING *FIRE!*
I KNEW IT!
HOLD STILL, YE ROTTEN WEE CHIMNEY SQUIRRELS!
THE POINT OF SWEEPING IS TO GET IT *INTO* THE BUCKET, MERIDA...

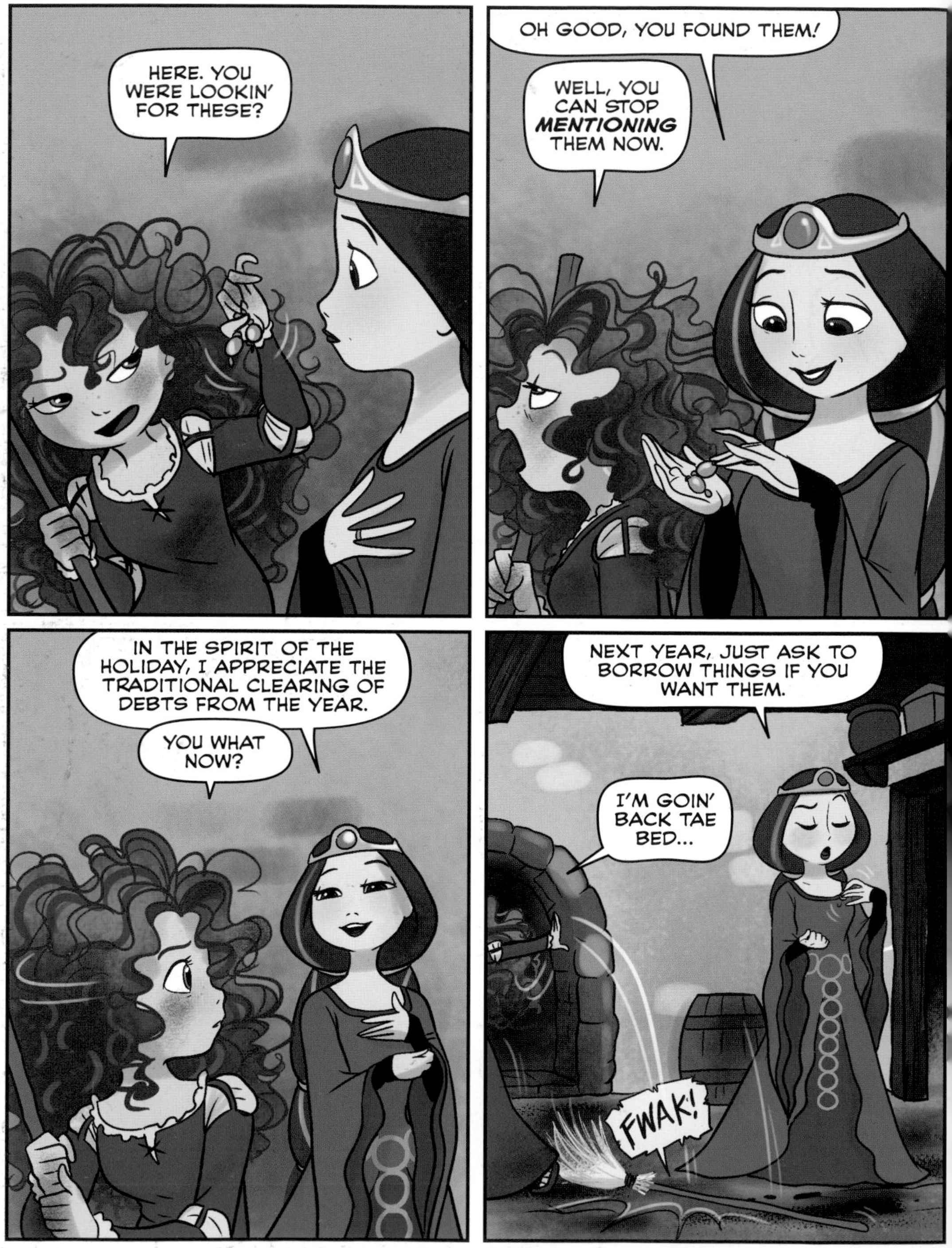
HERE. YOU WERE LOOKIN' FOR THESE?
OH GOOD, YOU FOUND THEM!
WELL, YOU CAN STOP *MENTIONING* THEM NOW.
IN THE SPIRIT OF THE HOLIDAY, I APPRECIATE THE TRADITIONAL CLEARING OF DEBTS FROM THE YEAR.
YOU WHAT NOW?
NEXT YEAR, JUST ASK TO BORROW THINGS IF YOU WANT THEM.
I'M GOIN' BACK TAE BED...
FWAK!

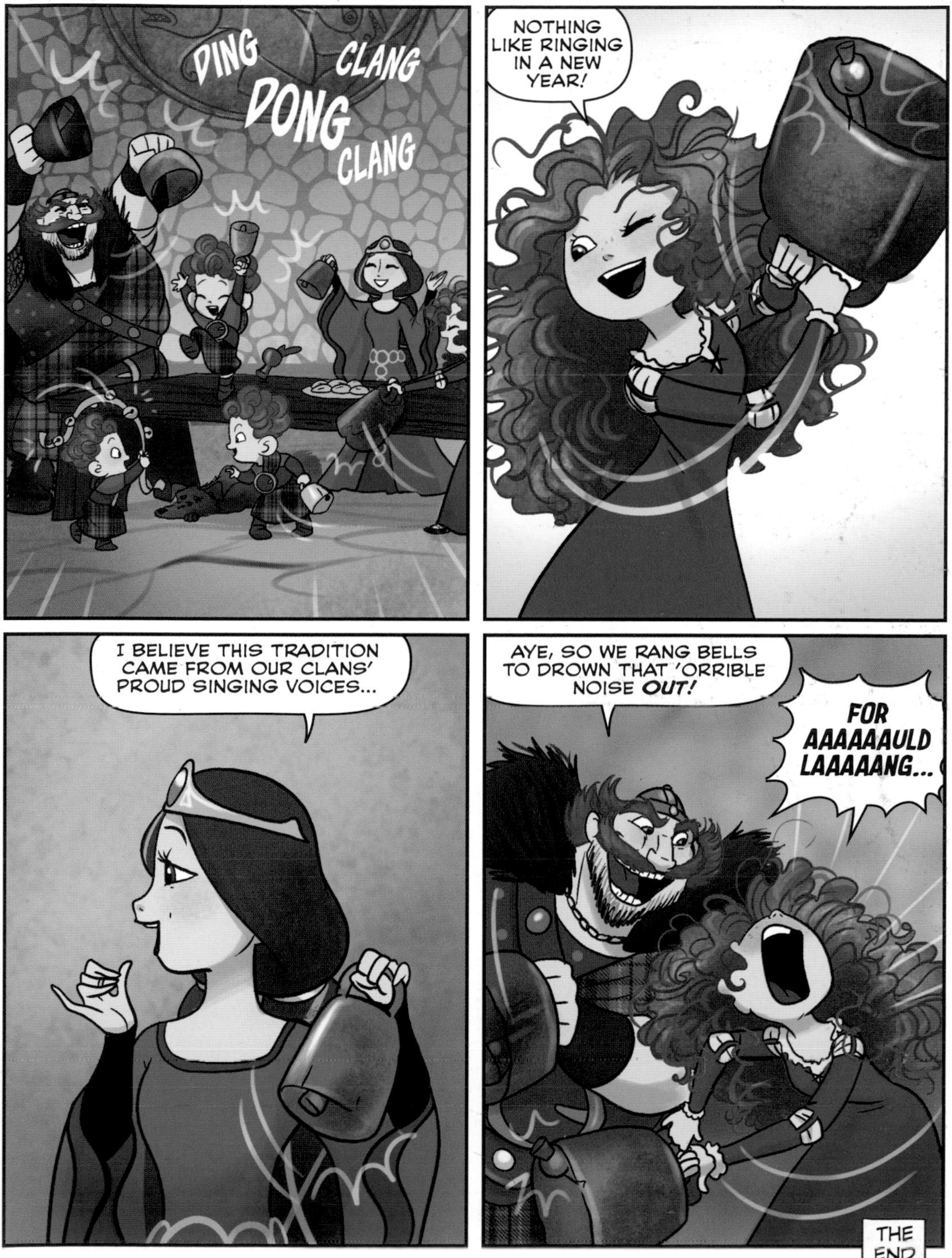
DING
DONG
CLANG
CLANG
NOTHING LIKE RINGING IN A NEW YEAR!
I BELIEVE THIS TRADITION CAME FROM OUR CLANS' PROUD SINGING VOICES...
AYE, SO WE RANG BELLS TO DROWN THAT 'ORRIBLE NOISE OUT!
FOR AAAAAAULD LAAAAANG...
THE END

"FORK IN THE RIVER"

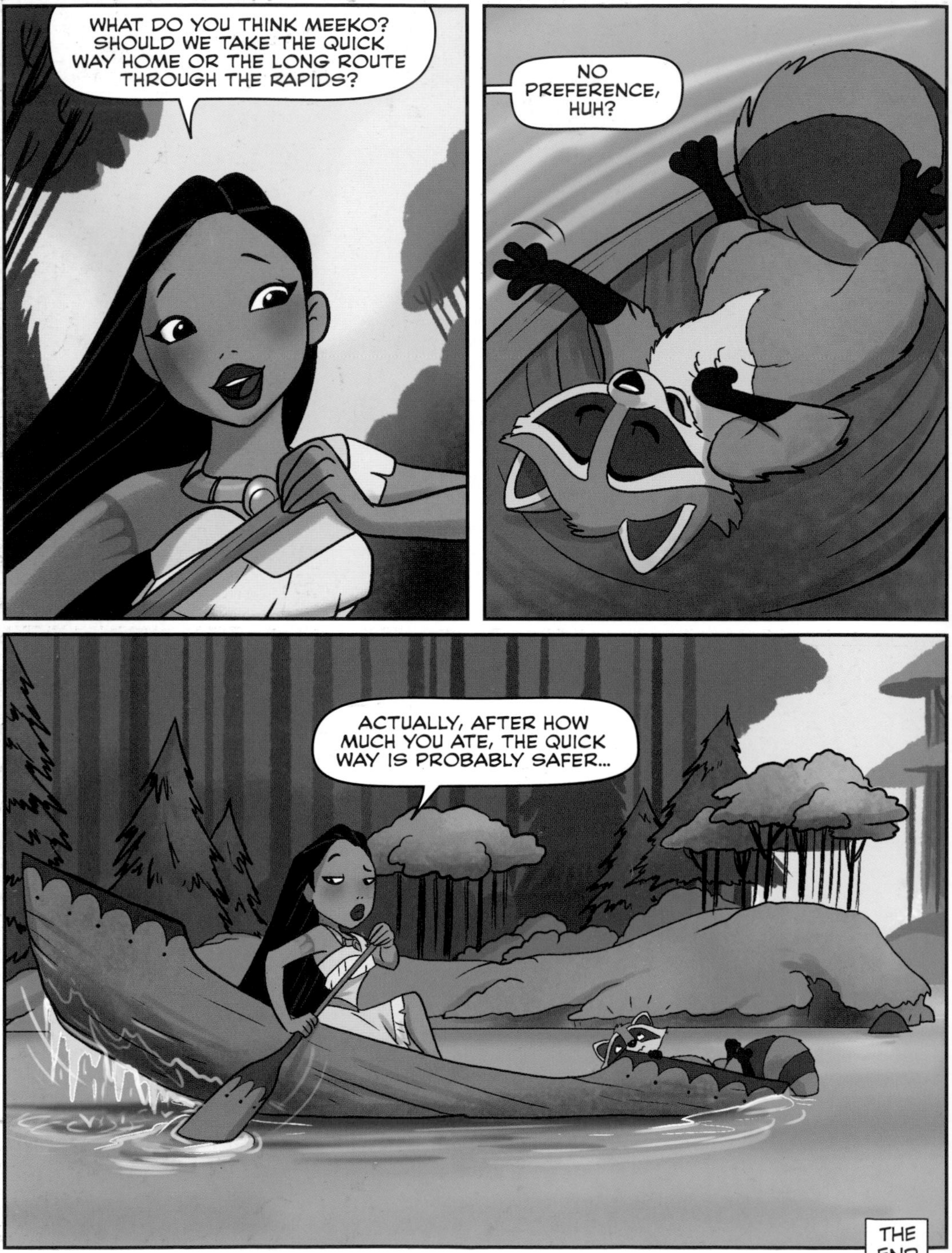
WHAT DO YOU THINK MEEKO? SHOULD WE TAKE THE QUICK WAY HOME OR THE LONG ROUTE THROUGH THE RAPIDS?
NO PREFERENCE, HUH?
ACTUALLY, AFTER HOW MUCH YOU ATE, THE QUICK WAY IS PROBABLY SAFER...
THE END

"FIREWORKS"

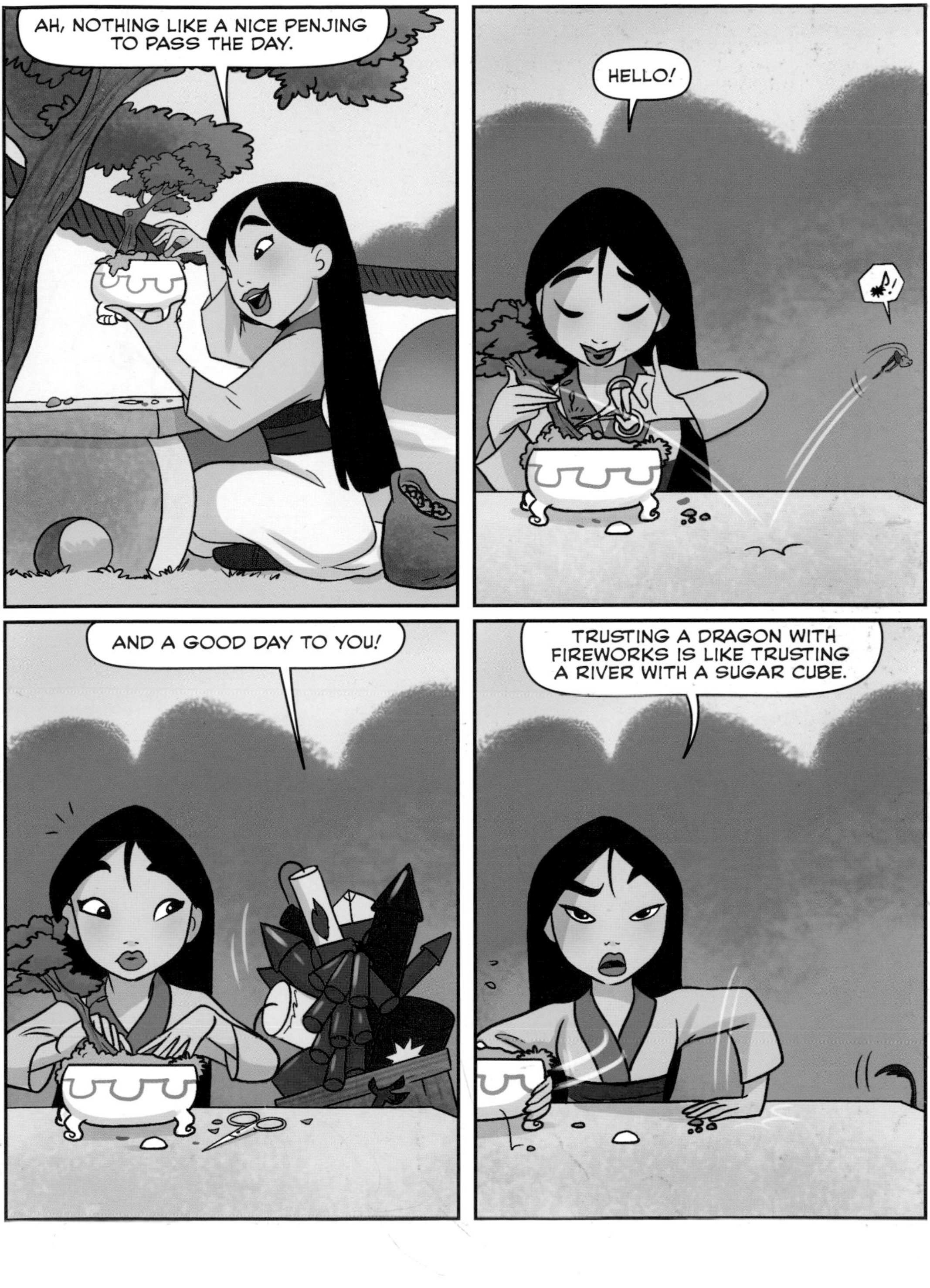
AH, NOTHING LIKE A NICE PENJING TO PASS THE DAY.
HELLO!
AND A GOOD DAY TO YOU!
TRUSTING A DRAGON WITH FIREWORKS IS LIKE TRUSTING A RIVER WITH A SUGAR CUBE.

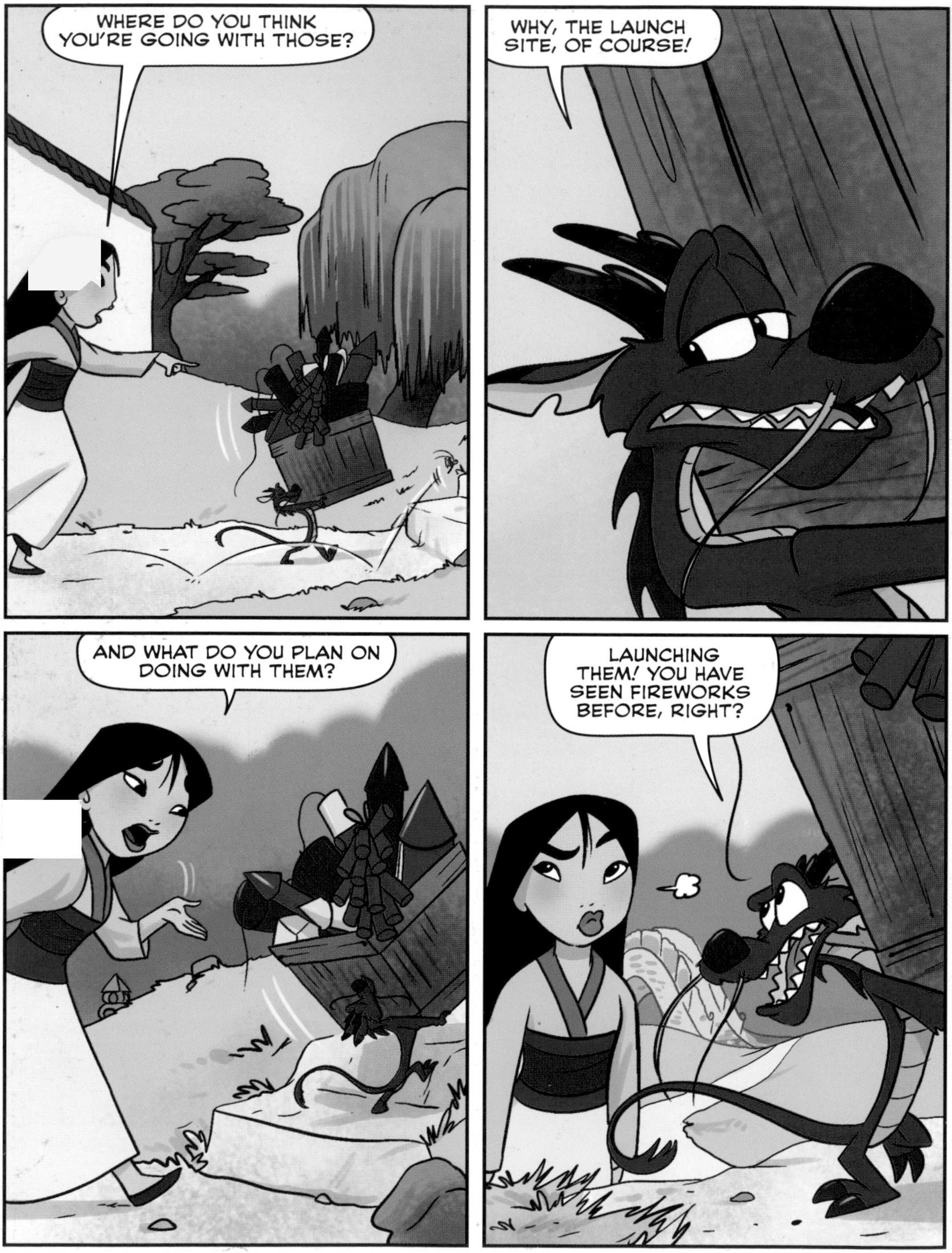
WHERE DO YOU THINK YOU'RE GOING WITH THOSE?
WHY, THE LAUNCH SITE, OF COURSE!
AND WHAT DO YOU PLAN ON DOING WITH THEM?
LAUNCHING THEM! YOU HAVE SEEN FIREWORKS BEFORE, RIGHT?

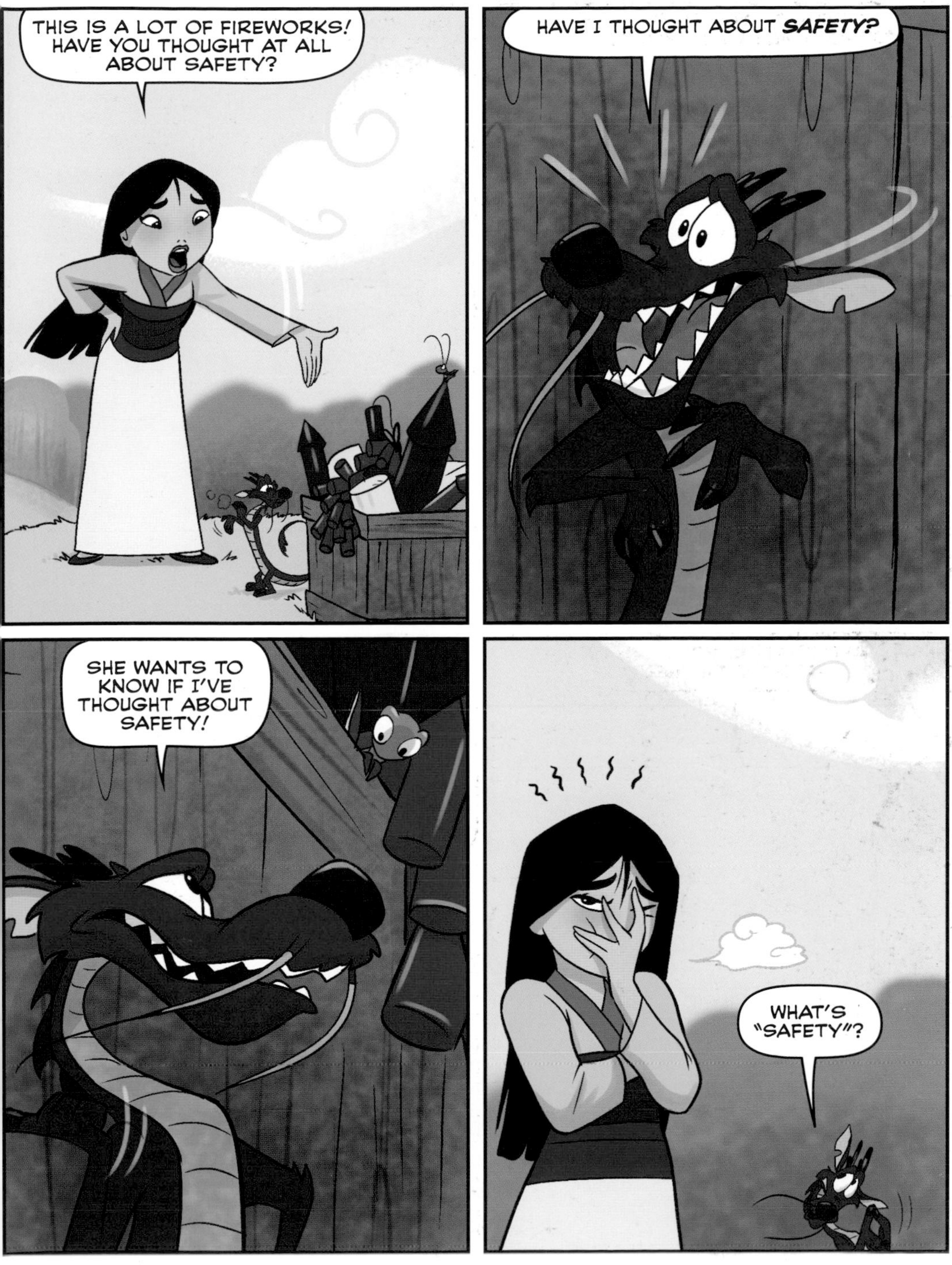
THIS IS A LOT OF FIREWORKS! HAVE YOU THOUGHT AT ALL ABOUT SAFETY?
HAVE I THOUGHT ABOUT **SAFETY?**
SHE WANTS TO KNOW IF I'VE THOUGHT ABOUT SAFETY!
WHAT'S "SAFETY"?

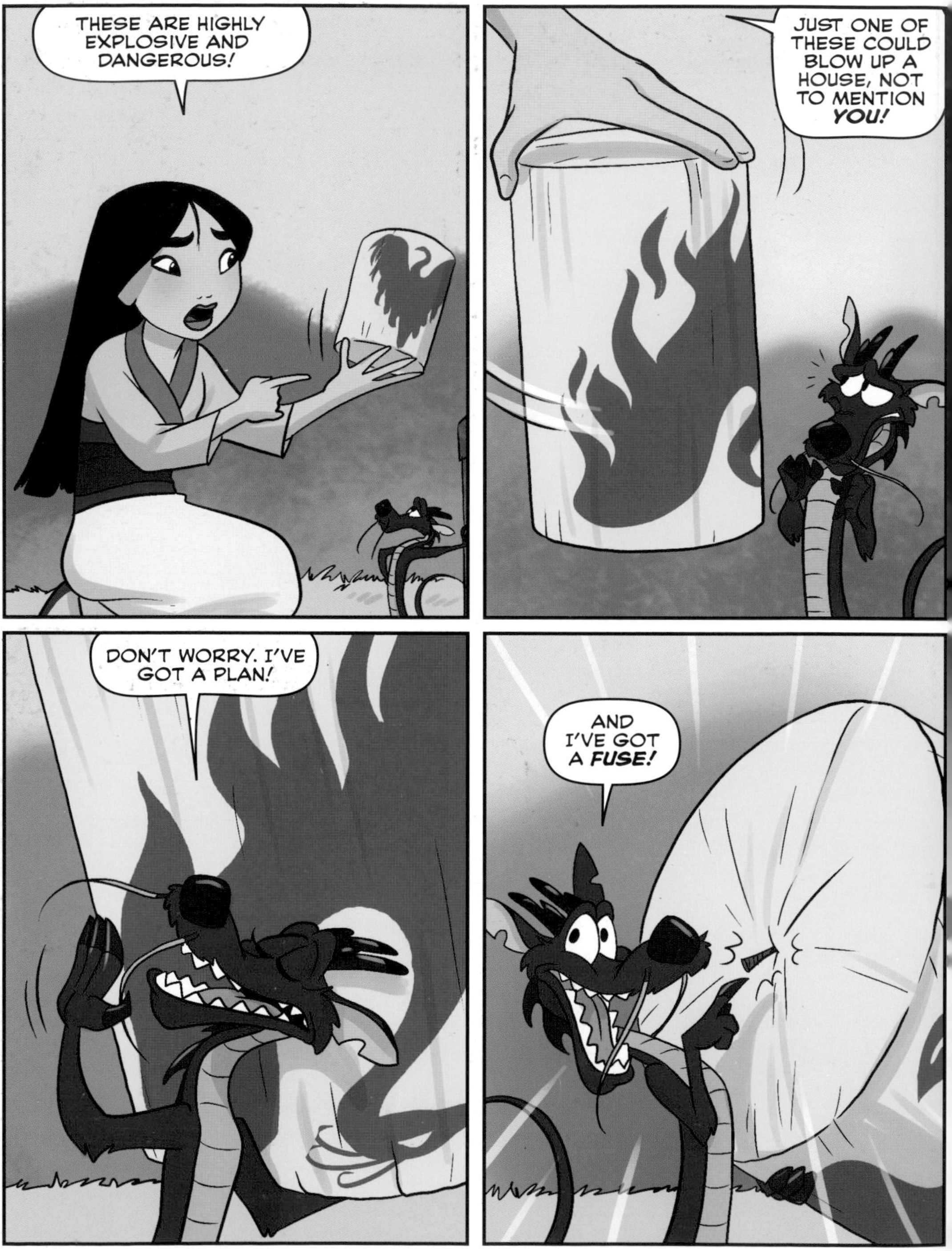
THESE ARE HIGHLY EXPLOSIVE AND DANGEROUS!
JUST ONE OF THESE COULD BLOW UP A HOUSE, NOT TO MENTION *YOU!*
DON'T WORRY. I'VE GOT A PLAN!
AND I'VE GOT A *FUSE!*

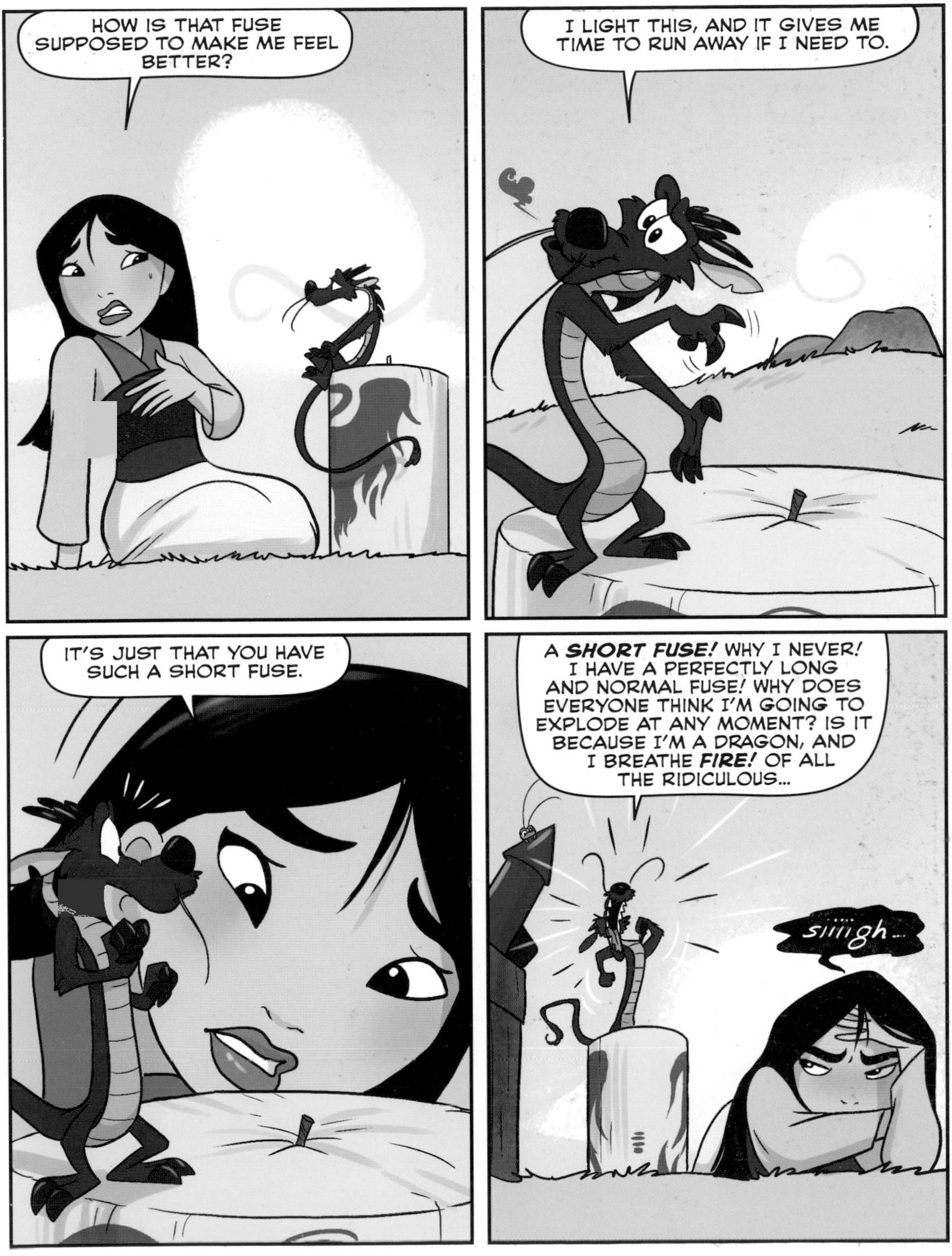
HOW IS THAT FUSE SUPPOSED TO MAKE ME FEEL BETTER?
I LIGHT THIS, AND IT GIVES ME TIME TO RUN AWAY IF I NEED TO.
IT'S JUST THAT YOU HAVE SUCH A SHORT FUSE.
A **SHORT FUSE!** WHY I NEVER! I HAVE A PERFECTLY LONG AND NORMAL FUSE! WHY DOES EVERYONE THINK I'M GOING TO EXPLODE AT ANY MOMENT? IS IT BECAUSE I'M A DRAGON, AND I BREATHE **FIRE!** OF ALL THE RIDICULOUS...
siiiigh...

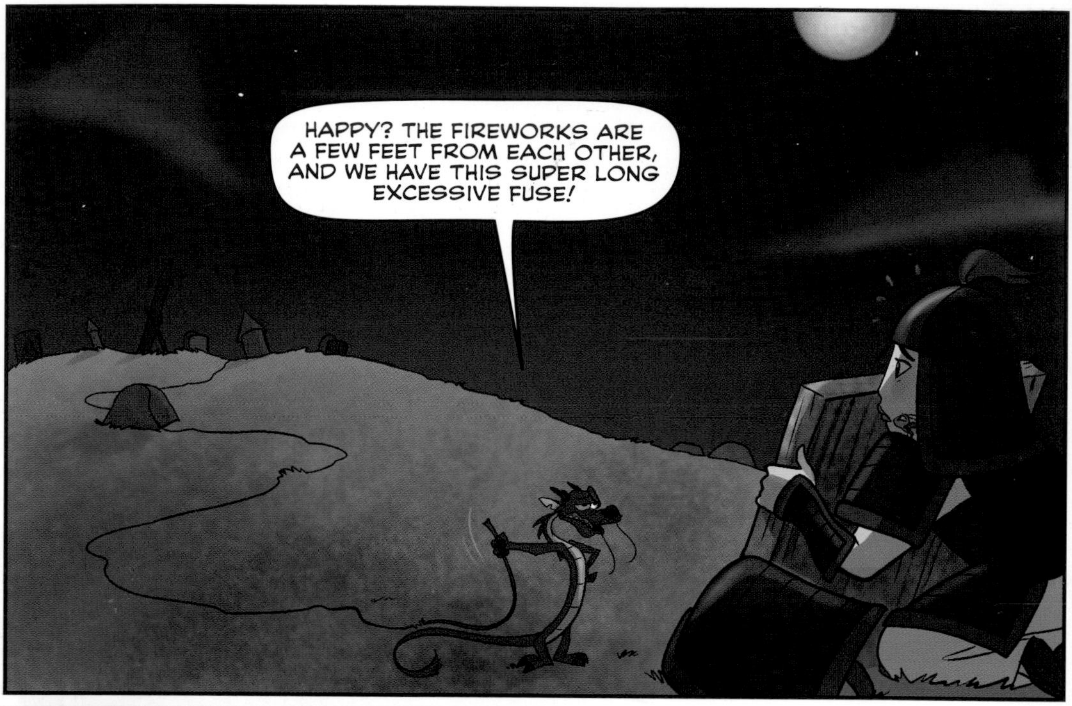
HAPPY? THE FIREWORKS ARE A FEW FEET FROM EACH OTHER, AND WE HAVE THIS SUPER LONG EXCESSIVE FUSE!

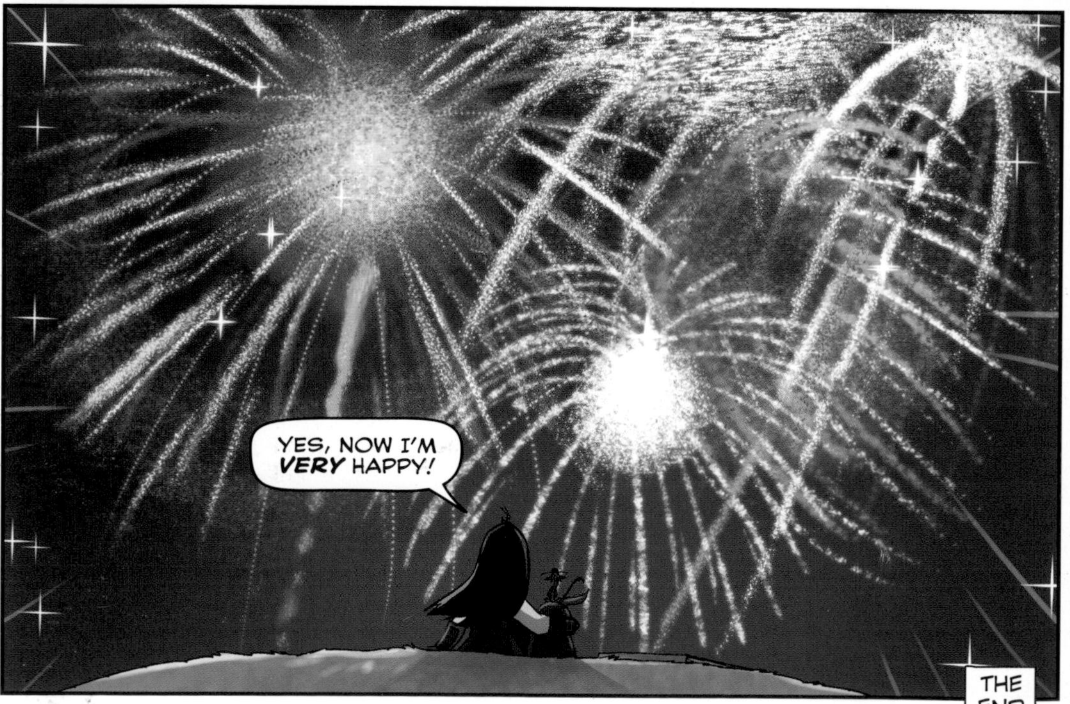
YES, NOW I'M **VERY** HAPPY!
THE END

"RISE AND SHINE"

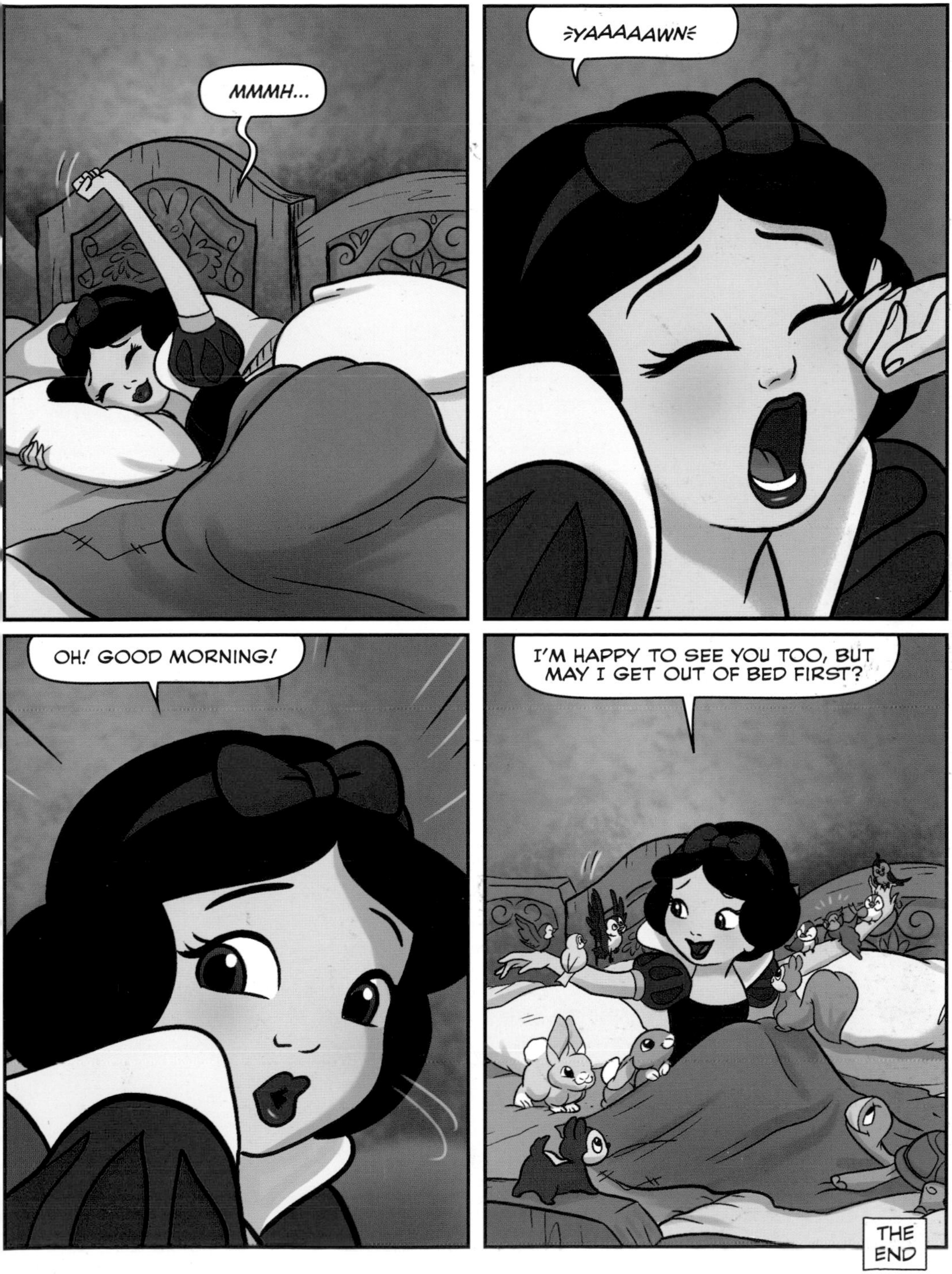
MMMH...
≡YAAAAAWN≡
OH! GOOD MORNING!
I'M HAPPY TO SEE YOU TOO, BUT MAY I GET OUT OF BED FIRST?
THE END

"PASCART"

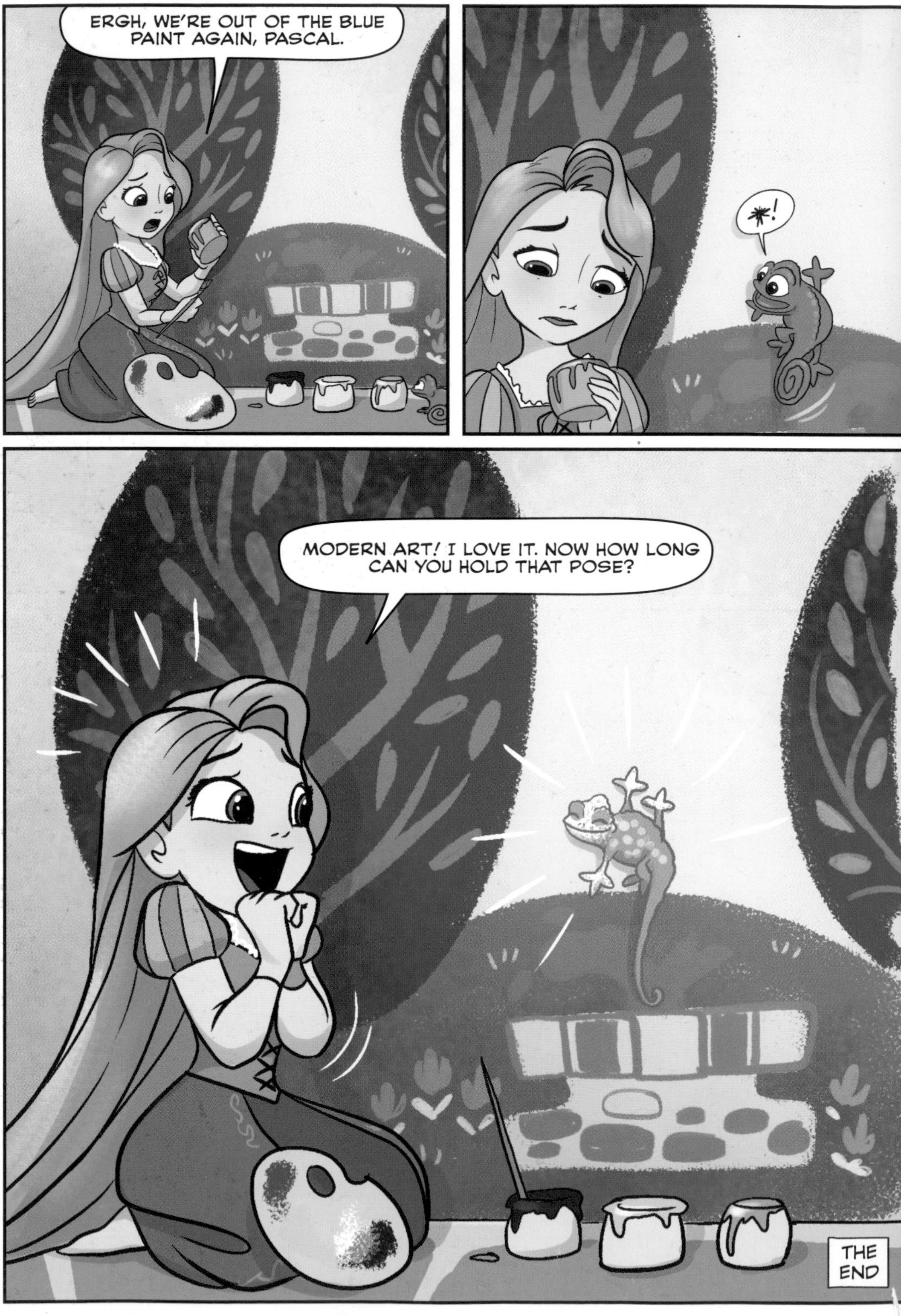
ERGH, WE'RE OUT OF THE BLUE PAINT AGAIN, PASCAL.
*!
MODERN ART! I LOVE IT. NOW HOW LONG CAN YOU HOLD THAT POSE?
THE END

"FIRST SNOWFALL"

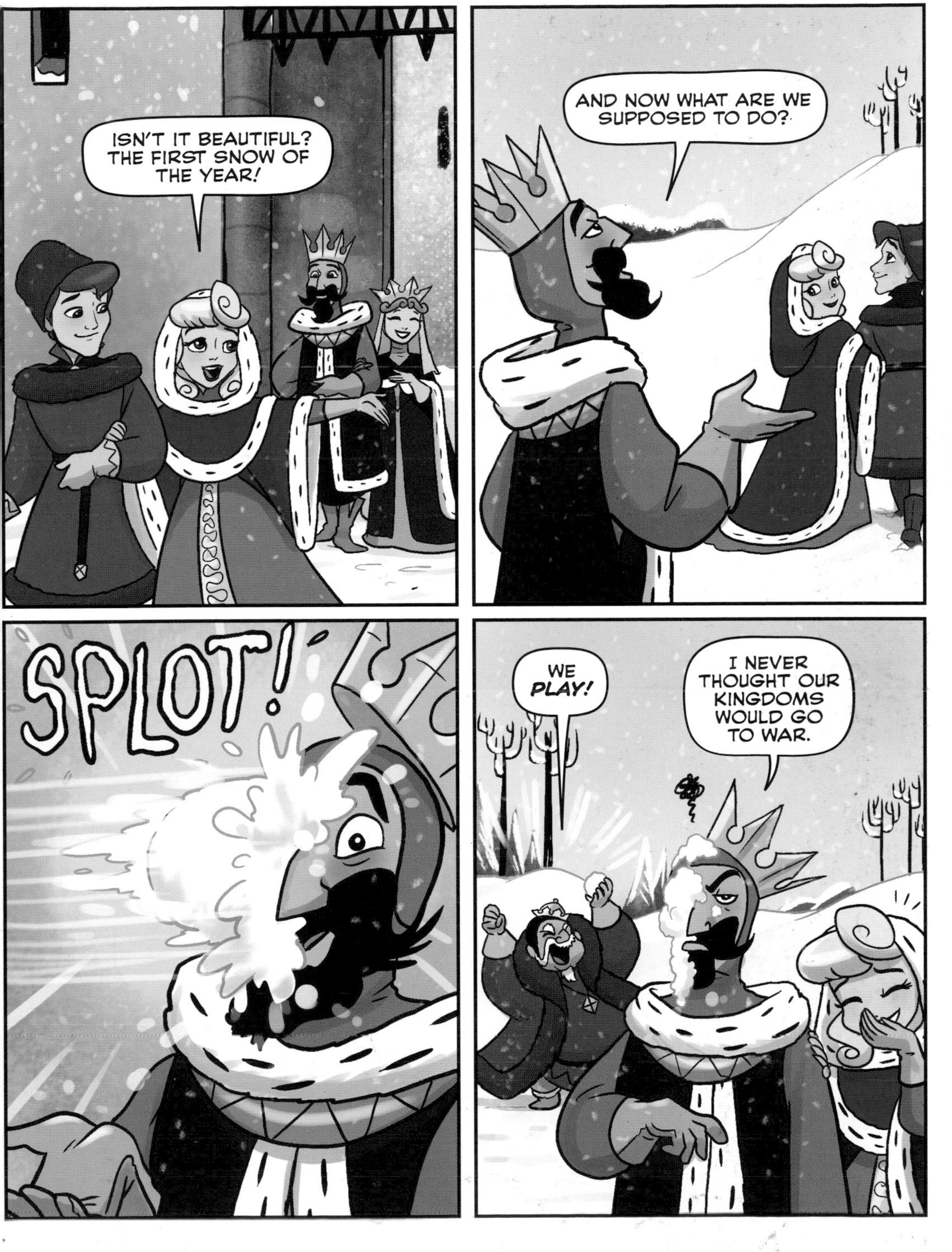

ISN'T IT BEAUTIFUL? THE FIRST SNOW OF THE YEAR!
AND NOW WHAT ARE WE SUPPOSED TO DO?
SPLOT!
WE *PLAY!*
I NEVER THOUGHT OUR KINGDOMS WOULD GO TO WAR.

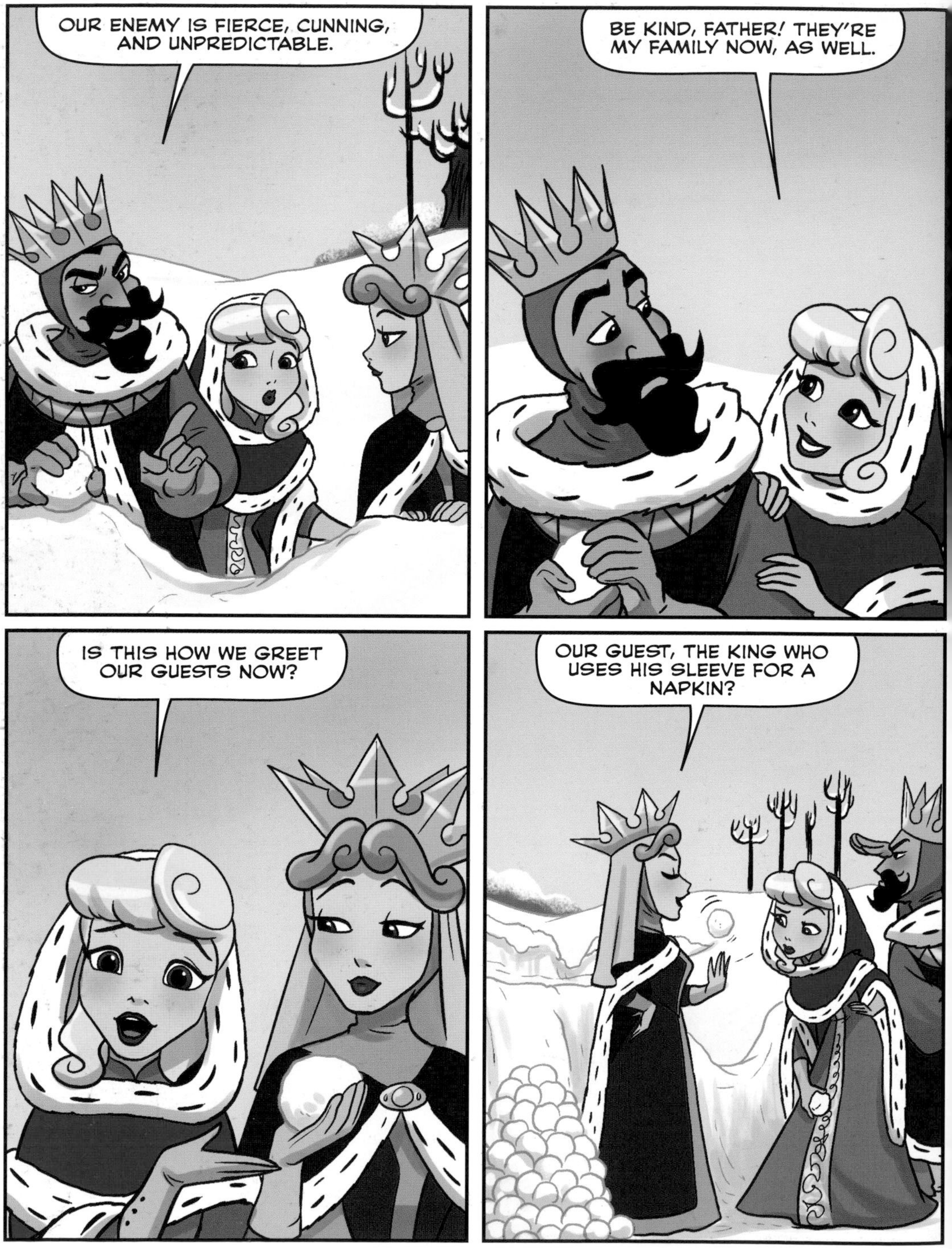
OUR ENEMY IS FIERCE, CUNNING, AND UNPREDICTABLE.
BE KIND, FATHER! THEY'RE MY FAMILY NOW, AS WELL.
IS THIS HOW WE GREET OUR GUESTS NOW?
OUR GUEST, THE KING WHO USES HIS SLEEVE FOR A NAPKIN?

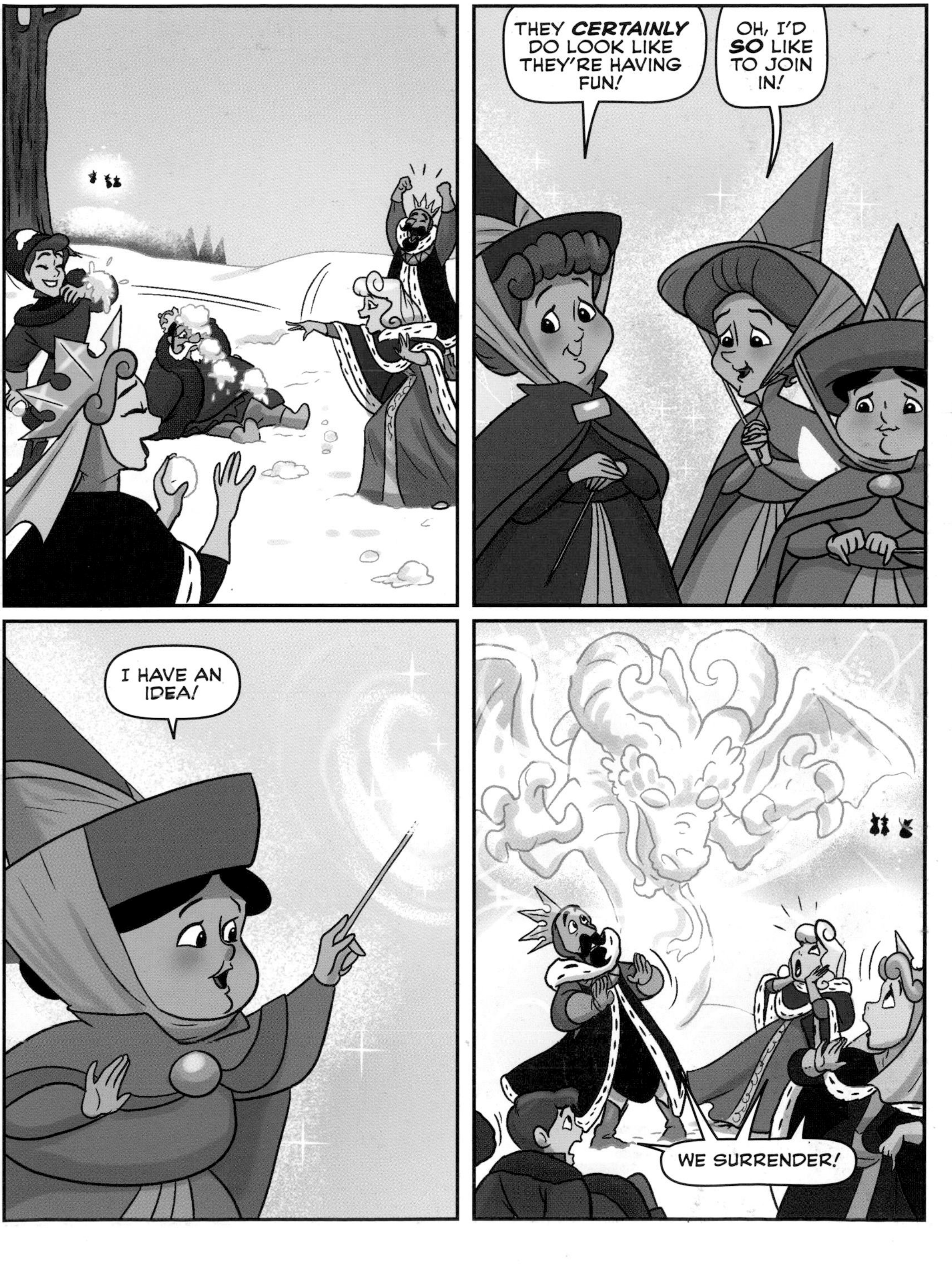
THEY *CERTAINLY* DO LOOK LIKE THEY'RE HAVING FUN!
OH, I'D *SO* LIKE TO JOIN IN!
I HAVE AN IDEA!
WE SURRENDER!

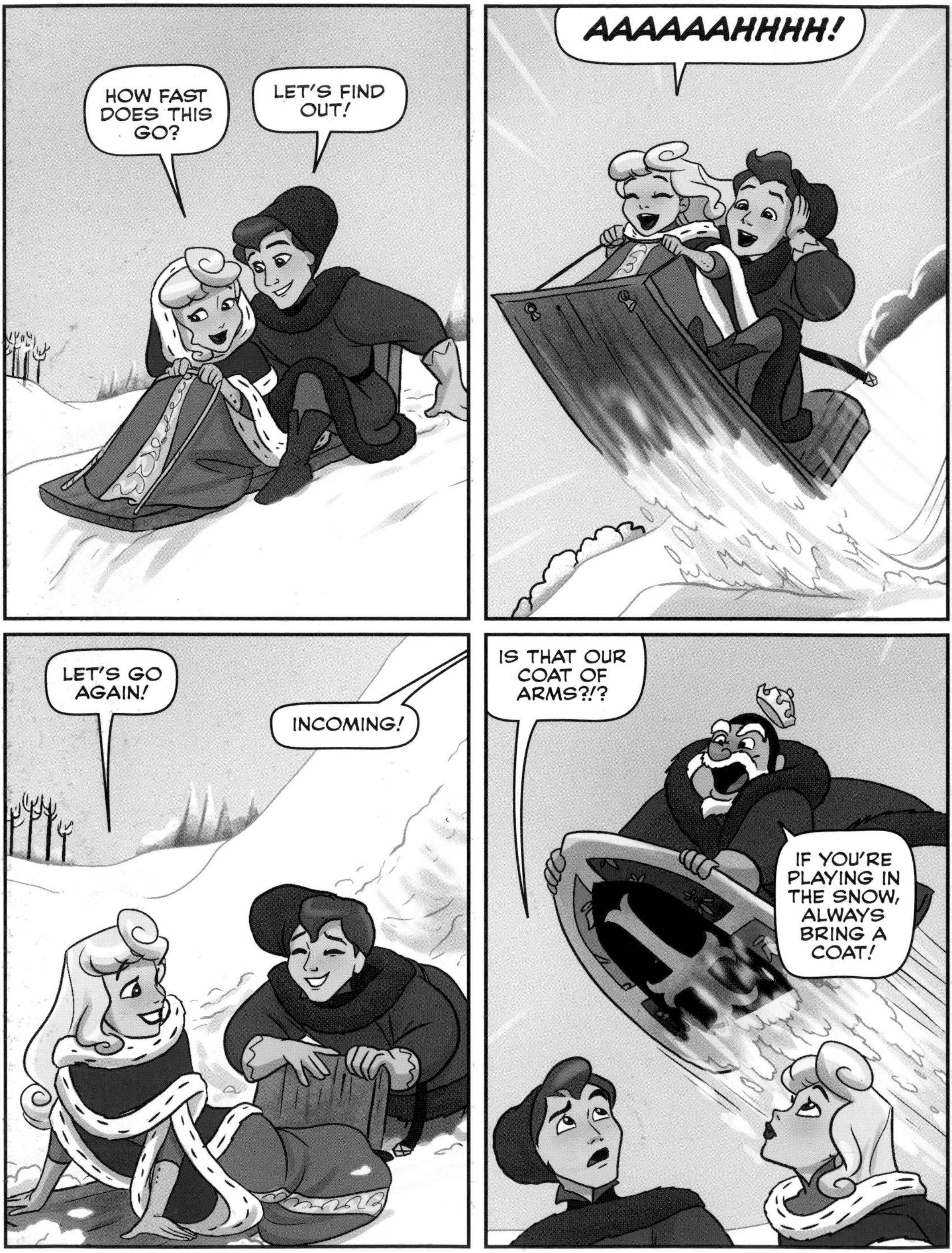
HOW FAST DOES THIS GO?
LET'S FIND OUT!
AAAAAAHHHH!
LET'S GO AGAIN!
INCOMING!
IS THAT OUR COAT OF ARMS?!?
IF YOU'RE PLAYING IN THE SNOW, ALWAYS BRING A COAT!

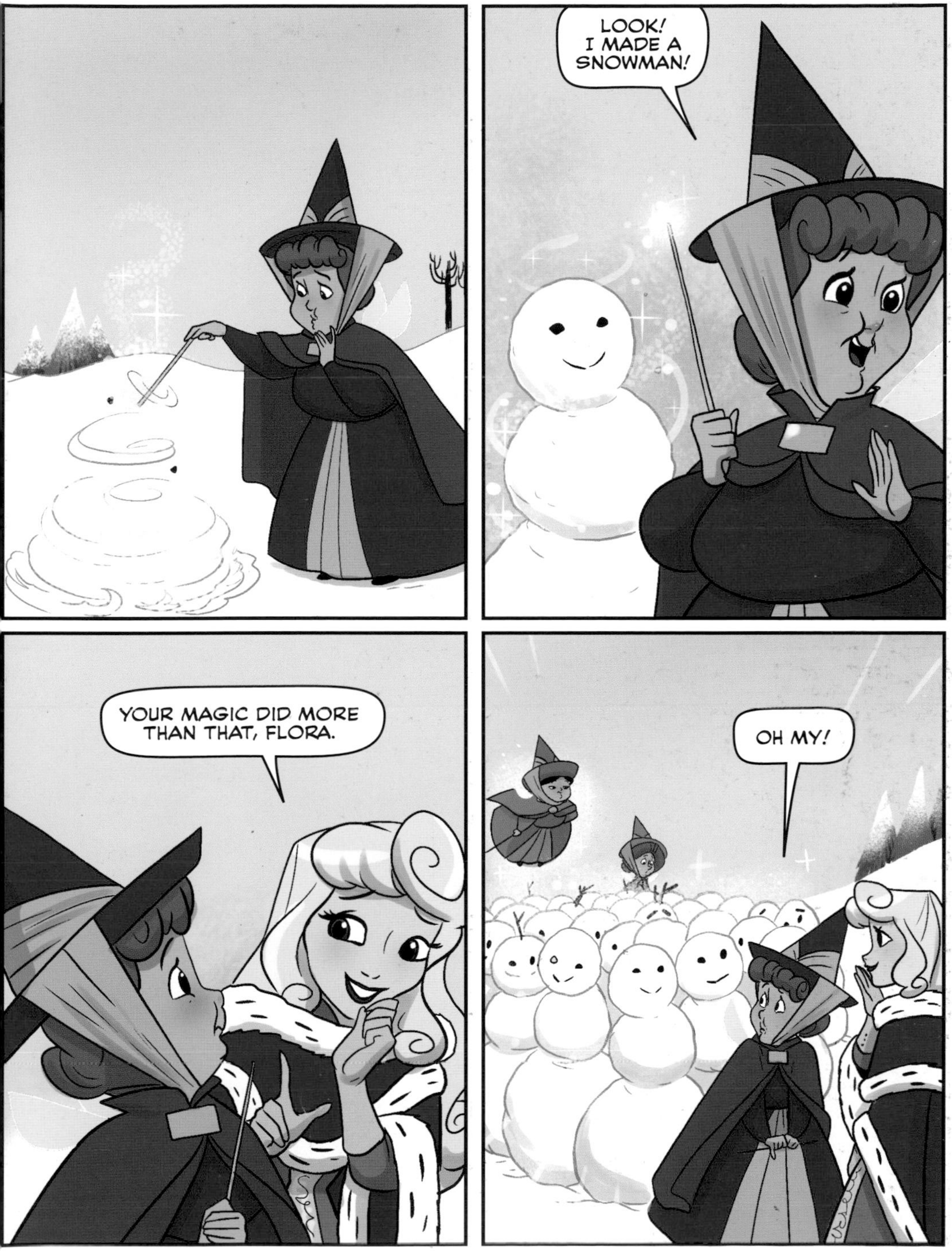
LOOK! I MADE A SNOWMAN!
YOUR MAGIC DID MORE THAN THAT, FLORA.
OH MY!

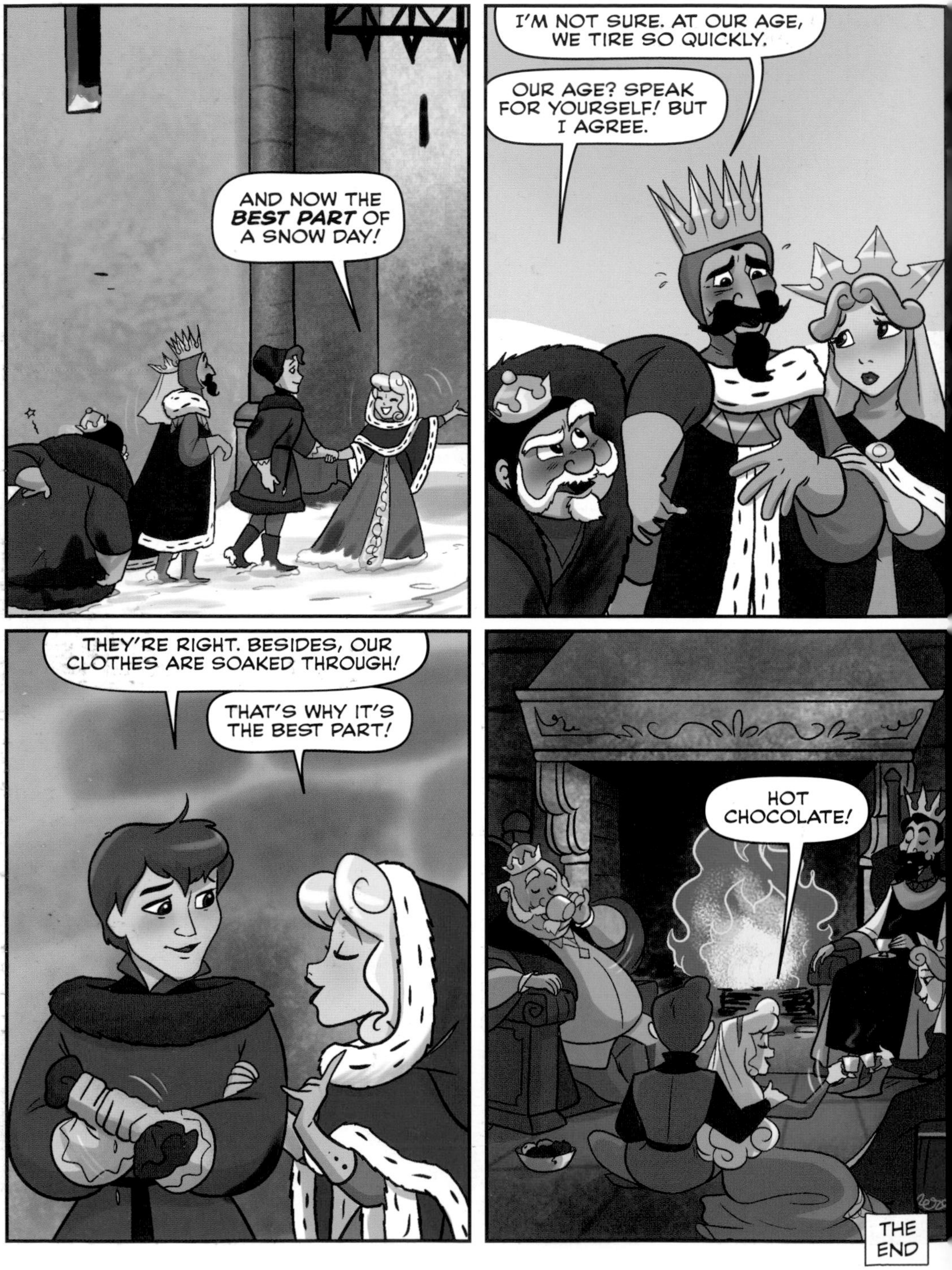
AND NOW THE **BEST PART** OF A SNOW DAY!
I'M NOT SURE. AT OUR AGE, WE TIRE SO QUICKLY.
OUR AGE? SPEAK FOR YOURSELF! BUT I AGREE.
THEY'RE RIGHT. BESIDES, OUR CLOTHES ARE SOAKED THROUGH!
THAT'S WHY IT'S THE BEST PART!
HOT CHOCOLATE!
THE END

"WHATEVER YOU WISH FOR"

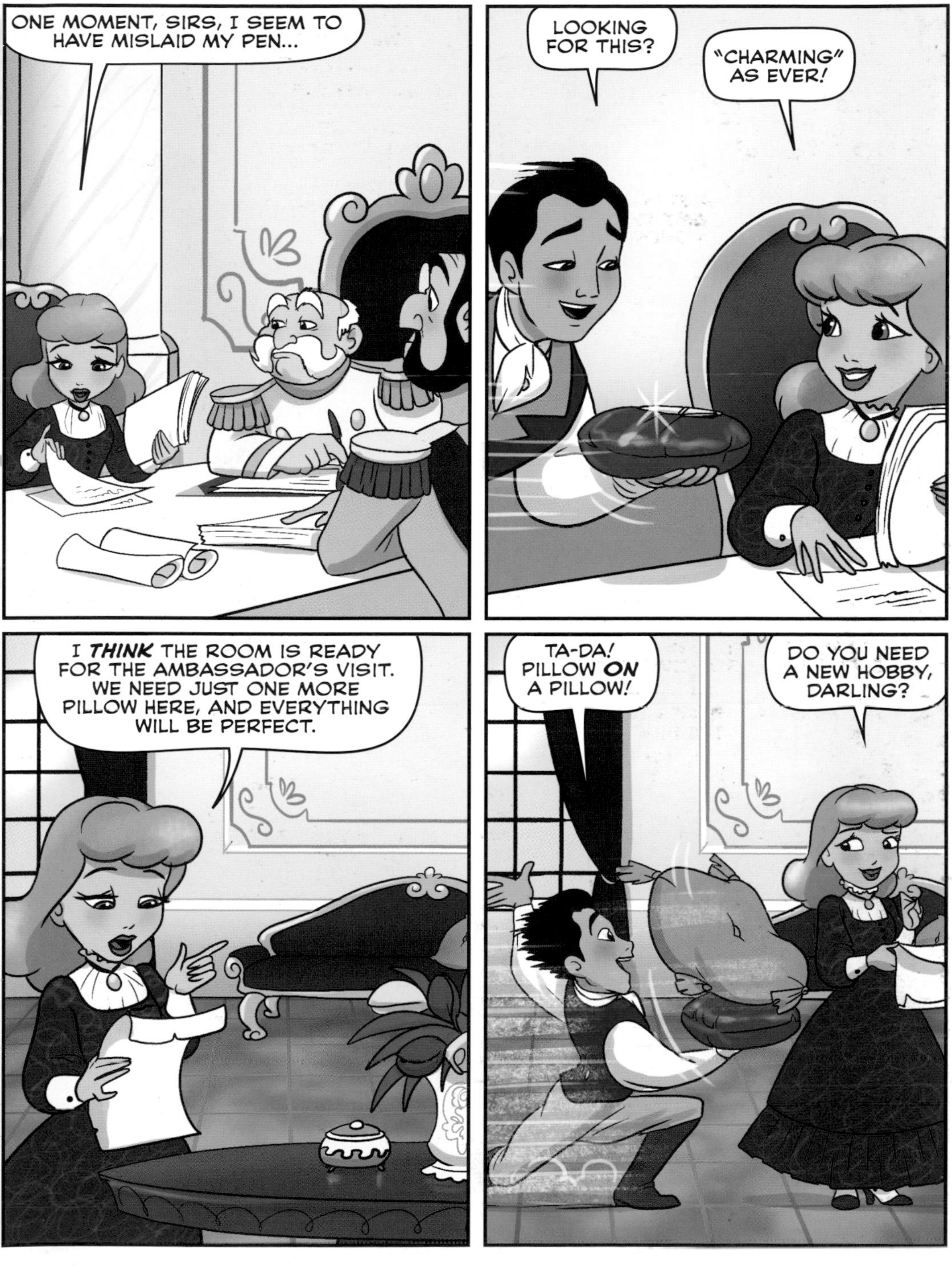
ONE MOMENT, SIRS, I SEEM TO HAVE MISLAID MY PEN...
LOOKING FOR THIS?
"CHARMING" AS EVER!
I *THINK* THE ROOM IS READY FOR THE AMBASSADOR'S VISIT. WE NEED JUST ONE MORE PILLOW HERE, AND EVERYTHING WILL BE PERFECT.
TA-DA! PILLOW *ON* A PILLOW!
DO YOU NEED A NEW HOBBY, DARLING?

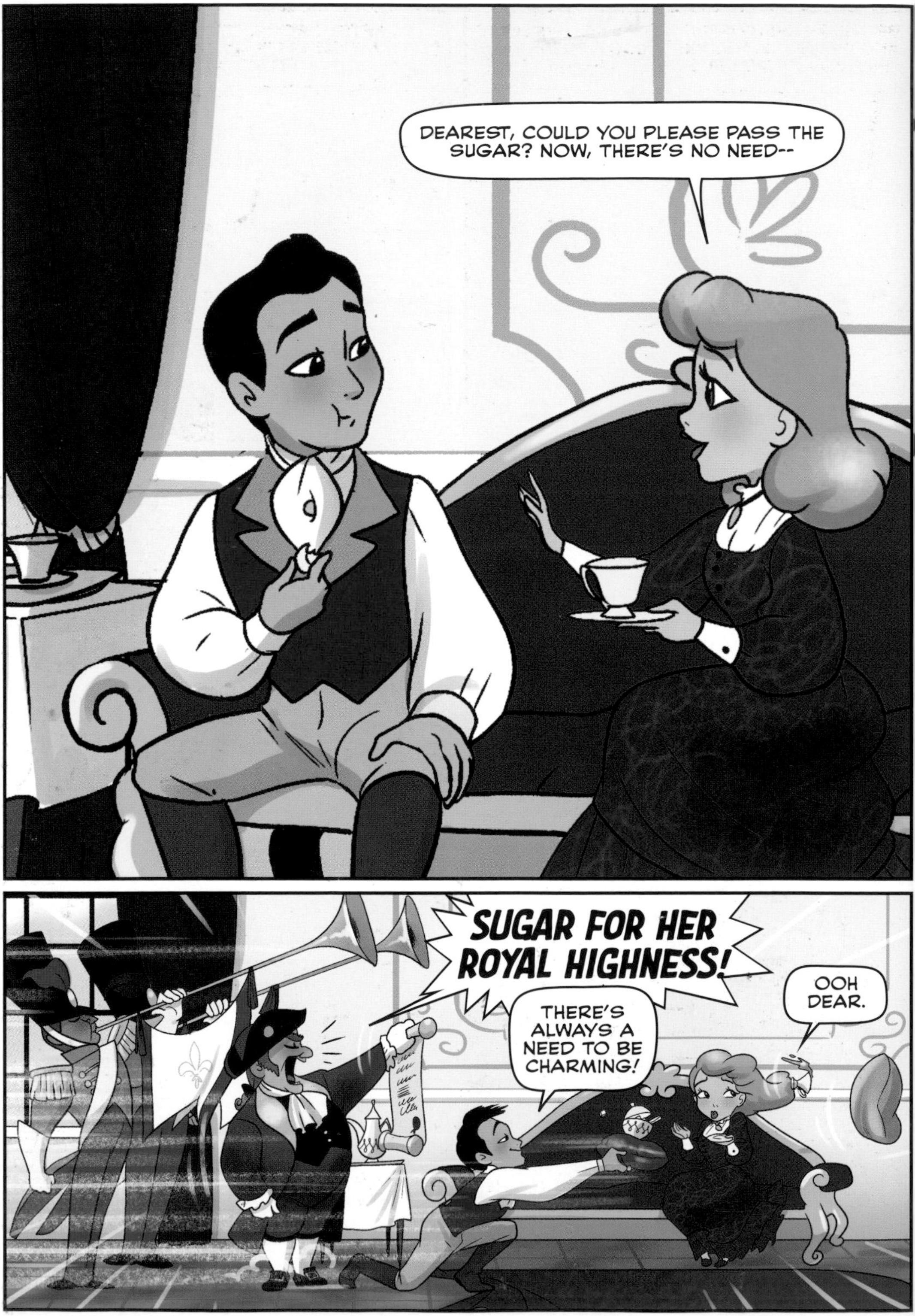
DEAREST, COULD YOU PLEASE PASS THE SUGAR? NOW, THERE'S NO NEED--
SUGAR FOR HER ROYAL HIGHNESS!
THERE'S ALWAYS A NEED TO BE CHARMING!
OOH DEAR.

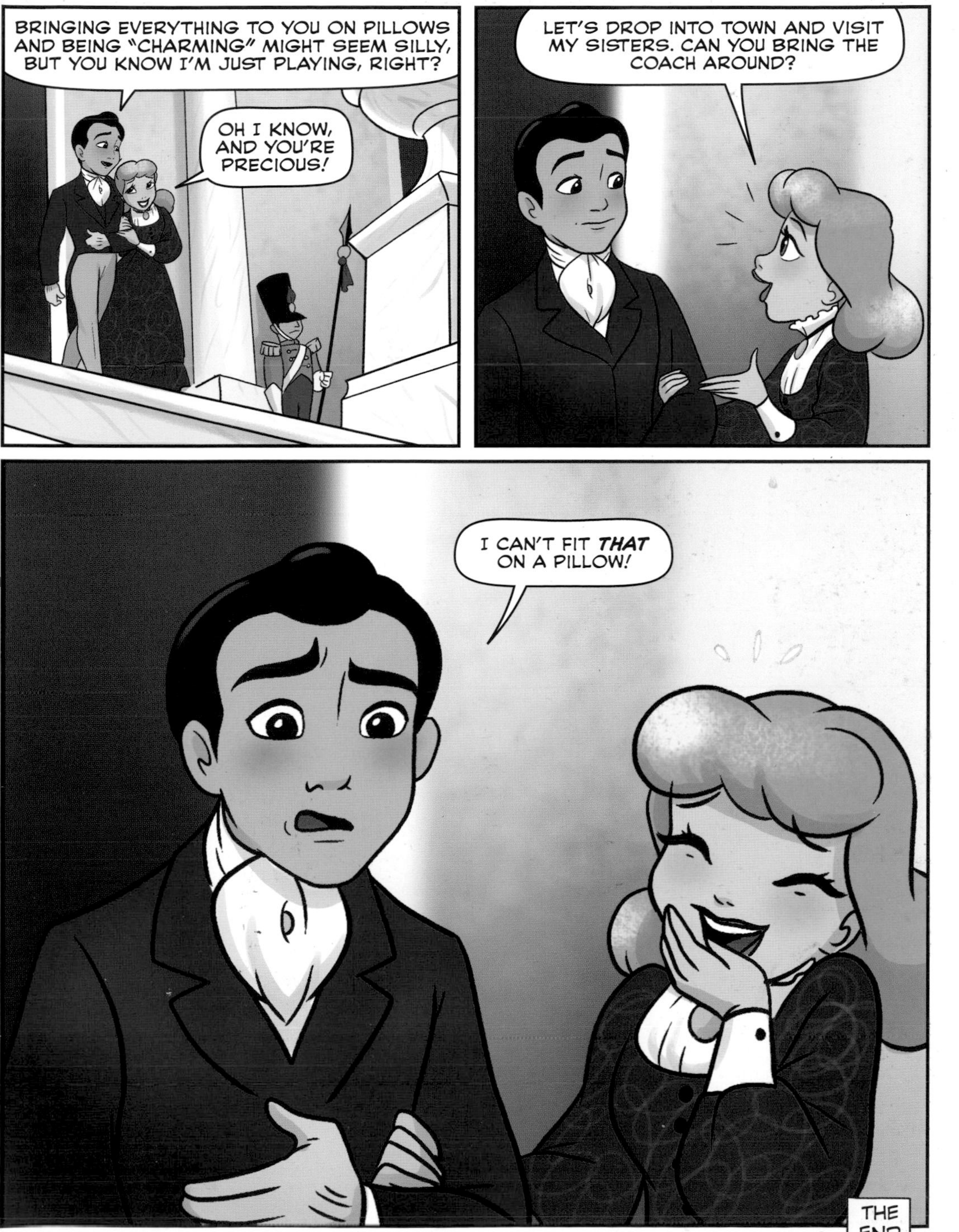
BRINGING EVERYTHING TO YOU ON PILLOWS AND BEING "CHARMING" MIGHT SEEM SILLY, BUT YOU KNOW I'M JUST PLAYING, RIGHT?
OH I KNOW, AND YOU'RE PRECIOUS!
LET'S DROP INTO TOWN AND VISIT MY SISTERS. CAN YOU BRING THE COACH AROUND?
I CAN'T FIT *THAT* ON A PILLOW!
THE END

"SAXOPHONE"

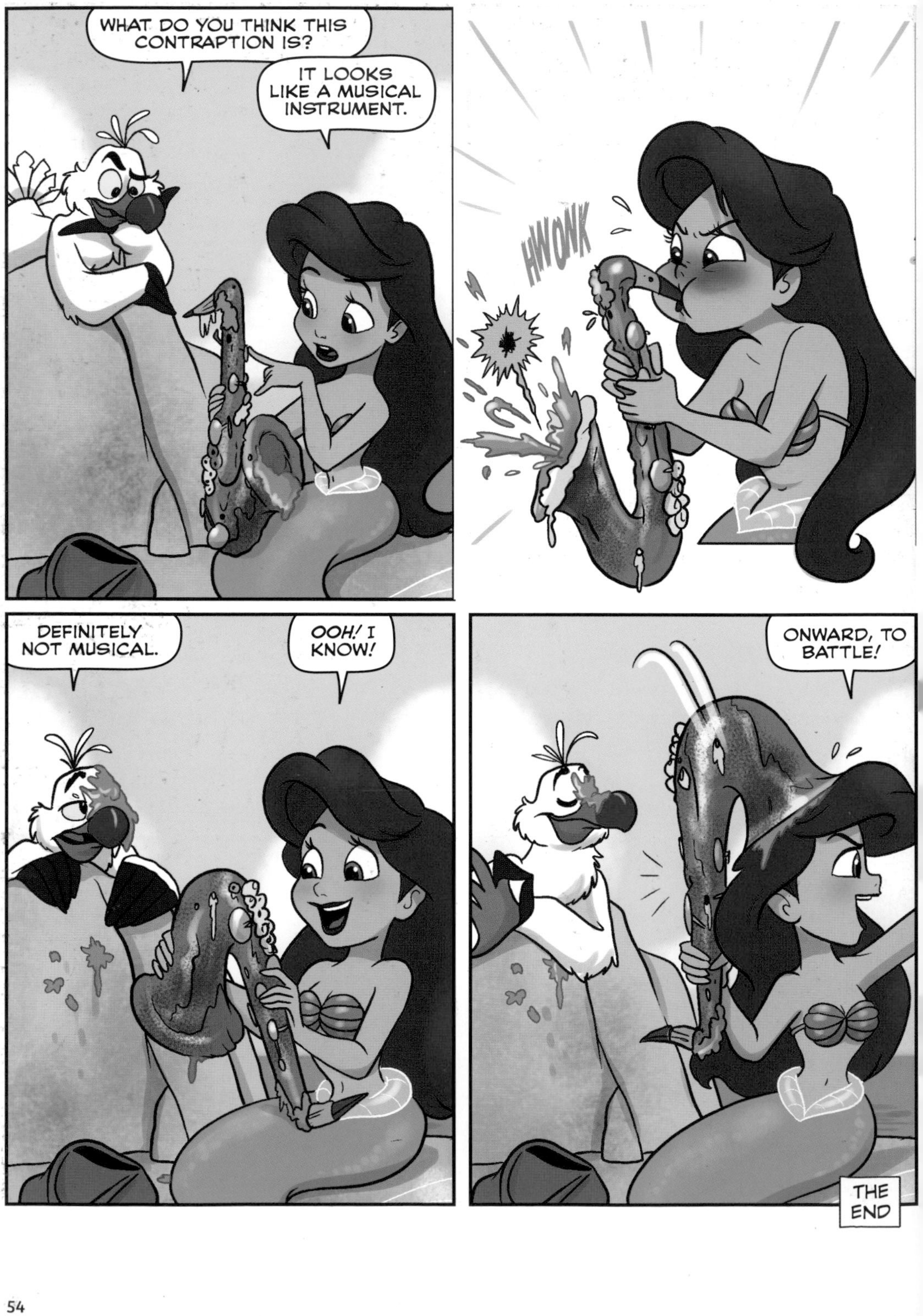
WHAT DO YOU THINK THIS CONTRAPTION IS?
IT LOOKS LIKE A MUSICAL INSTRUMENT.
HWONK
DEFINITELY NOT MUSICAL.
OOH! I KNOW!
ONWARD, TO BATTLE!
THE END

"TAG, YOU'RE IT!"

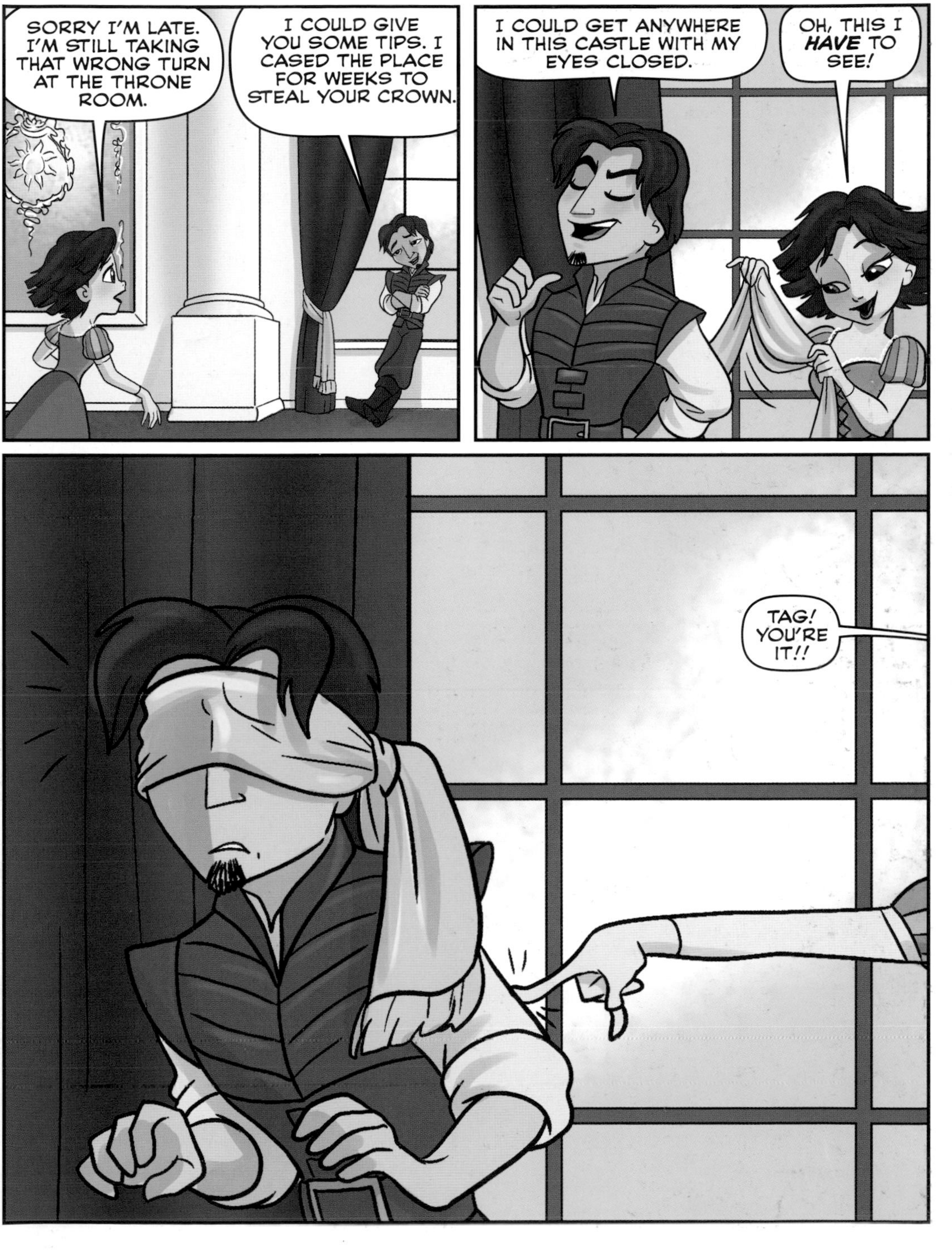
SORRY I'M LATE. I'M STILL TAKING THAT WRONG TURN AT THE THRONE ROOM.
I COULD GIVE YOU SOME TIPS. I CASED THE PLACE FOR WEEKS TO STEAL YOUR CROWN.
I COULD GET ANYWHERE IN THIS CASTLE WITH MY EYES CLOSED.
OH, THIS I ***HAVE*** TO SEE!
TAG! YOU'RE IT!!

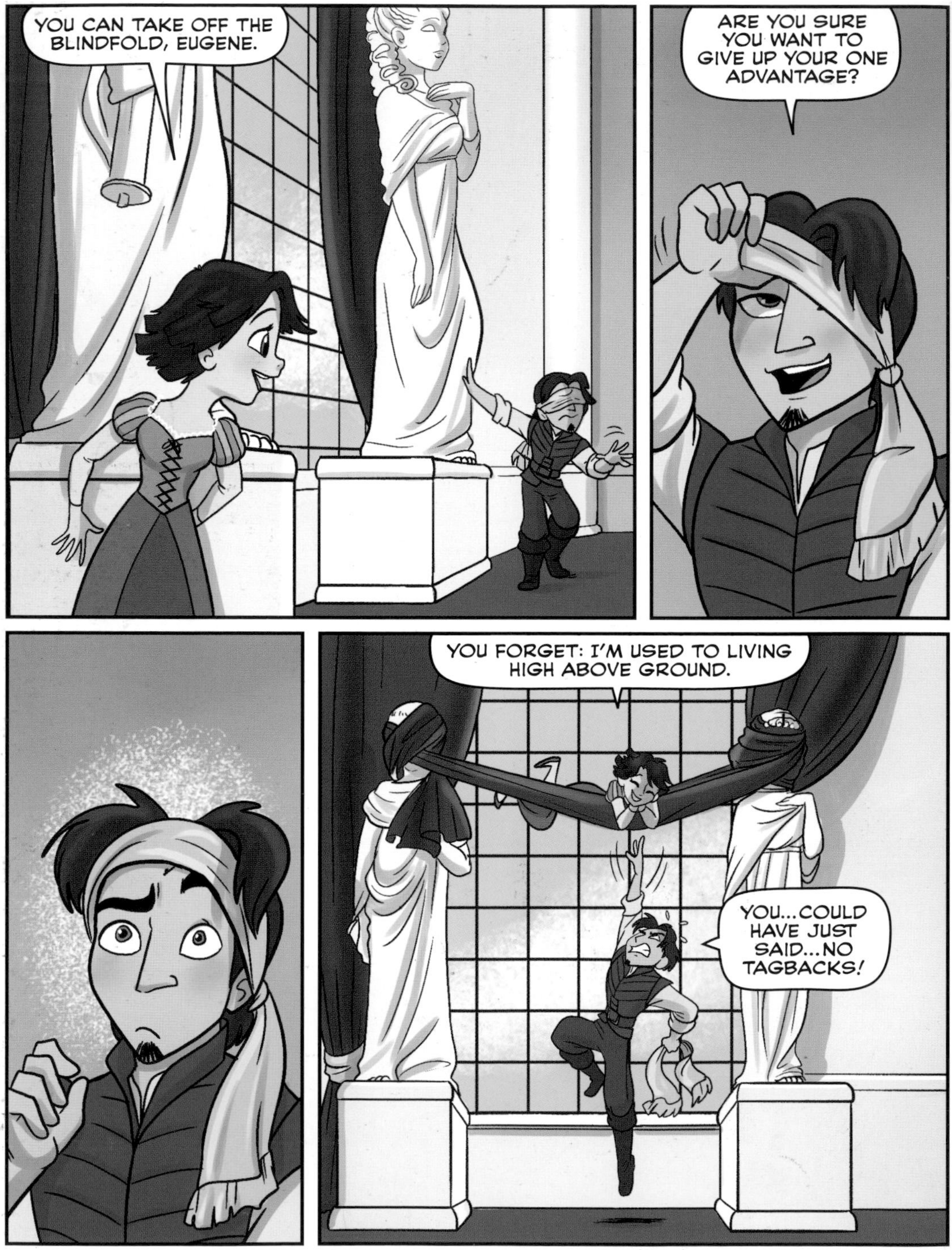
YOU CAN TAKE OFF THE BLINDFOLD, EUGENE.
ARE YOU SURE YOU WANT TO GIVE UP YOUR ONE ADVANTAGE?
YOU FORGET: I'M USED TO LIVING HIGH ABOVE GROUND.
YOU...COULD HAVE JUST SAID...NO TAGBACKS!

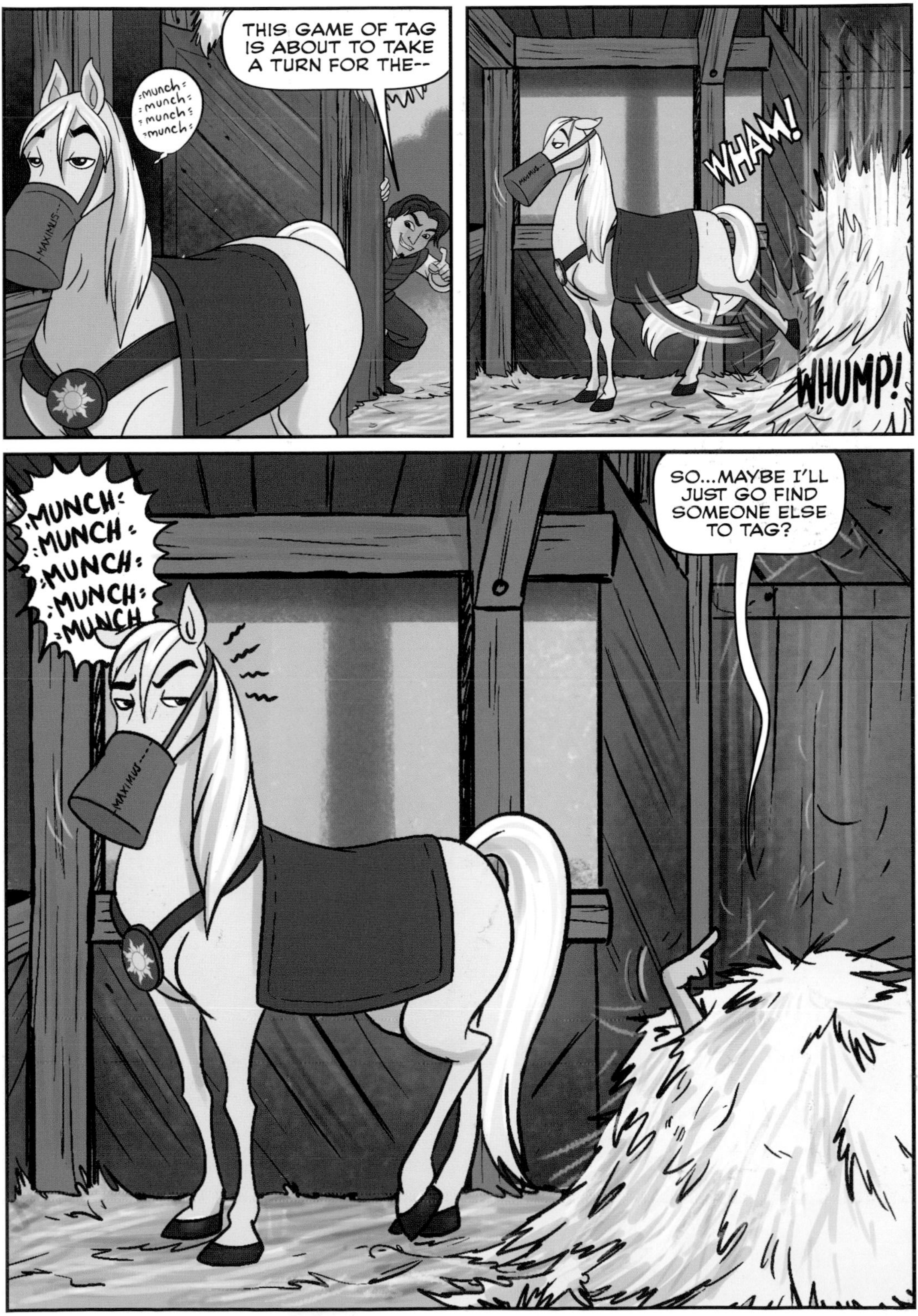
THIS GAME OF TAG IS ABOUT TO TAKE A TURN FOR THE--
munch munch munch munch
MAXIMUS
WHAM!
WHUMP!
MUNCH MUNCH MUNCH MUNCH MUNCH
MAXIMUS
SO...MAYBE I'LL JUST GO FIND SOMEONE ELSE TO TAG?

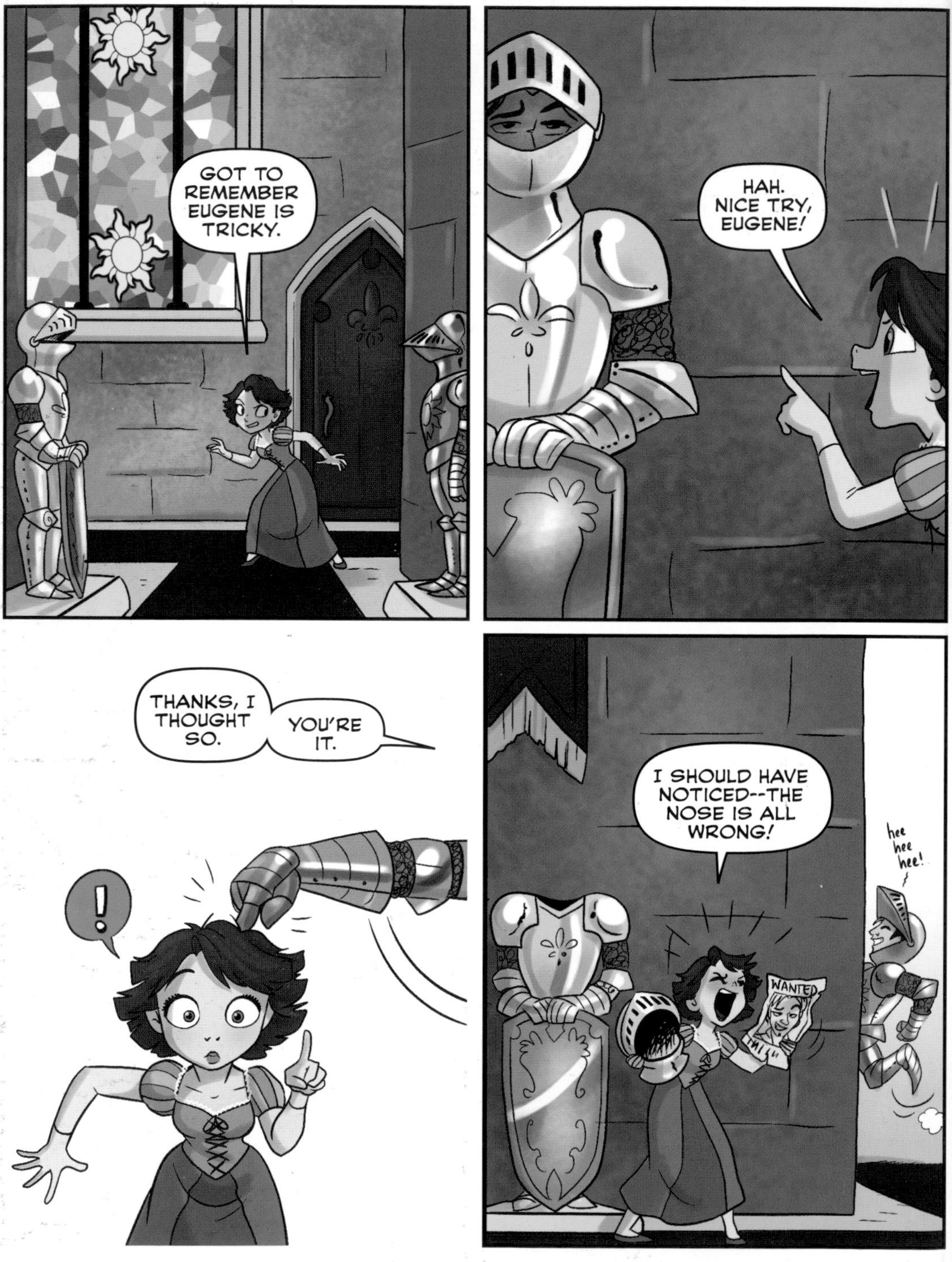
GOT TO REMEMBER EUGENE IS TRICKY.
HAH. NICE TRY, EUGENE!
THANKS, I THOUGHT SO.
YOU'RE IT.
!
I SHOULD HAVE NOTICED--THE NOSE IS ALL WRONG!
WANTED
hee hee hee!

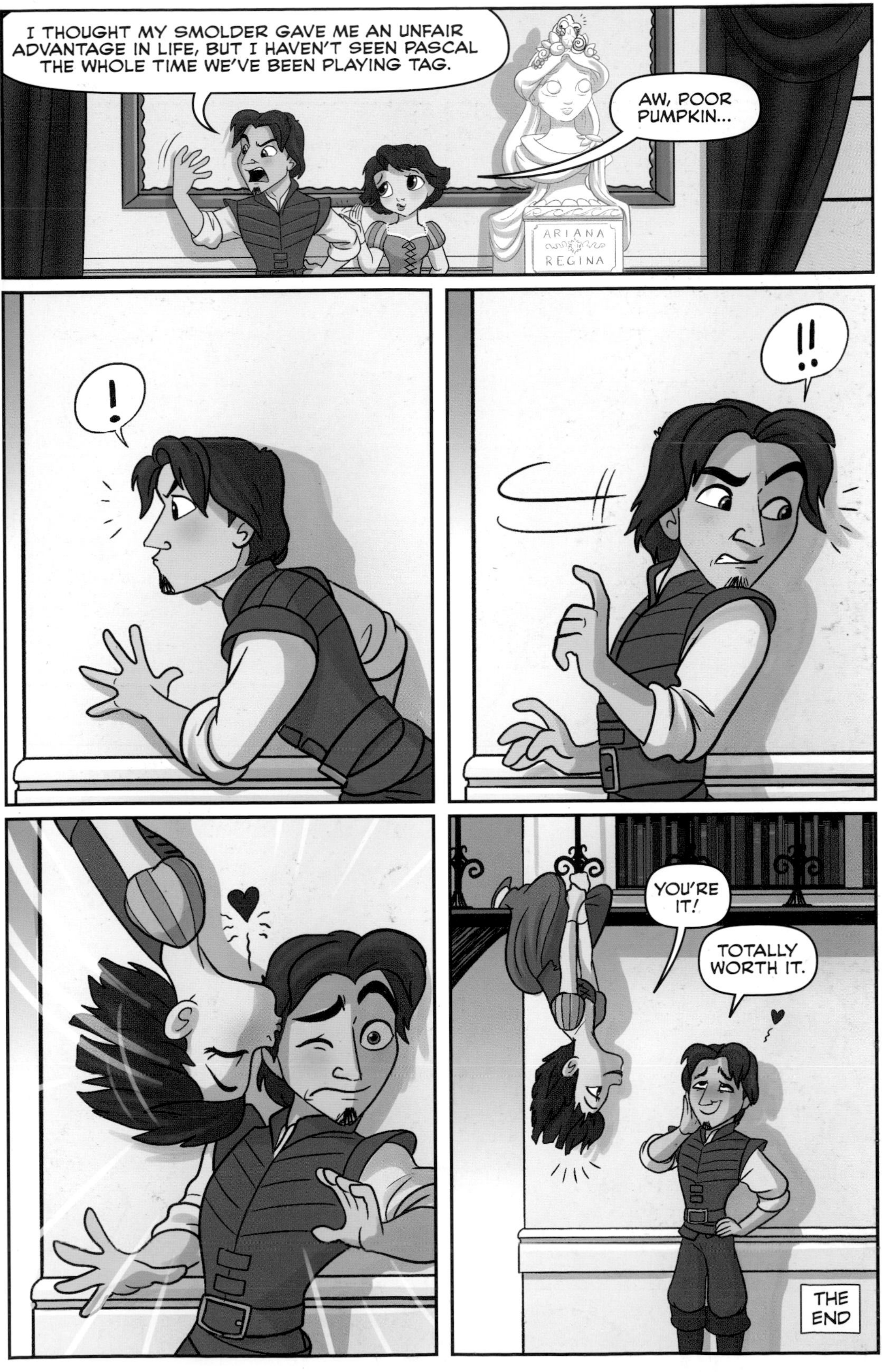
I THOUGHT MY SMOLDER GAVE ME AN UNFAIR ADVANTAGE IN LIFE, BUT I HAVEN'T SEEN PASCAL THE WHOLE TIME WE'VE BEEN PLAYING TAG.
AW, POOR PUMPKIN...
ARIANA REGINA
!
!!
YOU'RE IT!
TOTALLY WORTH IT.
THE END

"DISGUISE"

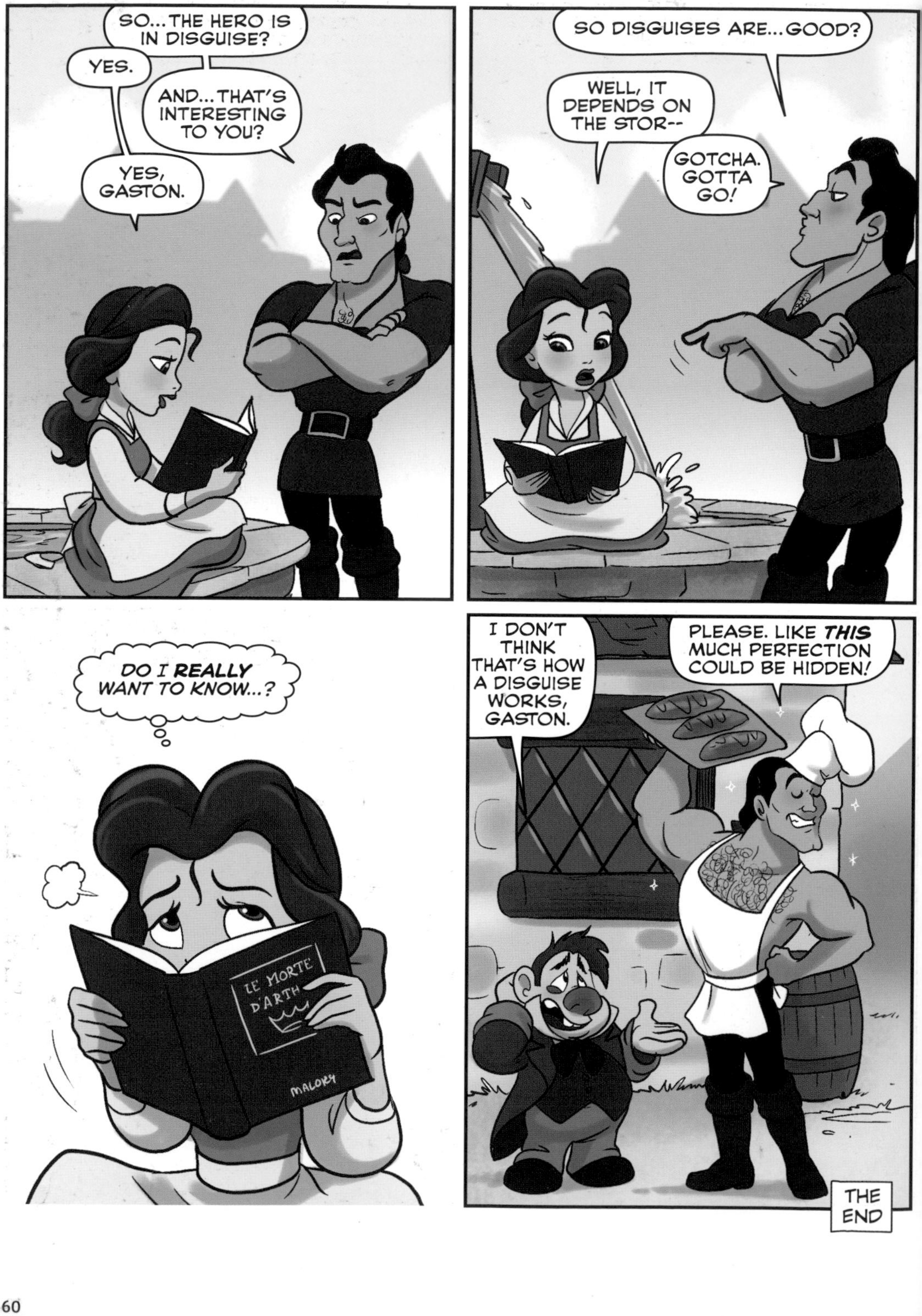

SO... THE HERO IS IN DISGUISE?
YES.
AND... THAT'S INTERESTING TO YOU?
YES, GASTON.
SO DISGUISES ARE... GOOD?
WELL, IT DEPENDS ON THE STOR--
GOTCHA. GOTTA GO!
DO I **REALLY** WANT TO KNOW...?
LE MORTE D'ARTH
MALORY
I DON'T THINK THAT'S HOW A DISGUISE WORKS, GASTON.
PLEASE. LIKE ***THIS*** MUCH PERFECTION COULD BE HIDDEN!
THE END

"BABYSITTING"

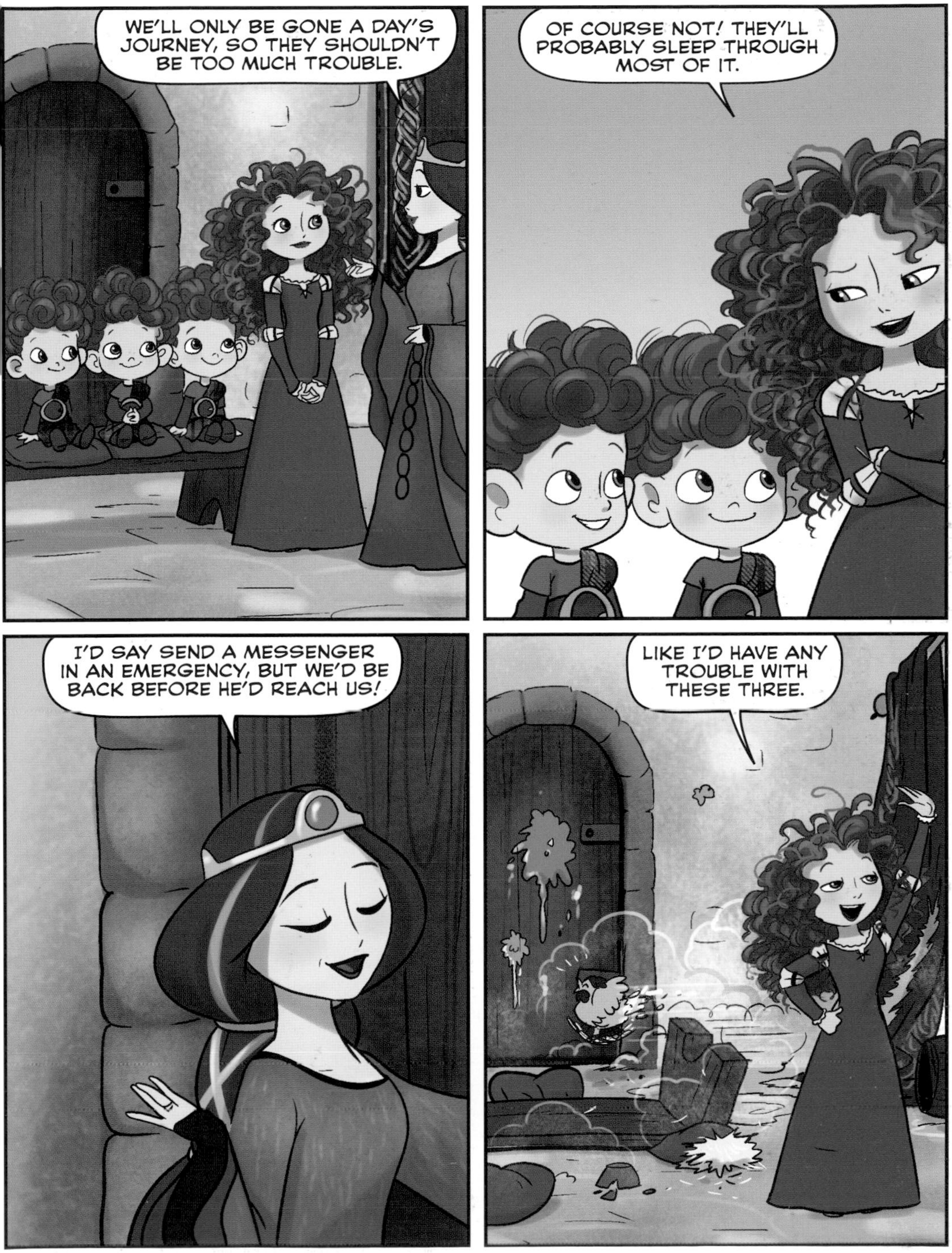
WE'LL ONLY BE GONE A DAY'S JOURNEY, SO THEY SHOULDN'T BE TOO MUCH TROUBLE.
OF COURSE NOT! THEY'LL PROBABLY SLEEP THROUGH MOST OF IT.
I'D SAY SEND A MESSENGER IN AN EMERGENCY, BUT WE'D BE BACK BEFORE HE'D REACH US!
LIKE I'D HAVE ANY TROUBLE WITH THESE THREE.

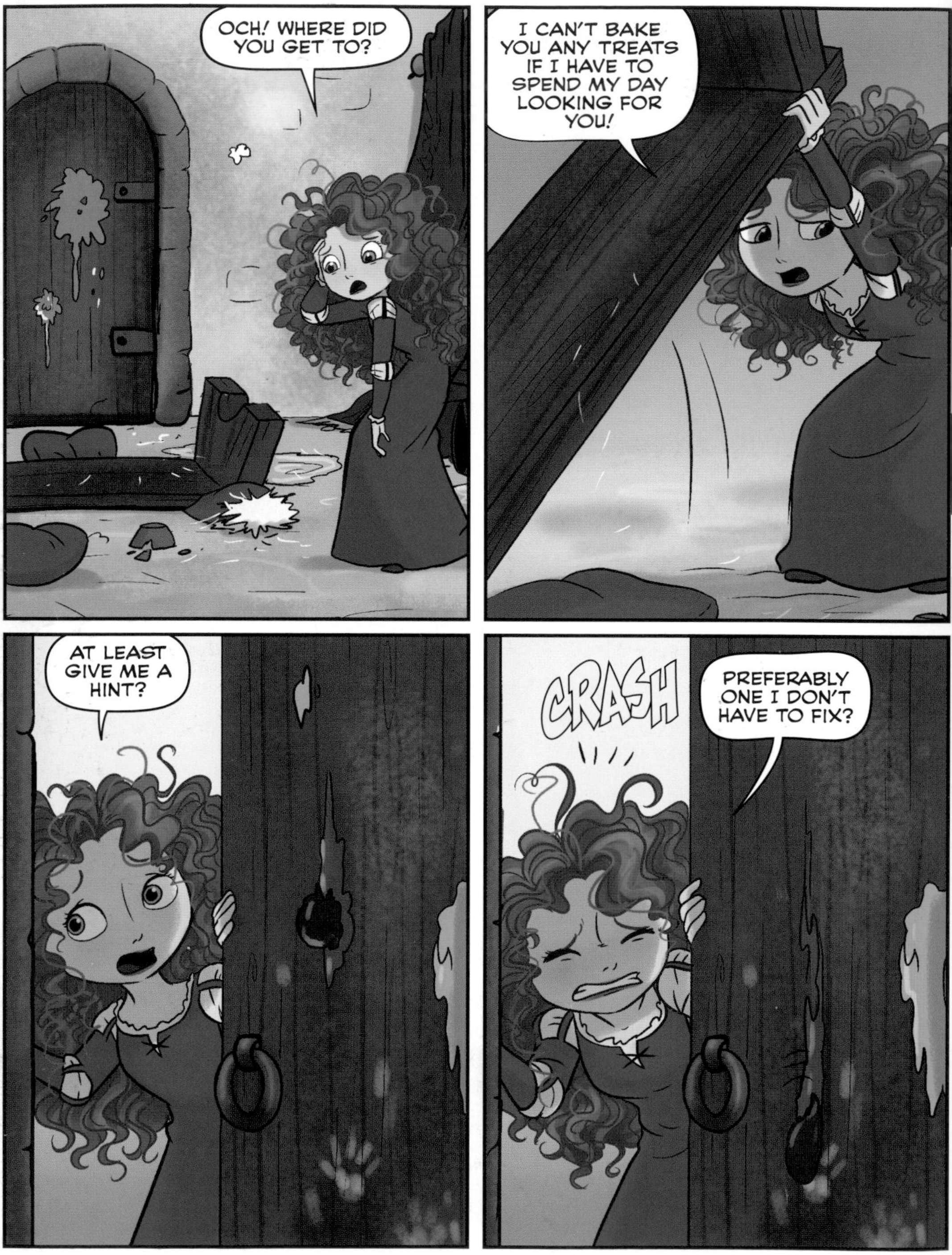
OCH! WHERE DID YOU GET TO?
I CAN'T BAKE YOU ANY TREATS IF I HAVE TO SPEND MY DAY LOOKING FOR YOU!
AT LEAST GIVE ME A HINT?
CRASH
PREFERABLY ONE I DON'T HAVE TO FIX?

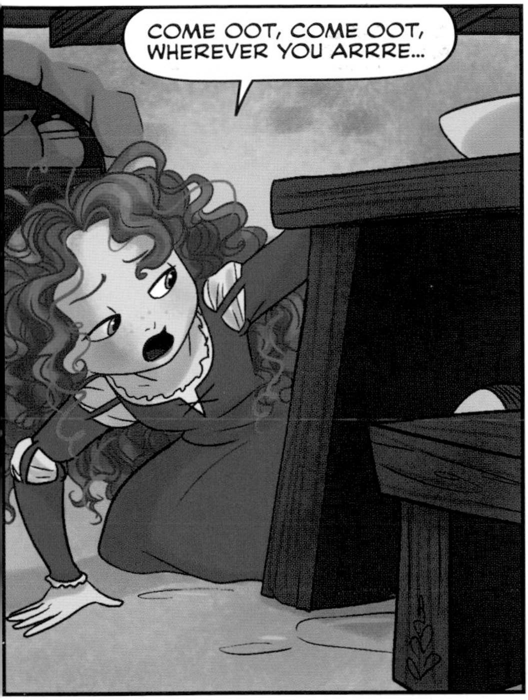
COME OOT, COME OOT, WHEREVER YOU ARRRE...

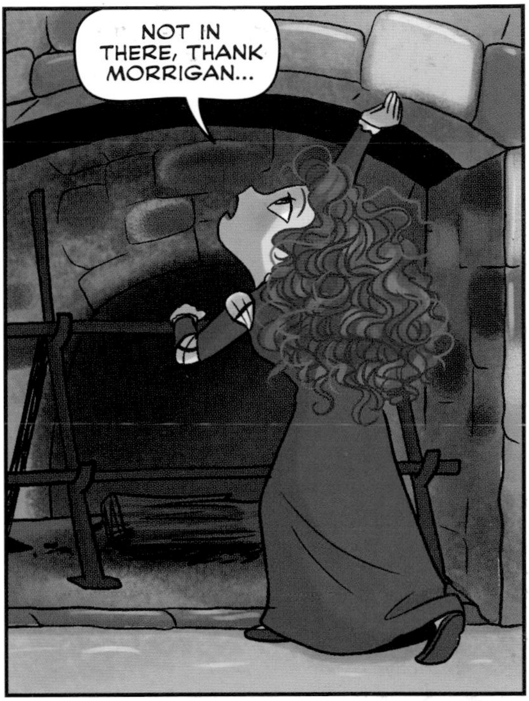
NOT IN THERE, THANK MORRIGAN...

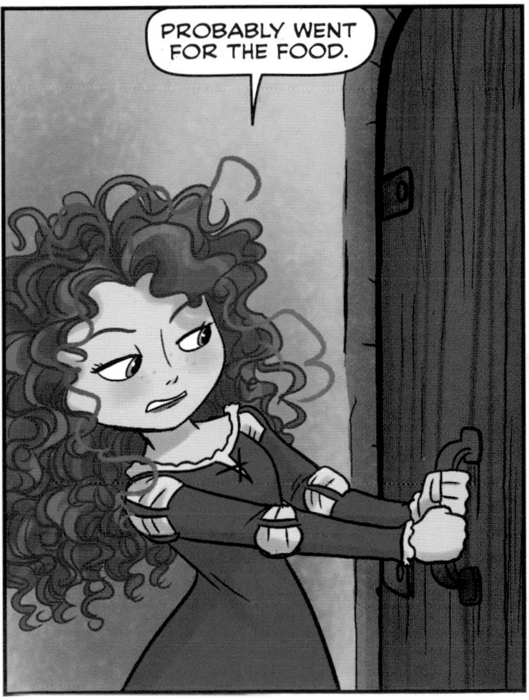
PROBABLY WENT FOR THE FOOD.

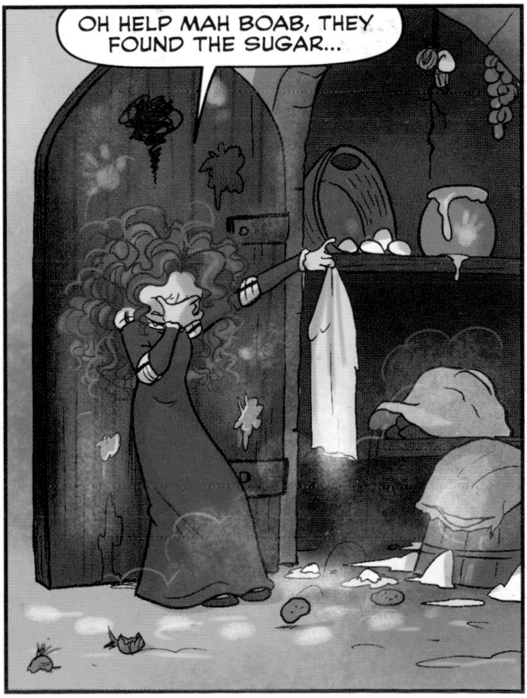
OH HELP MAH BOAB, THEY FOUND THE SUGAR...

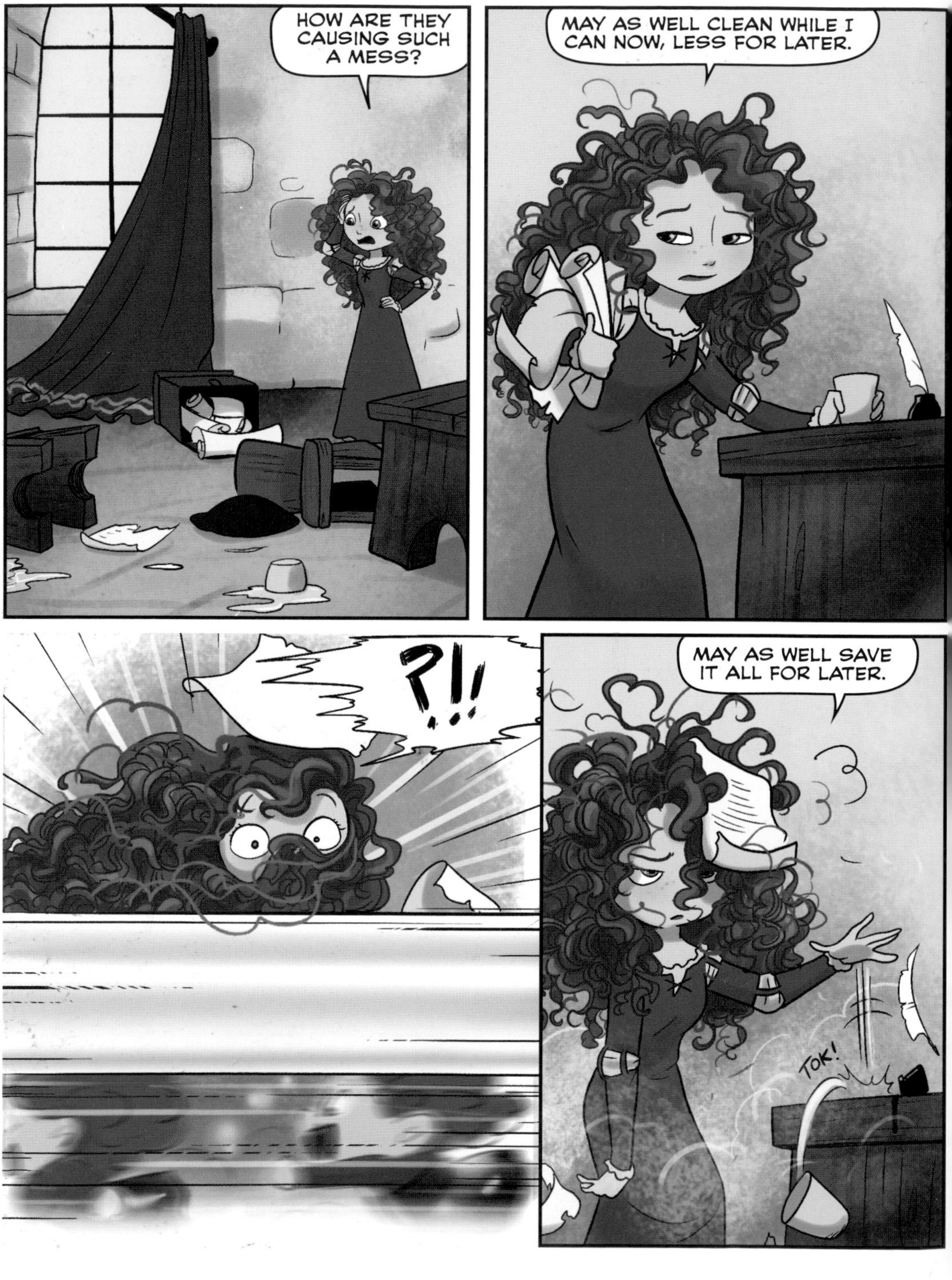
HOW ARE THEY CAUSING SUCH A MESS?
MAY AS WELL CLEAN WHILE I CAN NOW, LESS FOR LATER.
?!!
MAY AS WELL SAVE IT ALL FOR LATER.
TOK!

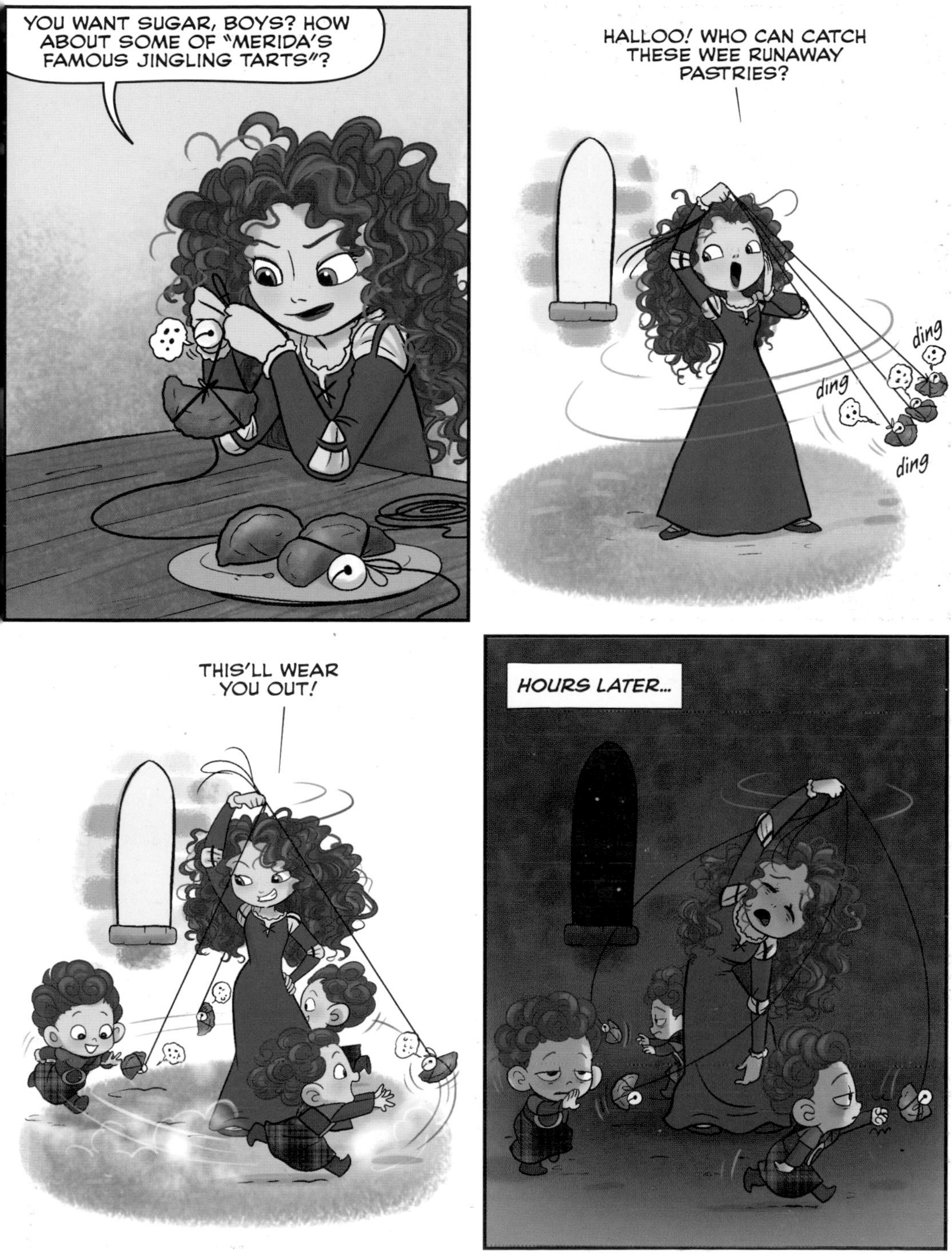
YOU WANT SUGAR, BOYS? HOW ABOUT SOME OF "MERIDA'S FAMOUS JINGLING TARTS"?
HALLOO! WHO CAN CATCH THESE WEE RUNAWAY PASTRIES?
ding
ding
ding
THIS'LL WEAR YOU OUT!
HOURS LATER...

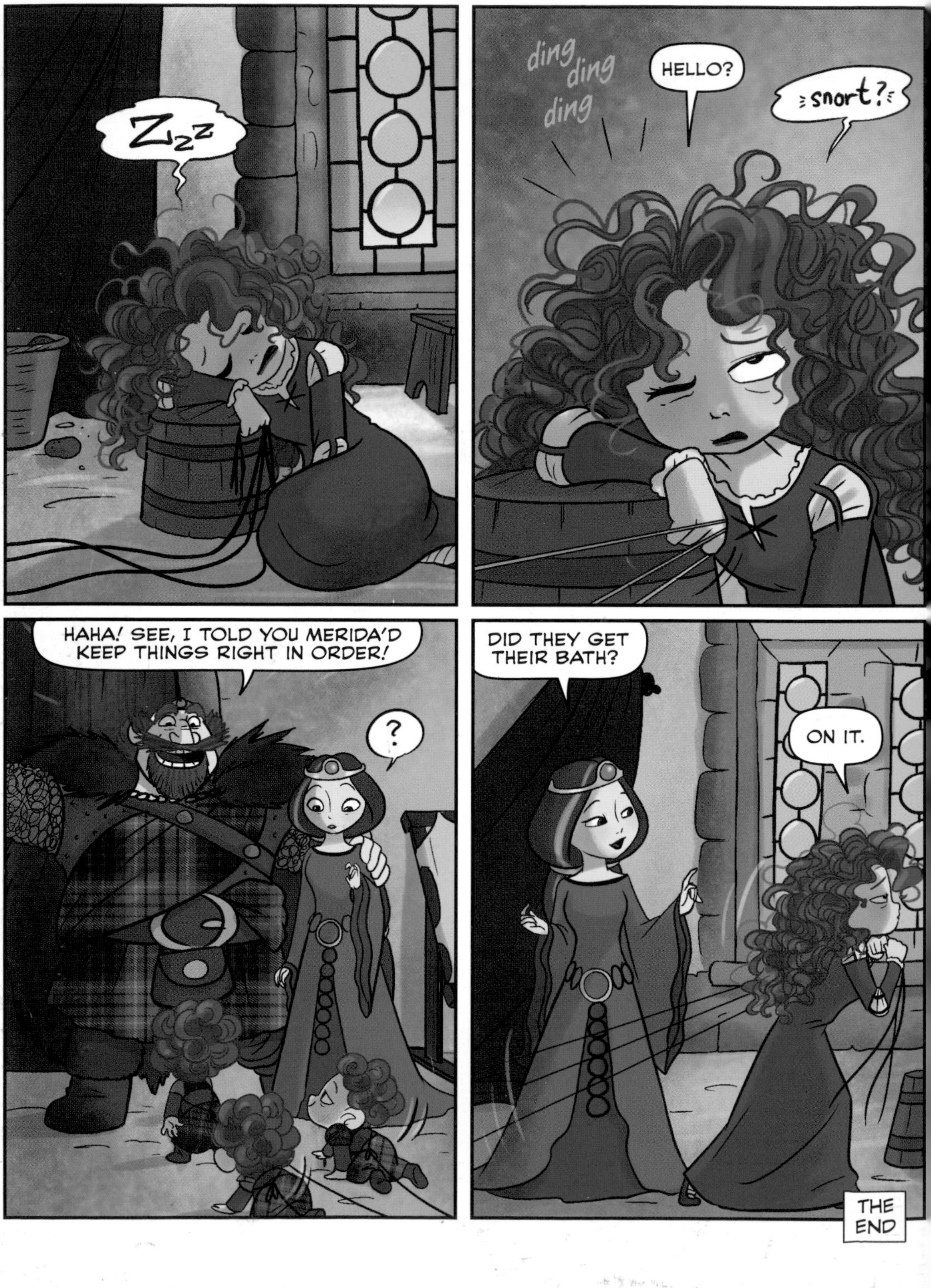
Z z z
ding ding ding
HELLO?
snort?
HAHA! SEE, I TOLD YOU MERIDA'D KEEP THINGS RIGHT IN ORDER!
?
DID THEY GET THEIR BATH?
ON IT.
THE END

"MARDI GRAS"

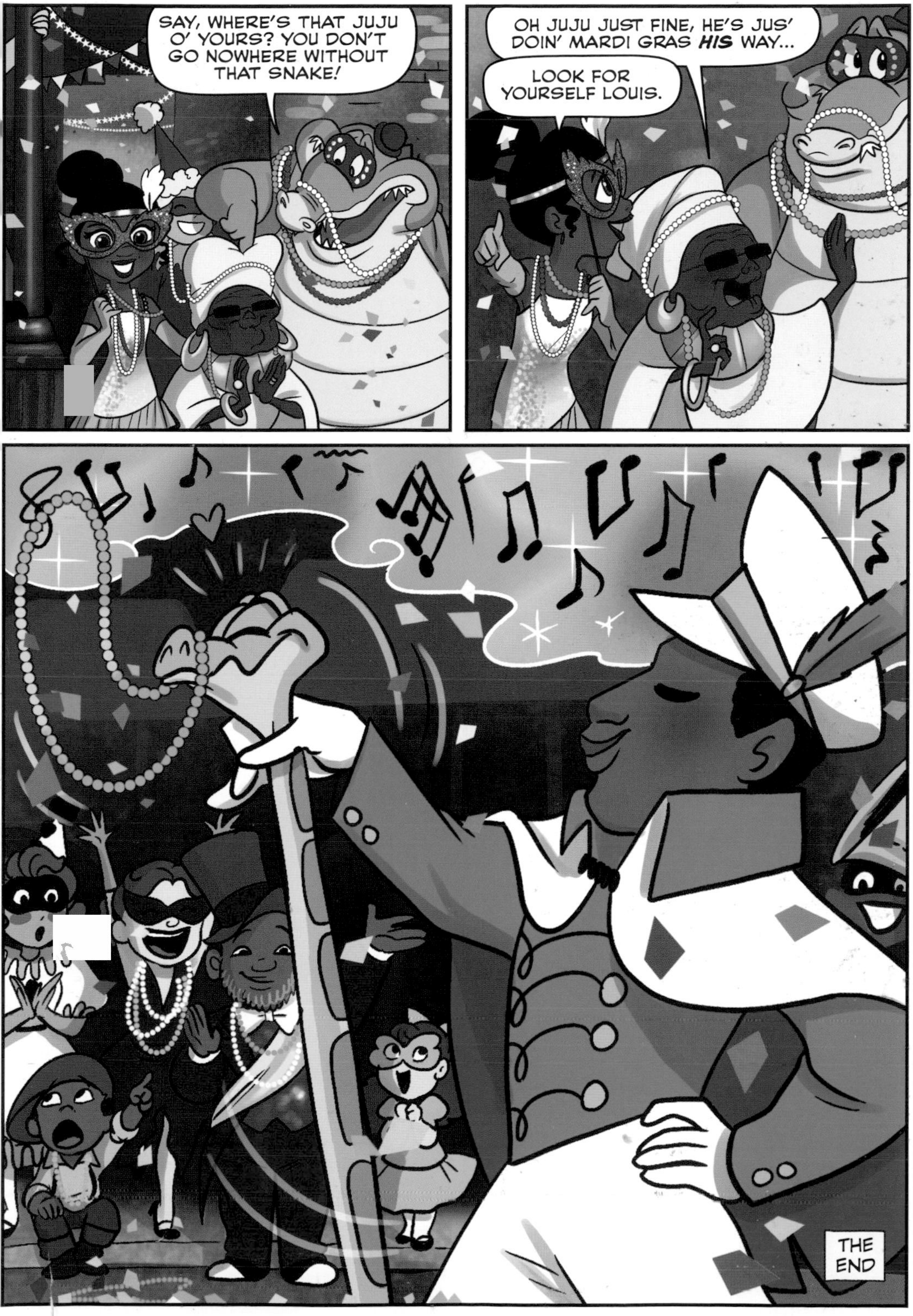

SAY, WHERE'S THAT JUJU O' YOURS? YOU DON'T GO NOWHERE WITHOUT THAT SNAKE!
OH JUJU JUST FINE, HE'S JUS' DOIN' MARDI GRAS ***HIS*** WAY...
LOOK FOR YOURSELF LOUIS.
THE END

"WHAT THE PEOPLE KNOW"

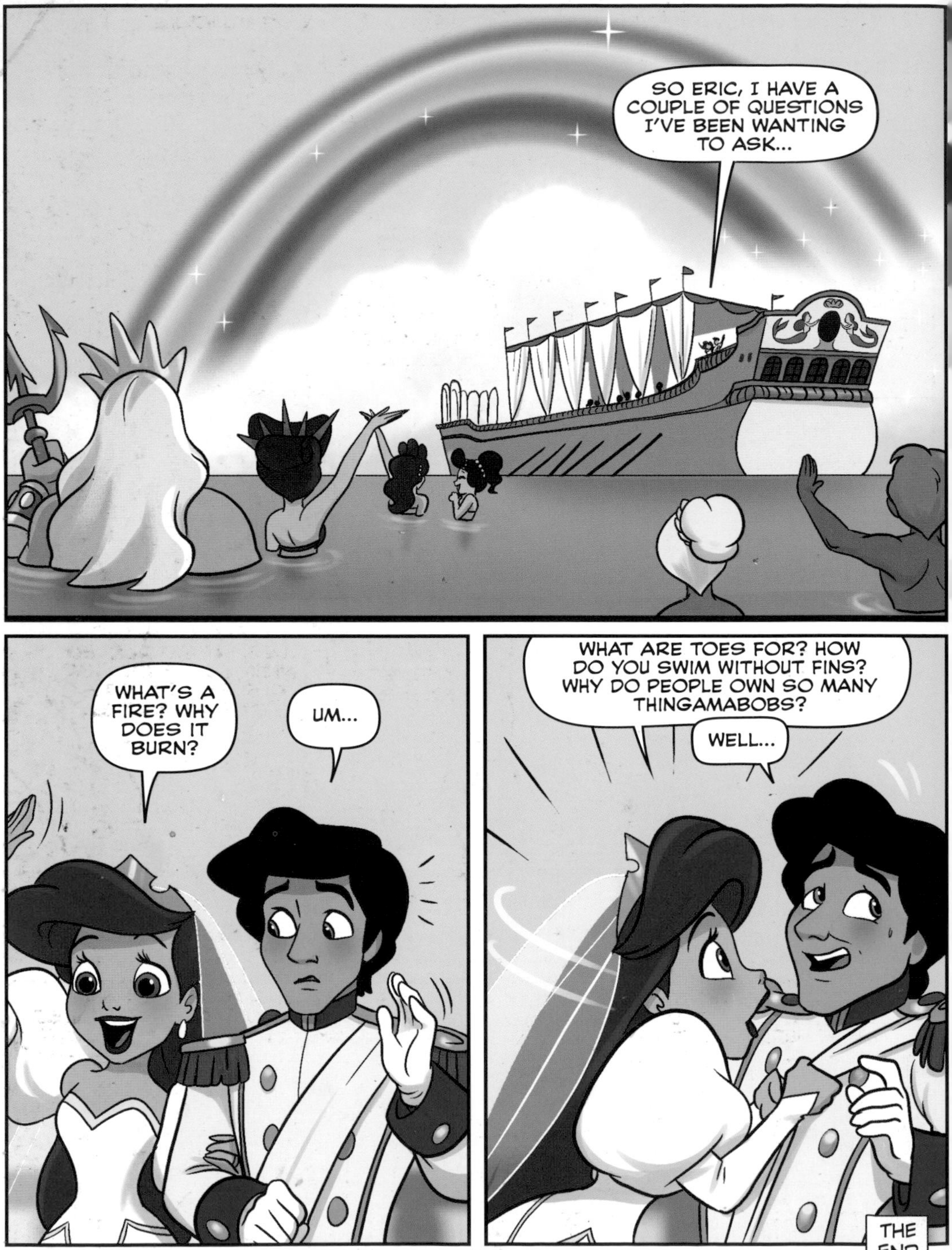

SO ERIC, I HAVE A COUPLE OF QUESTIONS I'VE BEEN WANTING TO ASK...
WHAT'S A FIRE? WHY DOES IT BURN?
UM...
WHAT ARE TOES FOR? HOW DO YOU SWIM WITHOUT FINS? WHY DO PEOPLE OWN SO MANY THINGAMABOBS?
WELL...
THE END

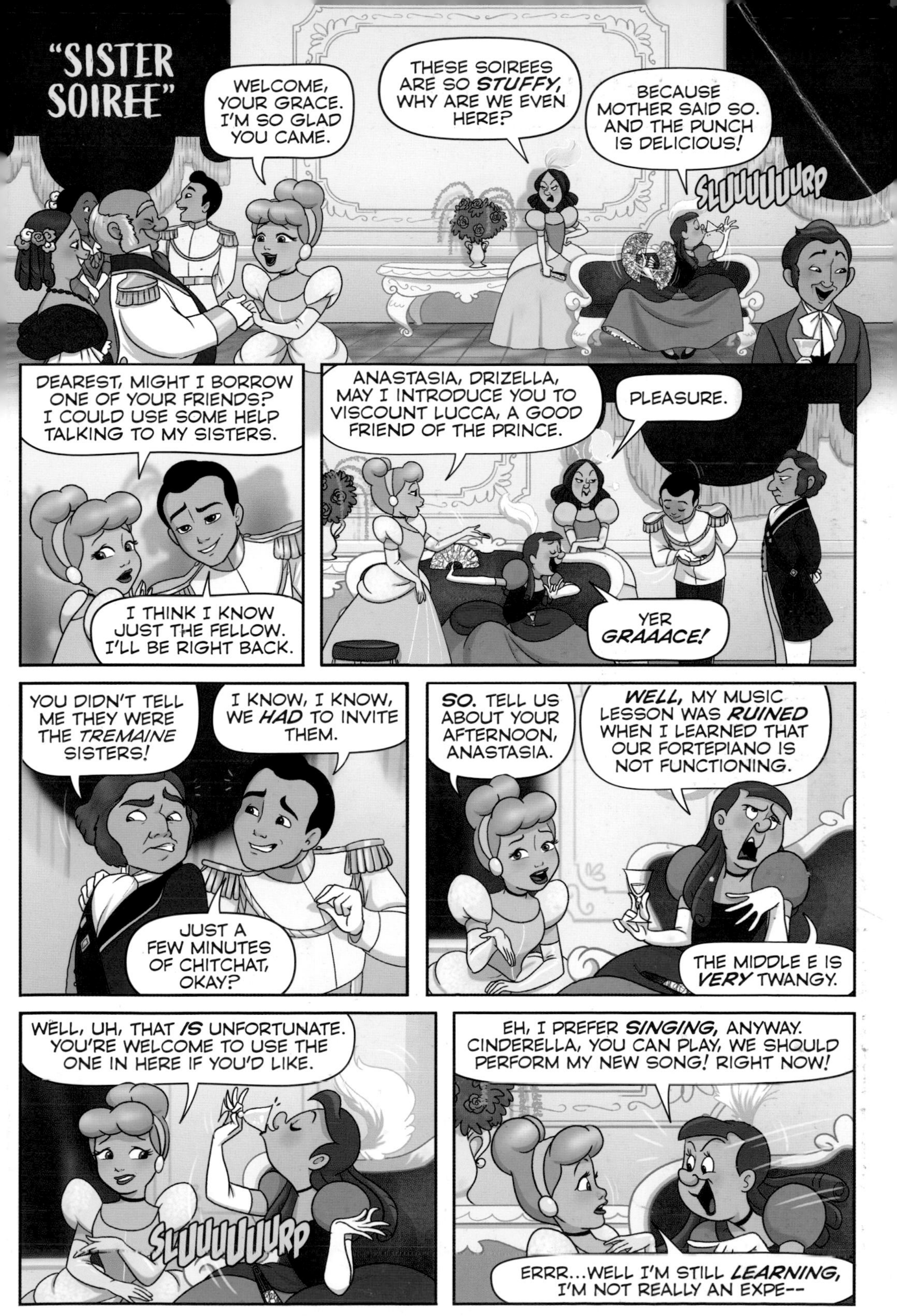
"SISTER SOIREE"
WELCOME, YOUR GRACE. I'M SO GLAD YOU CAME.
THESE SOIREES ARE SO STUFFY, WHY ARE WE EVEN HERE?
BECAUSE MOTHER SAID SO. AND THE PUNCH IS DELICIOUS!
SLUUUUUURP
DEAREST, MIGHT I BORROW ONE OF YOUR FRIENDS? I COULD USE SOME HELP TALKING TO MY SISTERS.
I THINK I KNOW JUST THE FELLOW. I'LL BE RIGHT BACK.
ANASTASIA, DRIZELLA, MAY I INTRODUCE YOU TO VISCOUNT LUCCA, A GOOD FRIEND OF THE PRINCE.
PLEASURE.
YER GRAAACE!
YOU DIDN'T TELL ME THEY WERE THE TREMAINE SISTERS!
I KNOW, I KNOW, WE HAD TO INVITE THEM.
JUST A FEW MINUTES OF CHITCHAT, OKAY?
SO. TELL US ABOUT YOUR AFTERNOON, ANASTASIA.
WELL, MY MUSIC LESSON WAS RUINED WHEN I LEARNED THAT OUR FORTEPIANO IS NOT FUNCTIONING.
THE MIDDLE E IS VERY TWANGY.
WELL, UH, THAT IS UNFORTUNATE. YOU'RE WELCOME TO USE THE ONE IN HERE IF YOU'D LIKE.
SLUUUUUURP
EH, I PREFER SINGING, ANYWAY. CINDERELLA, YOU CAN PLAY, WE SHOULD PERFORM MY NEW SONG! RIGHT NOW!
ERRR...WELL I'M STILL LEARNING, I'M NOT REALLY AN EXPE--

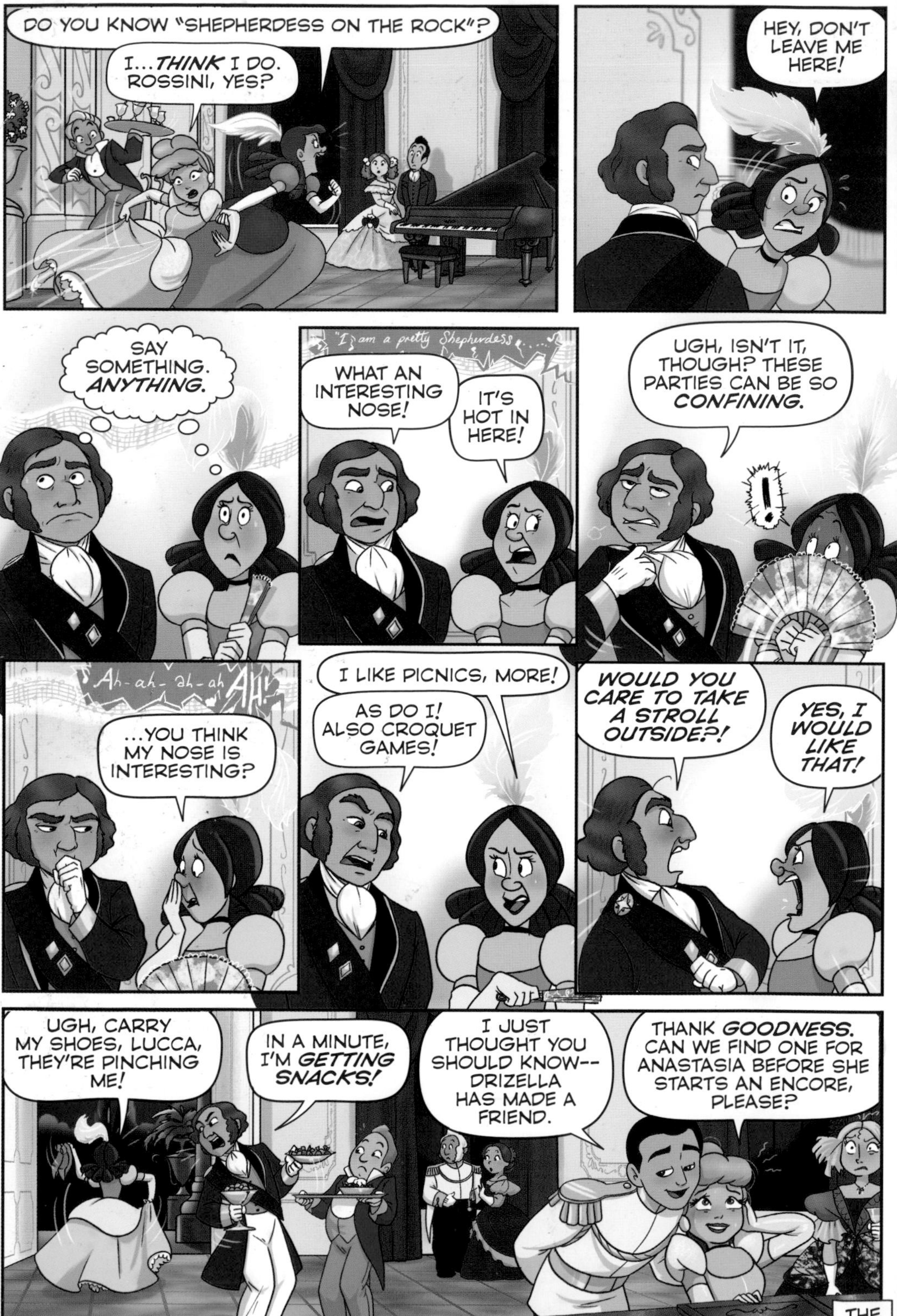
DO YOU KNOW "SHEPHERDESS ON THE ROCK"?
I...THINK I DO. ROSSINI, YES?
HEY, DON'T LEAVE ME HERE!
SAY SOMETHING. ANYTHING.
"I am a pretty Shepherdess...
WHAT AN INTERESTING NOSE!
IT'S HOT IN HERE!
UGH, ISN'T IT, THOUGH? THESE PARTIES CAN BE SO CONFINING.
!
Ah-ah-ah-ah AH!
...YOU THINK MY NOSE IS INTERESTING?
I LIKE PICNICS, MORE!
AS DO I! ALSO CROQUET GAMES!
WOULD YOU CARE TO TAKE A STROLL OUTSIDE?!
YES, I WOULD LIKE THAT!
UGH, CARRY MY SHOES, LUCCA, THEY'RE PINCHING ME!
IN A MINUTE, I'M GETTING SNACKS!
I JUST THOUGHT YOU SHOULD KNOW-- DRIZELLA HAS MADE A FRIEND.
THANK GOODNESS. CAN WE FIND ONE FOR ANASTASIA BEFORE SHE STARTS AN ENCORE, PLEASE?
THE END

"MYSTERY CAVE"

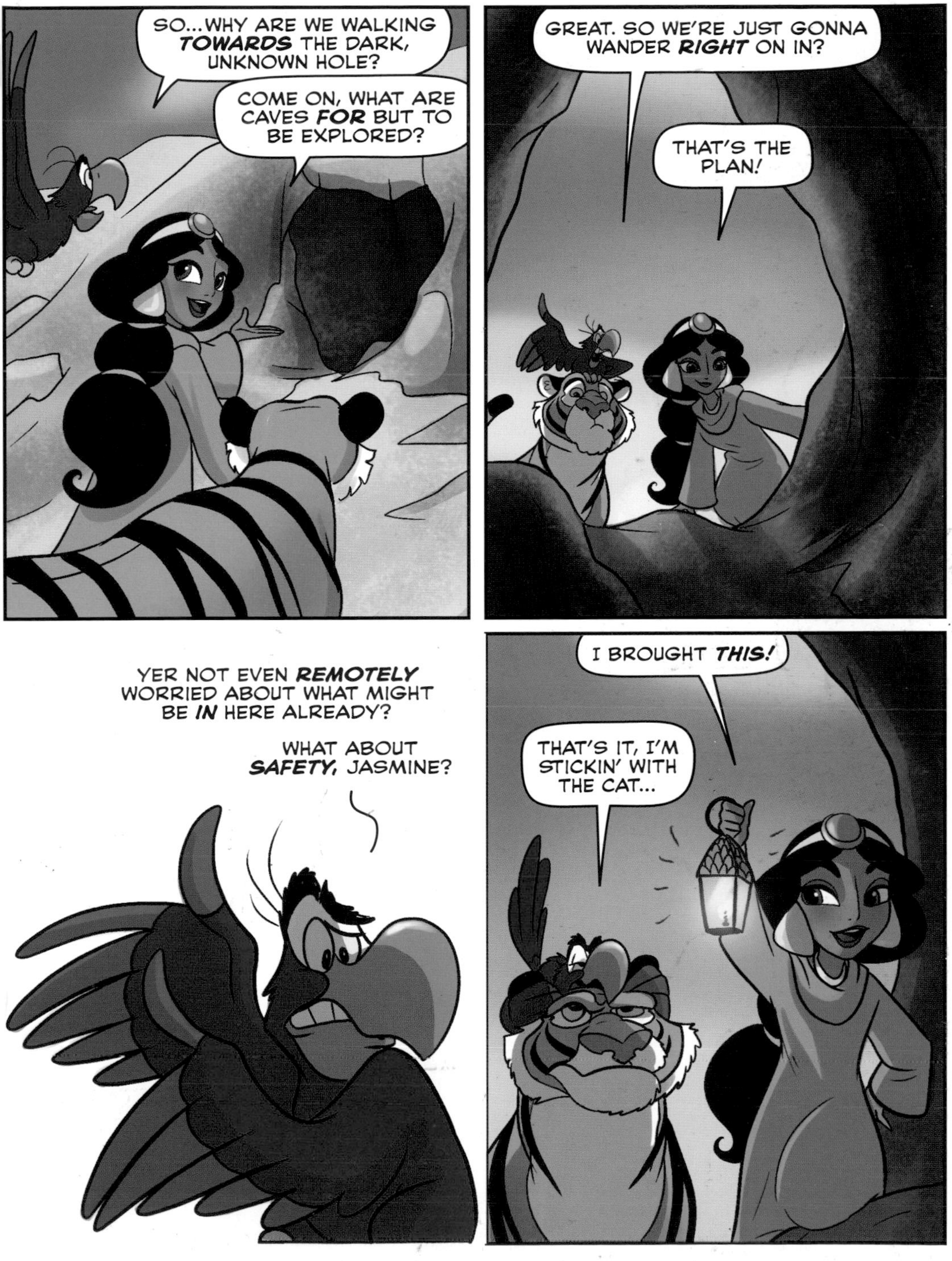
SO...WHY ARE WE WALKING TOWARDS THE DARK, UNKNOWN HOLE?
COME ON, WHAT ARE CAVES FOR BUT TO BE EXPLORED?
GREAT. SO WE'RE JUST GONNA WANDER RIGHT ON IN?
THAT'S THE PLAN!
YER NOT EVEN REMOTELY WORRIED ABOUT WHAT MIGHT BE IN HERE ALREADY?
WHAT ABOUT SAFETY, JASMINE?
I BROUGHT THIS!
THAT'S IT, I'M STICKIN' WITH THE CAT...

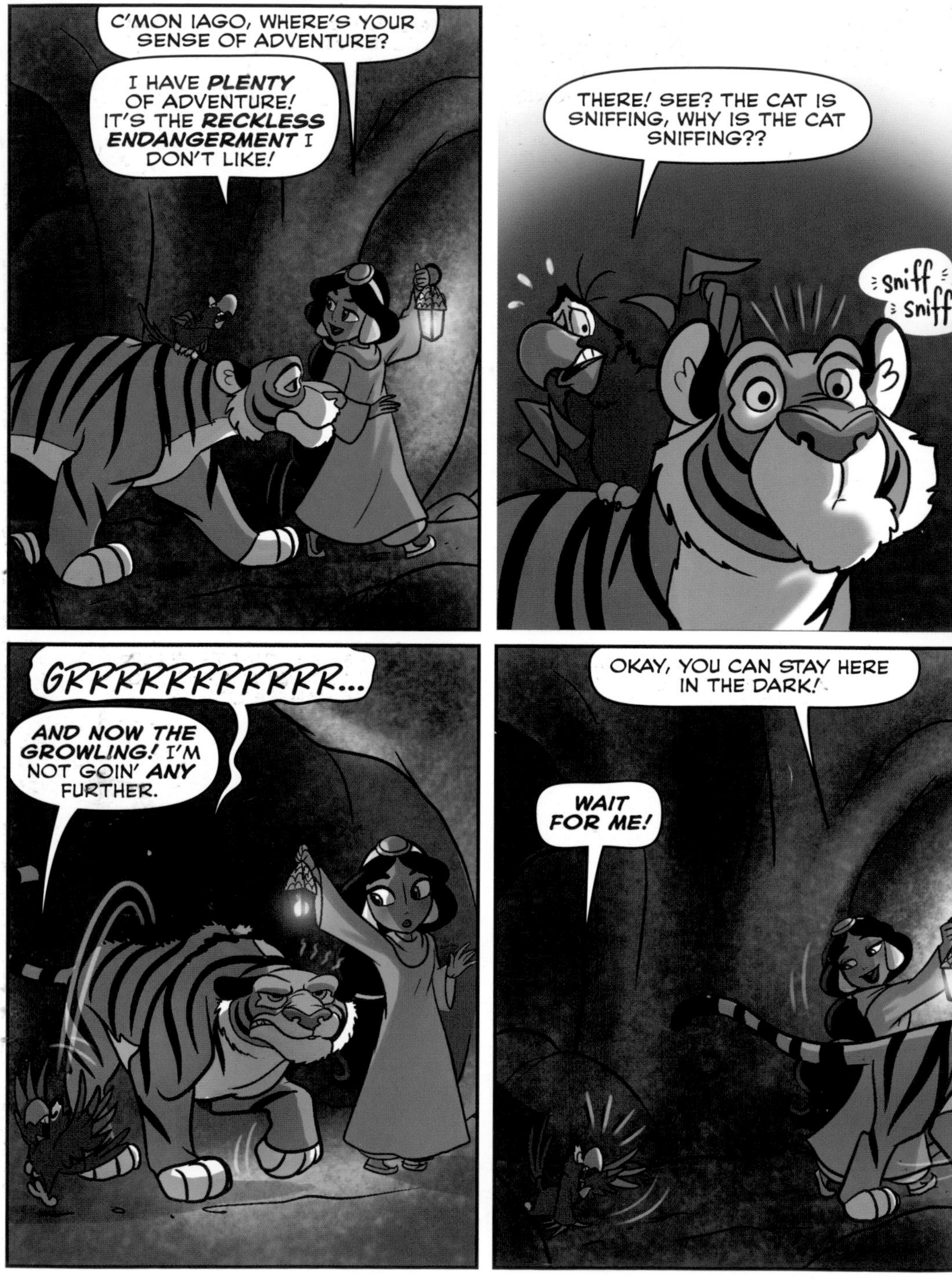
C'MON IAGO, WHERE'S YOUR SENSE OF ADVENTURE?
I HAVE PLENTY OF ADVENTURE! IT'S THE RECKLESS ENDANGERMENT I DON'T LIKE!
THERE! SEE? THE CAT IS SNIFFING, WHY IS THE CAT SNIFFING??
sniff sniff
GRKKKKKKKKKKR...
AND NOW THE GROWLING! I'M NOT GOIN' ANY FURTHER.
OKAY, YOU CAN STAY HERE IN THE DARK!
WAIT FOR ME!

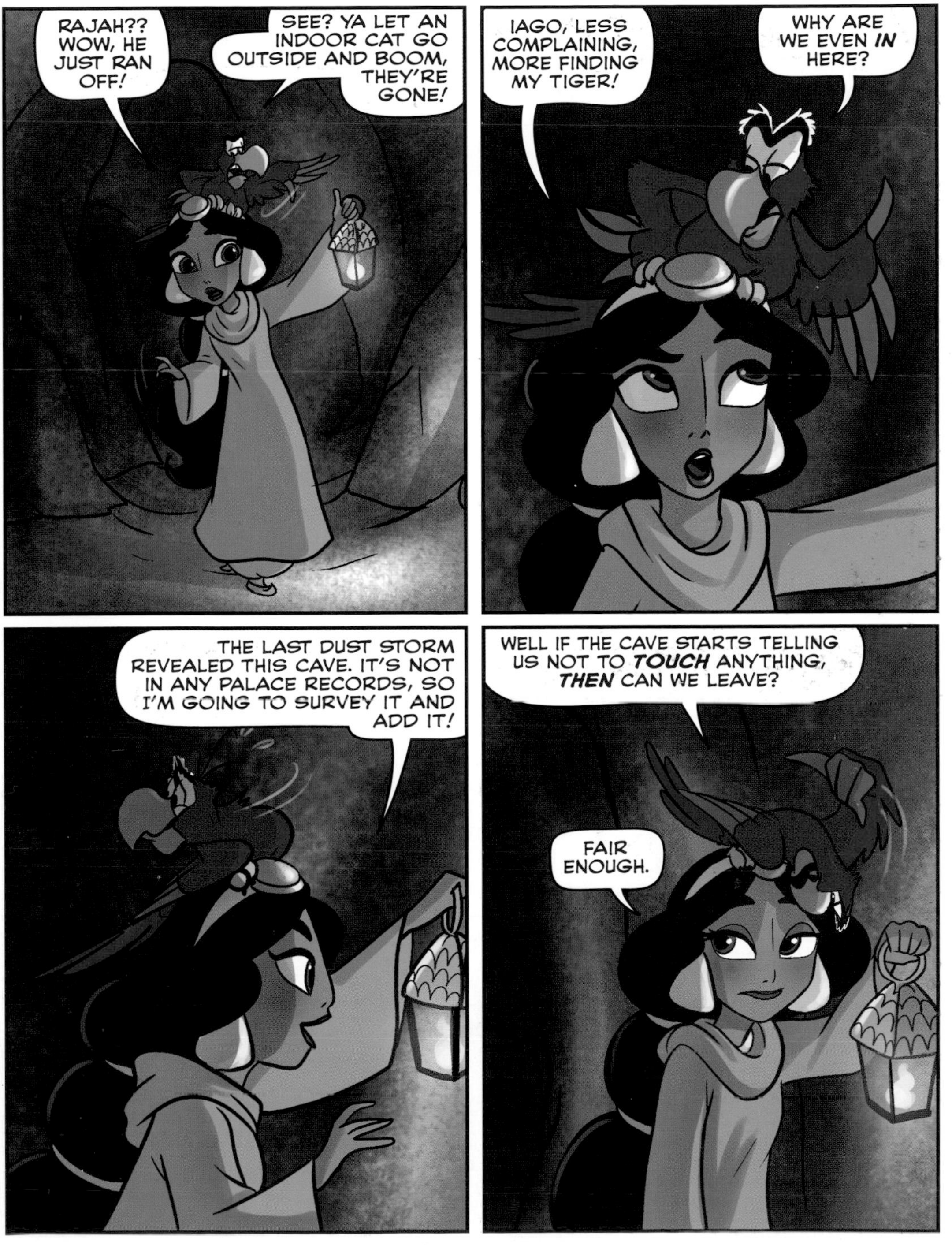
RAJAH?? WOW, HE JUST RAN OFF!
SEE? YA LET AN INDOOR CAT GO OUTSIDE AND BOOM, THEY'RE GONE!
IAGO, LESS COMPLAINING, MORE FINDING MY TIGER!
WHY ARE WE EVEN *IN* HERE?
THE LAST DUST STORM REVEALED THIS CAVE. IT'S NOT IN ANY PALACE RECORDS, SO I'M GOING TO SURVEY IT AND ADD IT!
WELL IF THE CAVE STARTS TELLING US NOT TO *TOUCH* ANYTHING, *THEN* CAN WE LEAVE?
FAIR ENOUGH.

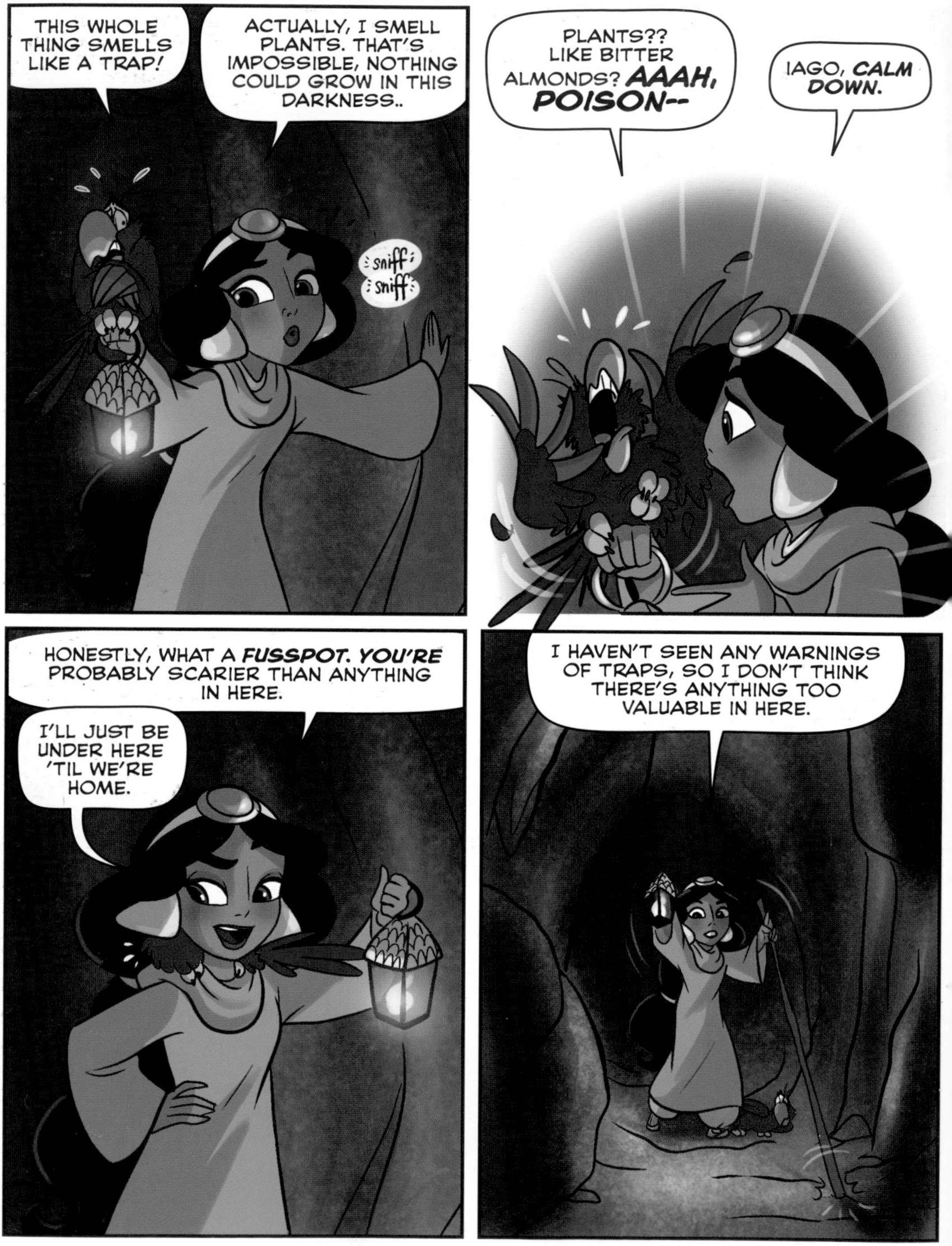
THIS WHOLE THING SMELLS LIKE A TRAP!
ACTUALLY, I SMELL PLANTS. THAT'S IMPOSSIBLE, NOTHING COULD GROW IN THIS DARKNESS..
sniff sniff
PLANTS?? LIKE BITTER ALMONDS? AAAH, POISON--
IAGO, CALM DOWN.
HONESTLY, WHAT A FUSSPOT. YOU'RE PROBABLY SCARIER THAN ANYTHING IN HERE.
I'LL JUST BE UNDER HERE 'TIL WE'RE HOME.
I HAVEN'T SEEN ANY WARNINGS OF TRAPS, SO I DON'T THINK THERE'S ANYTHING TOO VALUABLE IN HERE.

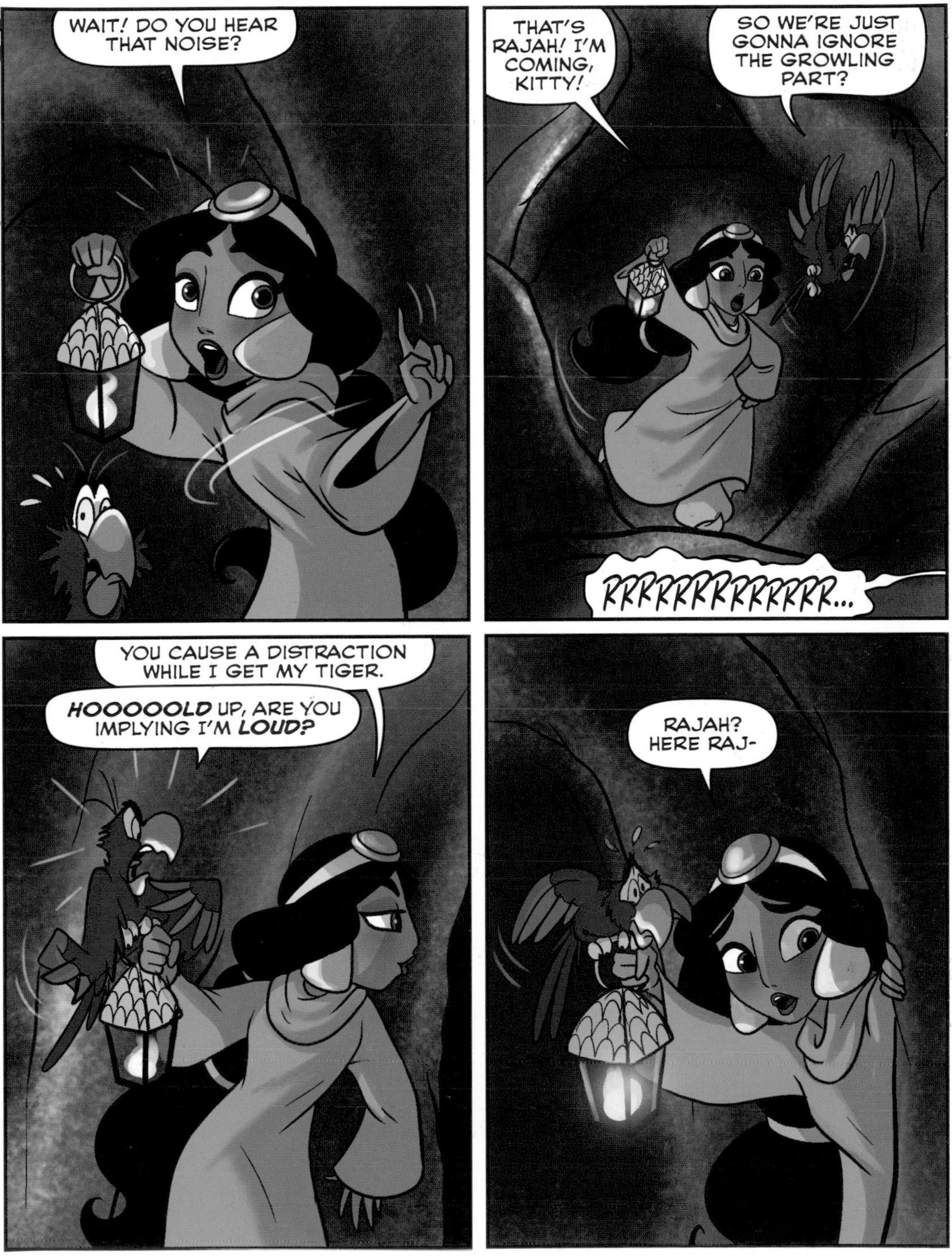
WAIT! DO YOU HEAR THAT NOISE?
THAT'S RAJAH! I'M COMING, KITTY!
SO WE'RE JUST GONNA IGNORE THE GROWLING PART?
RRRRRRRRRRRRR...
YOU CAUSE A DISTRACTION WHILE I GET MY TIGER.
HOOOOOLD UP, ARE YOU IMPLYING I'M **LOUD?**
RAJAH? HERE RAJ-

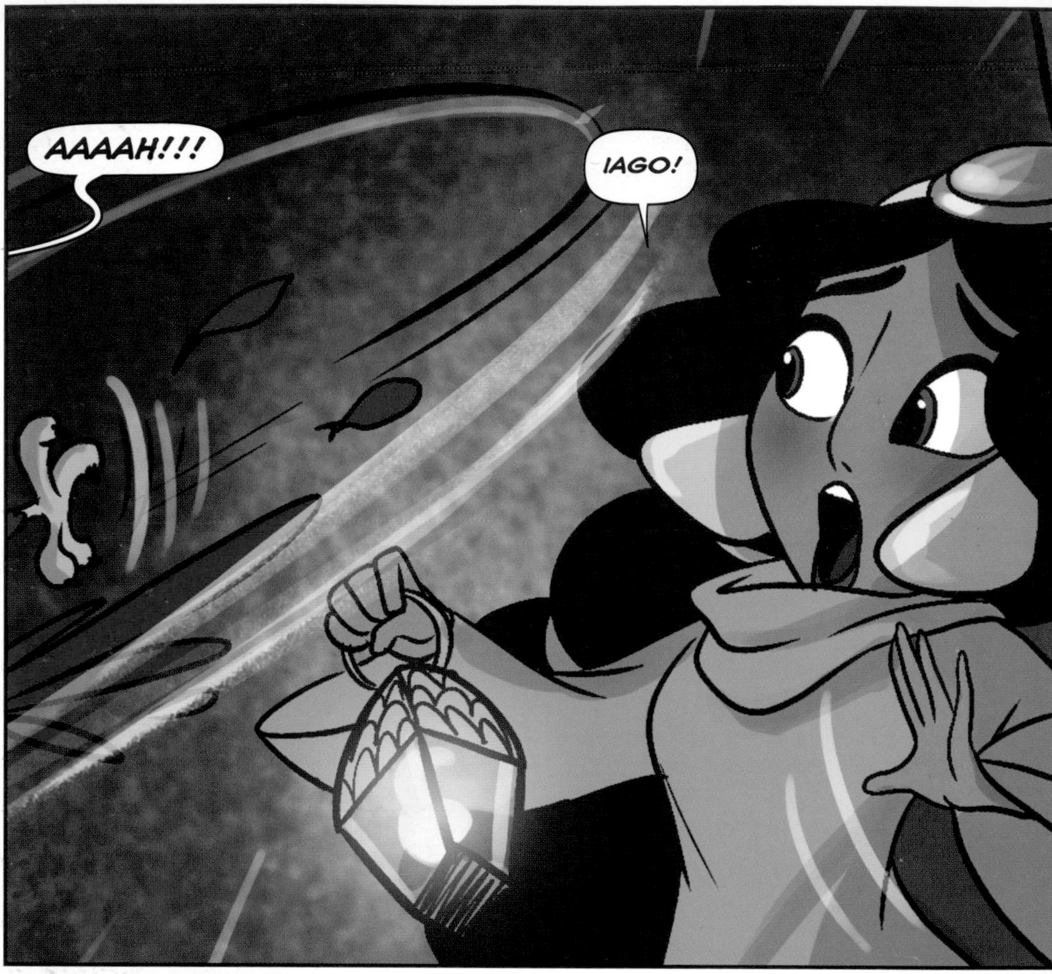
AAAAH!!!
IAGO!

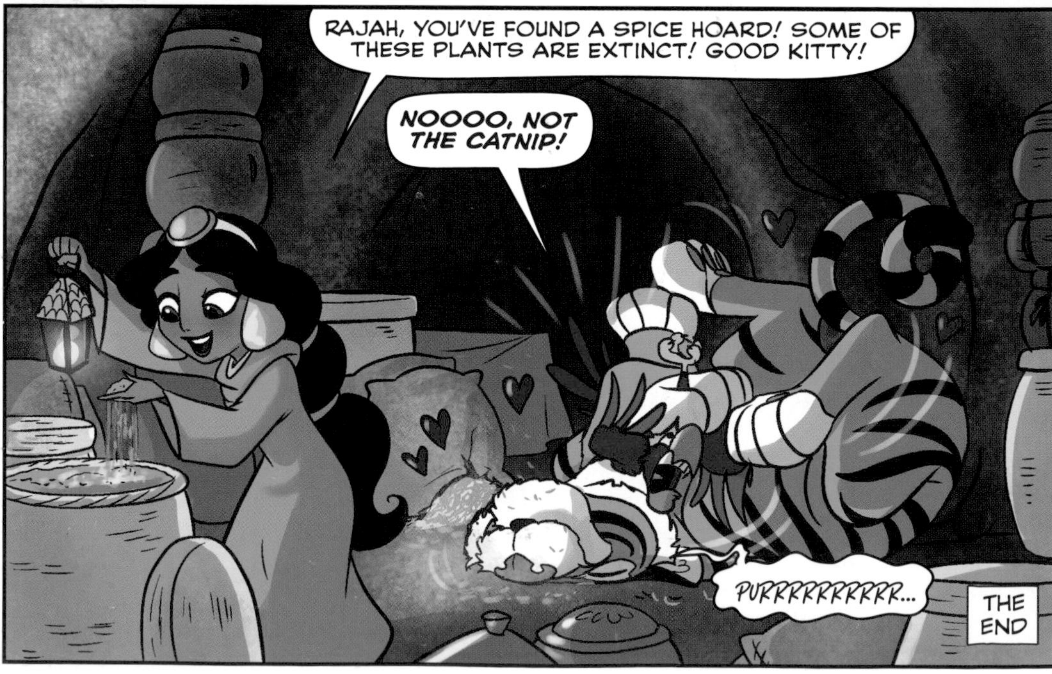
RAJAH, YOU'VE FOUND A SPICE HOARD! SOME OF THESE PLANTS ARE EXTINCT! GOOD KITTY!
NOOOO, NOT THE CATNIP!
PURRRRRRRRRR...
THE END

"DON'T BLINK"

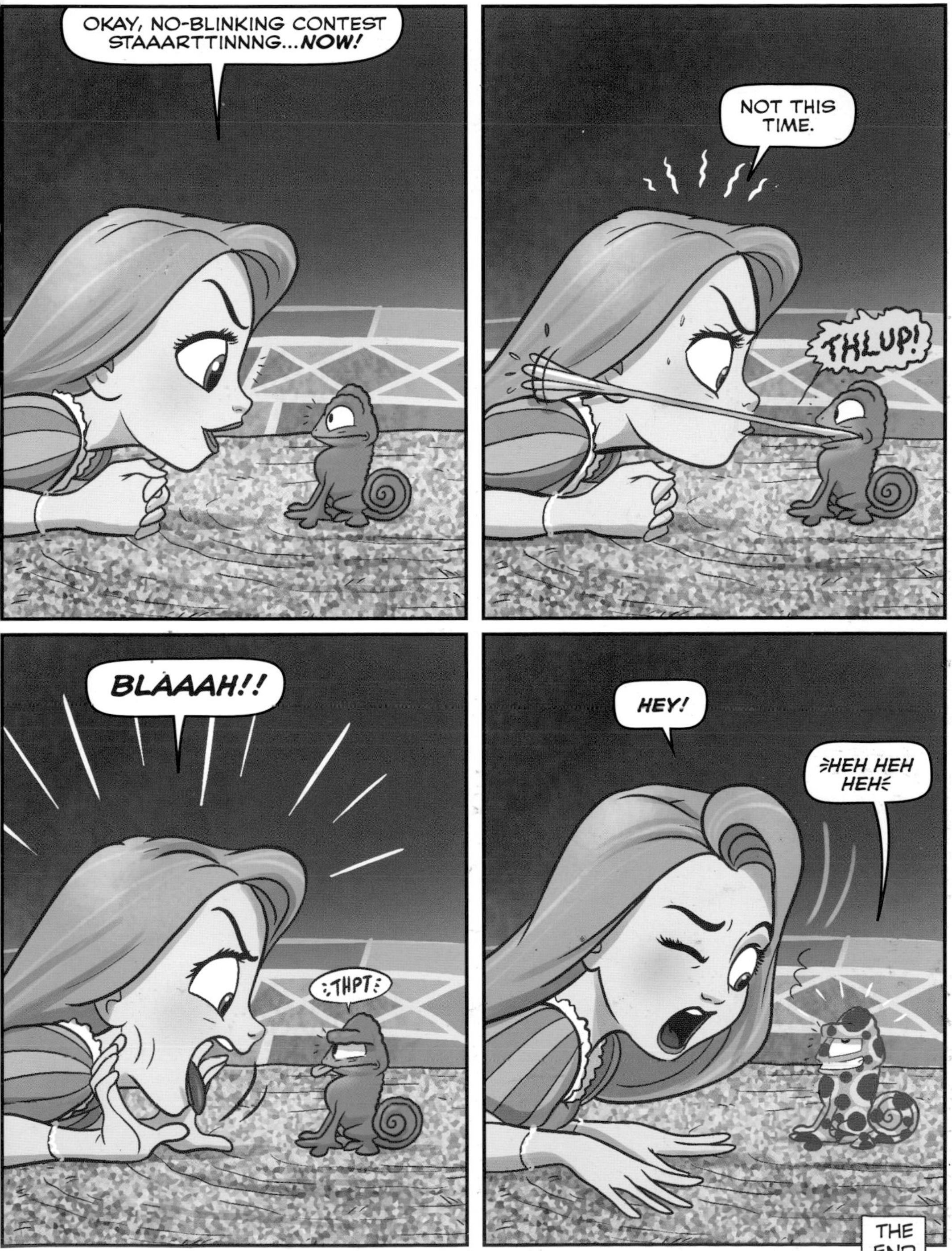
OKAY, NO-BLINKING CONTEST STAAARTTINNNG...*NOW!*
NOT THIS TIME.
THLUP!
BLAAAH!!
THPT
HEY!
HEH HEH HEH
THE END

"THEY COME IN THREES"

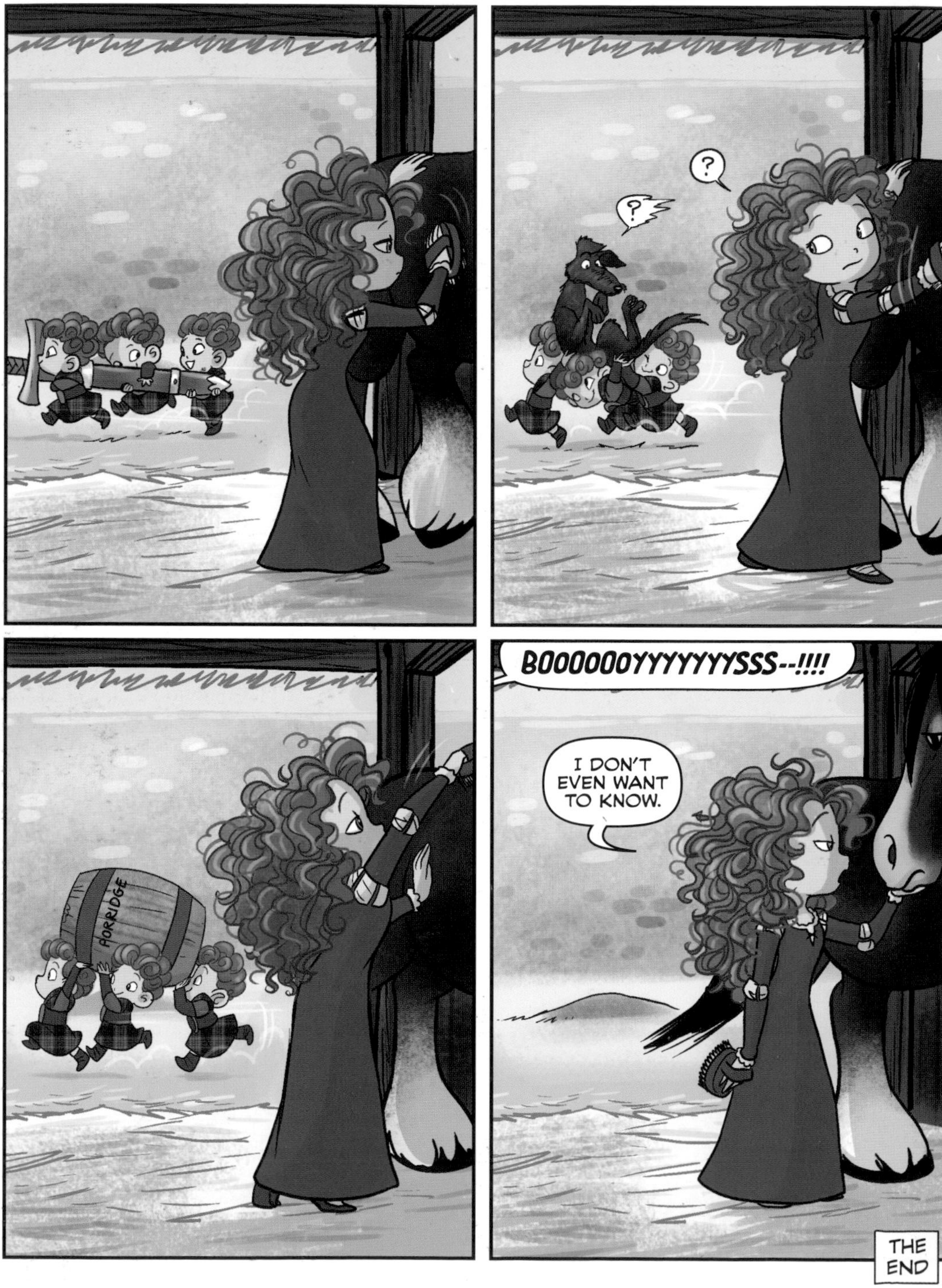
?
?
PORRIDGE
BOOOOOOYYYYYYYSSS--!!!!
I DON'T EVEN WANT TO KNOW.
THE END

"BEEF CAKE"

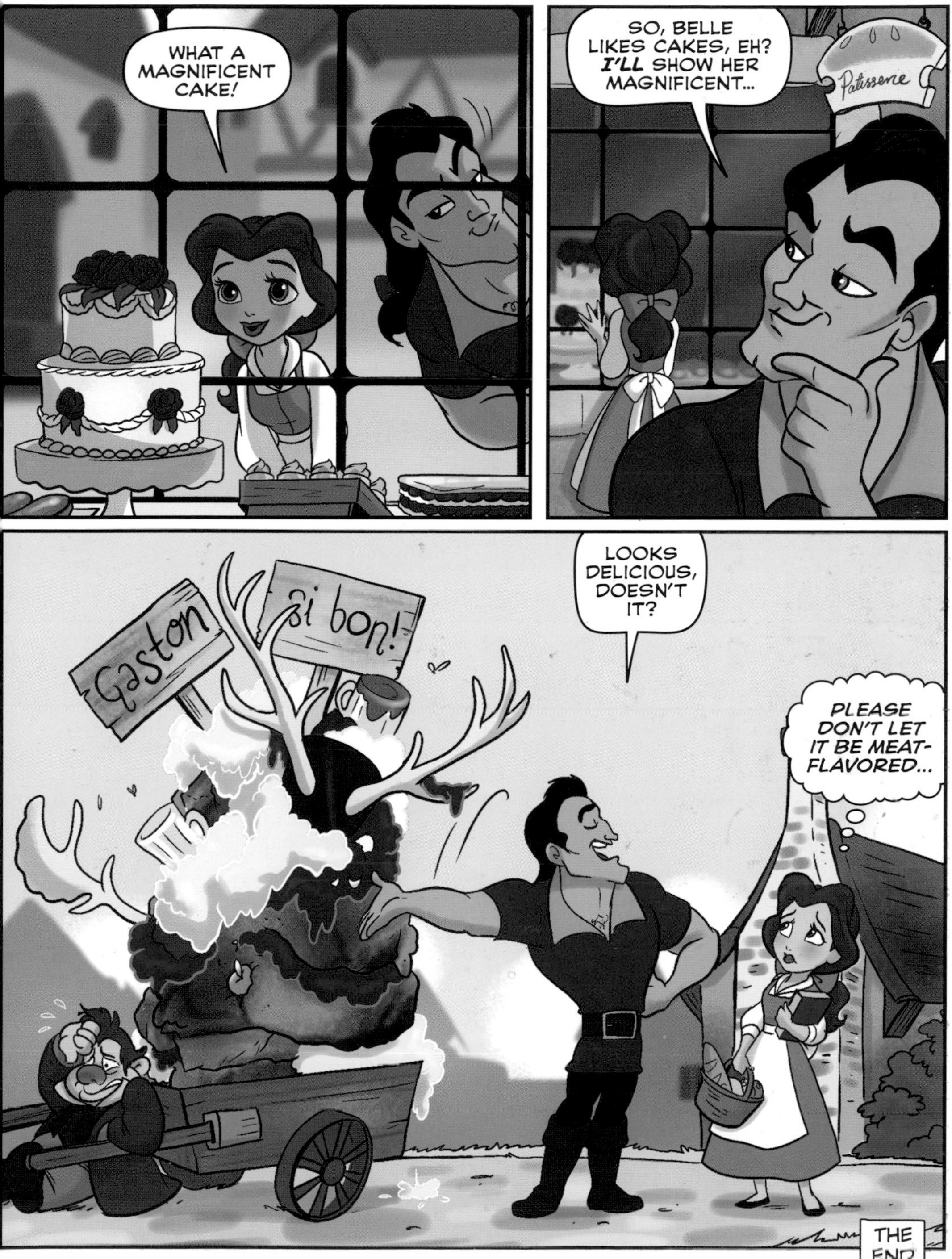

WHAT A MAGNIFICENT CAKE!
SO, BELLE LIKES CAKES, EH? *I'LL* SHOW HER MAGNIFICENT...
Patisserie
Gaston
Si bon!
LOOKS DELICIOUS, DOESN'T IT?
PLEASE DON'T LET IT BE MEAT-FLAVORED...
THE END

"INCENTIVES"

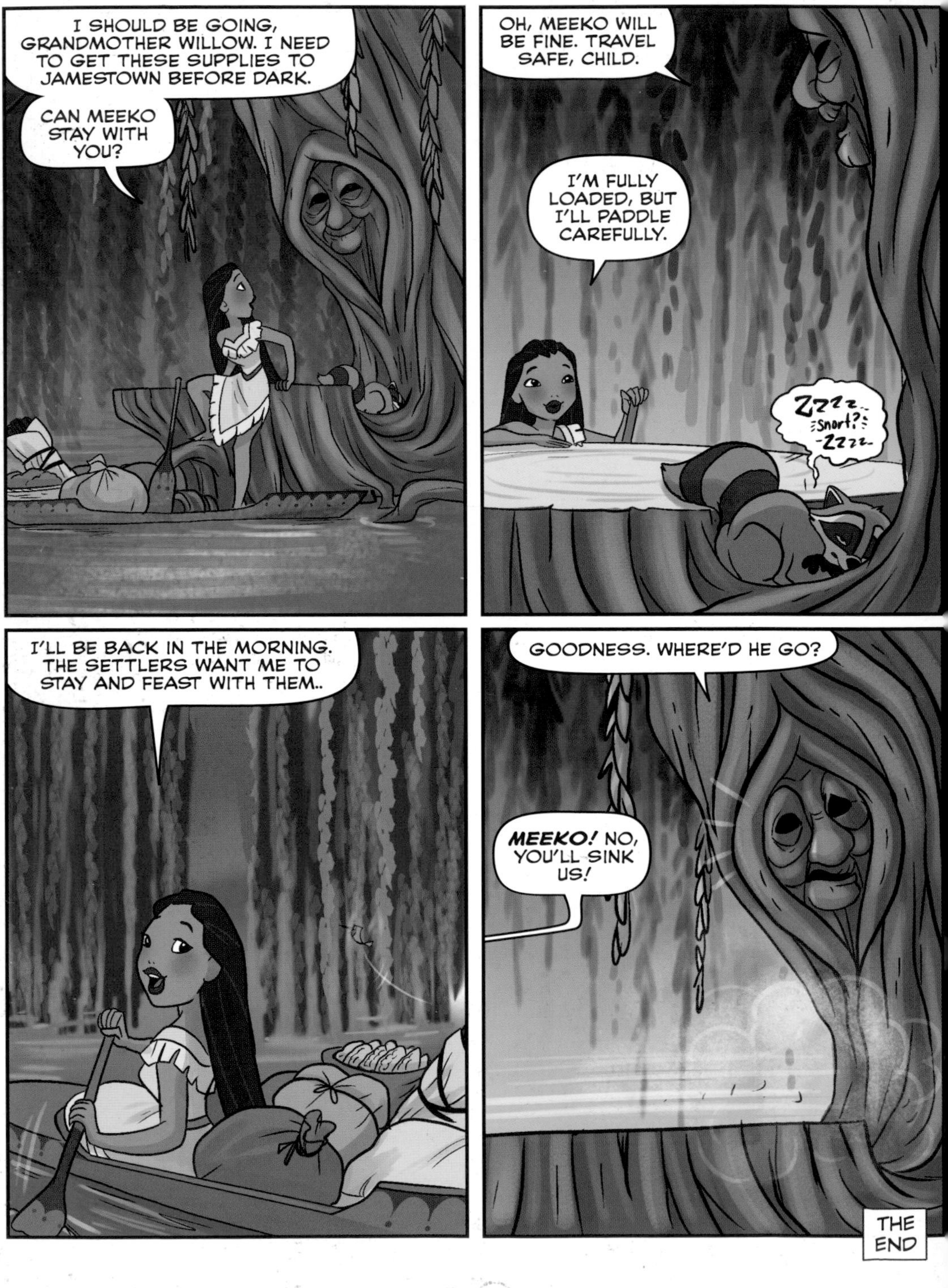

I SHOULD BE GOING, GRANDMOTHER WILLOW. I NEED TO GET THESE SUPPLIES TO JAMESTOWN BEFORE DARK.
CAN MEEKO STAY WITH YOU?
OH, MEEKO WILL BE FINE. TRAVEL SAFE, CHILD.
I'M FULLY LOADED, BUT I'LL PADDLE CAREFULLY.
ZZZZ...
SNORT?
ZZZZ...
I'LL BE BACK IN THE MORNING. THE SETTLERS WANT ME TO STAY AND FEAST WITH THEM..
GOODNESS. WHERE'D HE GO?
MEEKO! NO, YOU'LL SINK US!
THE END

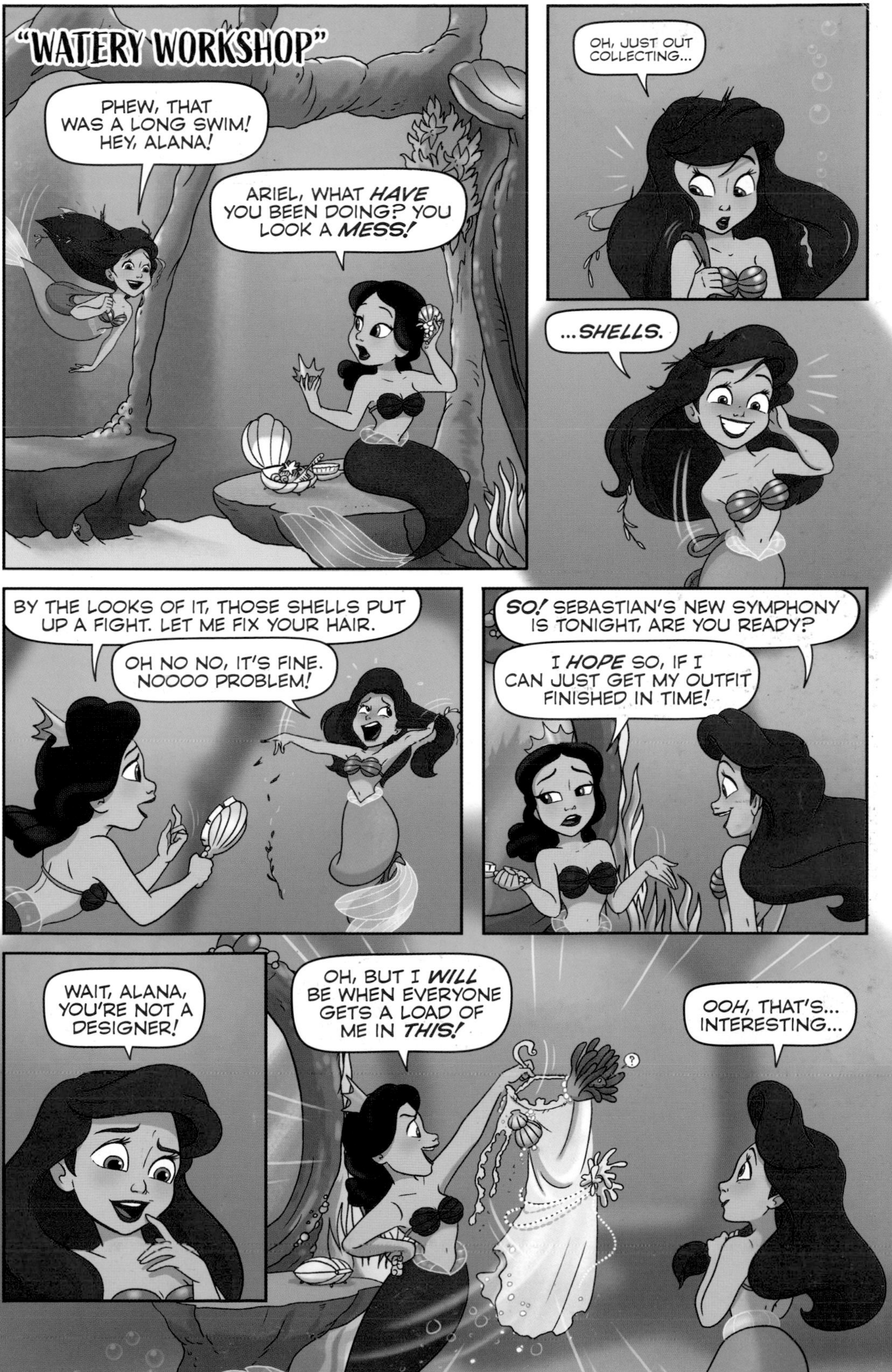
"WATERY WORKSHOP"
PHEW, THAT WAS A LONG SWIM! HEY, ALANA!
ARIEL, WHAT *HAVE* YOU BEEN DOING? YOU LOOK A *MESS!*
OH, JUST OUT COLLECTING...
...*SHELLS.*
BY THE LOOKS OF IT, THOSE SHELLS PUT UP A FIGHT. LET ME FIX YOUR HAIR.
OH NO NO, IT'S FINE. NOOOO PROBLEM!
SO! SEBASTIAN'S NEW SYMPHONY IS TONIGHT, ARE YOU READY?
I *HOPE* SO, IF I CAN JUST GET MY OUTFIT FINISHED IN TIME!
WAIT, ALANA, YOU'RE NOT A DESIGNER!
OH, BUT I *WILL* BE WHEN EVERYONE GETS A LOAD OF ME IN *THIS!*
?
OOH, THAT'S... INTERESTING...

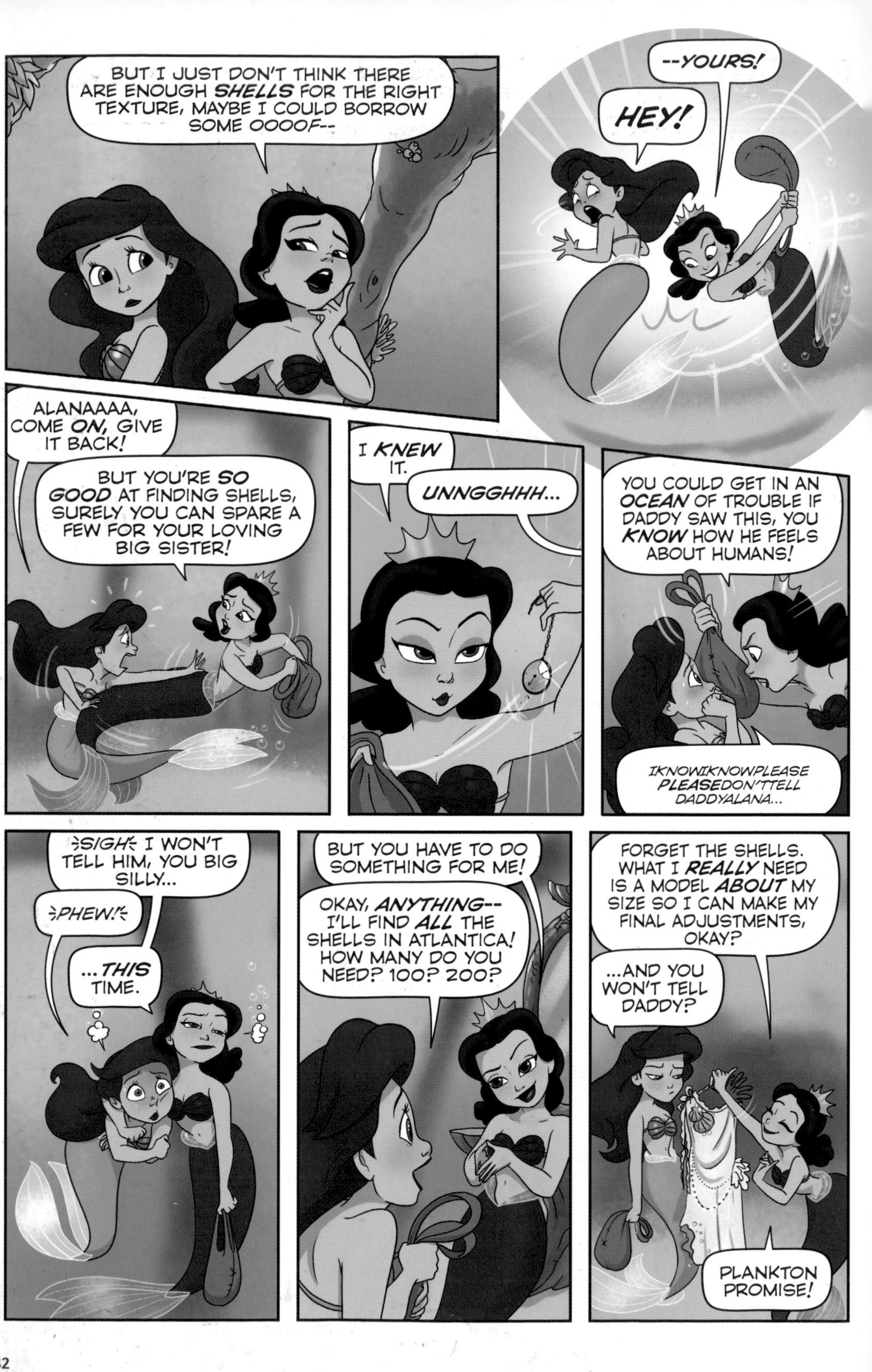
BUT I JUST DON'T THINK THERE ARE ENOUGH SHELLS FOR THE RIGHT TEXTURE, MAYBE I COULD BORROW SOME OOOOF--
HEY!
--YOURS!
ALANAAAA, COME ON, GIVE IT BACK!
BUT YOU'RE SO GOOD AT FINDING SHELLS, SURELY YOU CAN SPARE A FEW FOR YOUR LOVING BIG SISTER!
I KNEW IT.
UNNGGHHH...
YOU COULD GET IN AN OCEAN OF TROUBLE IF DADDY SAW THIS, YOU KNOW HOW HE FEELS ABOUT HUMANS!
IKNOWIKNOWPLEASE PLEASEDON'TTELL DADDYALANA...
SIGH I WON'T TELL HIM, YOU BIG SILLY...
PHEW!
...THIS TIME.
BUT YOU HAVE TO DO SOMETHING FOR ME!
OKAY, ANYTHING-- I'LL FIND ALL THE SHELLS IN ATLANTICA! HOW MANY DO YOU NEED? 100? 200?
FORGET THE SHELLS. WHAT I REALLY NEED IS A MODEL ABOUT MY SIZE SO I CAN MAKE MY FINAL ADJUSTMENTS, OKAY?
...AND YOU WON'T TELL DADDY?
PLANKTON PROMISE!

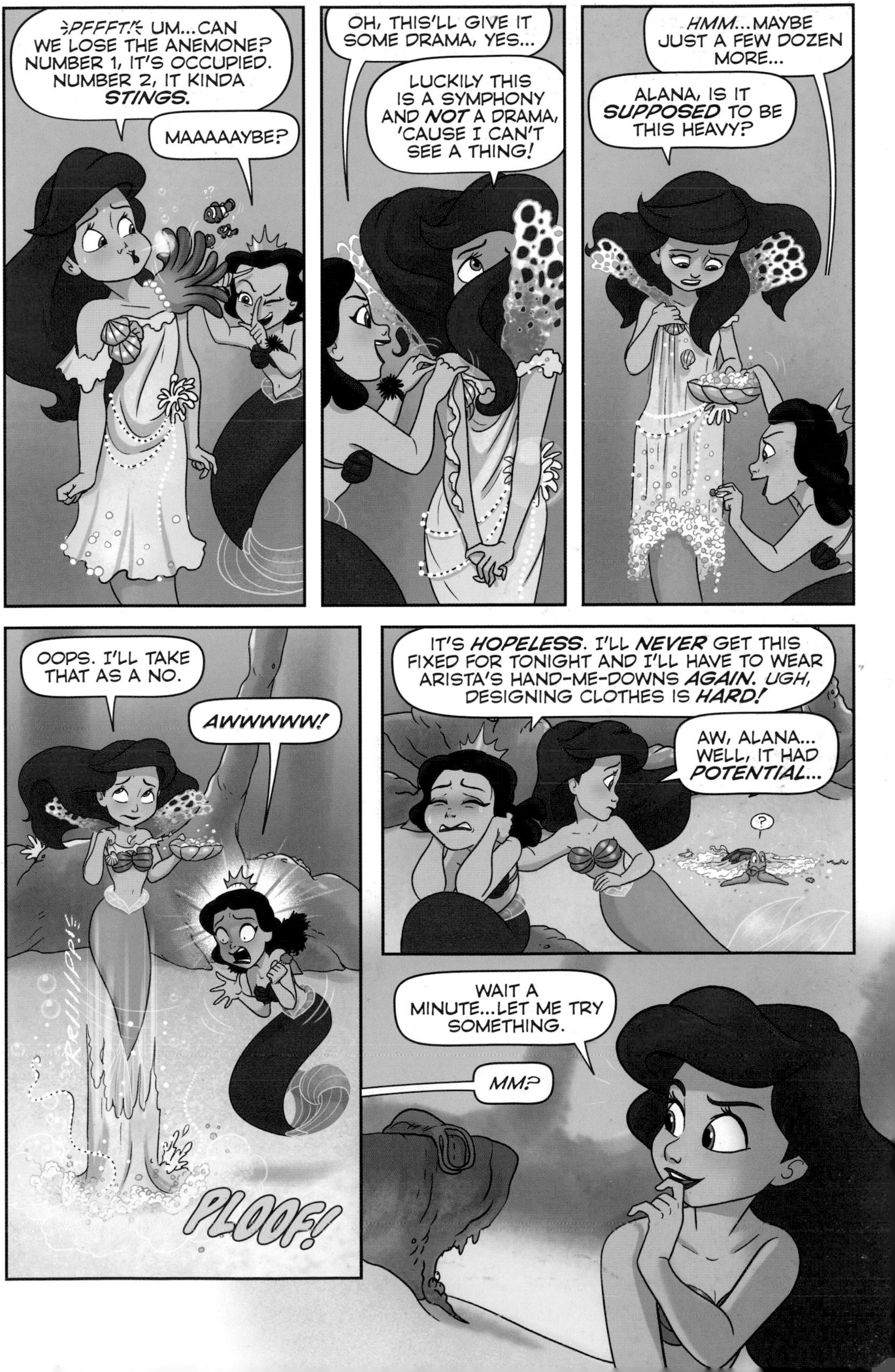
PFFFT! UM...CAN WE LOSE THE ANEMONE? NUMBER 1, IT'S OCCUPIED. NUMBER 2, IT KINDA *STINGS*.
MAAAAAYBE?
OH, THIS'LL GIVE IT SOME DRAMA, YES...
LUCKILY THIS IS A SYMPHONY AND *NOT* A DRAMA, 'CAUSE I CAN'T SEE A THING!
HMM...MAYBE JUST A FEW DOZEN MORE...
ALANA, IS IT *SUPPOSED* TO BE THIS HEAVY?
OOPS. I'LL TAKE THAT AS A NO.
AWWWWW!
RRIIIIPP!
PLOOF!
IT'S *HOPELESS*. I'LL *NEVER* GET THIS FIXED FOR TONIGHT AND I'LL HAVE TO WEAR ARISTA'S HAND-ME-DOWNS *AGAIN*. *UGH*, DESIGNING CLOTHES IS *HARD!*
AW, ALANA... WELL, IT HAD *POTENTIAL*...
?
WAIT A MINUTE...LET ME TRY SOMETHING.
MM?

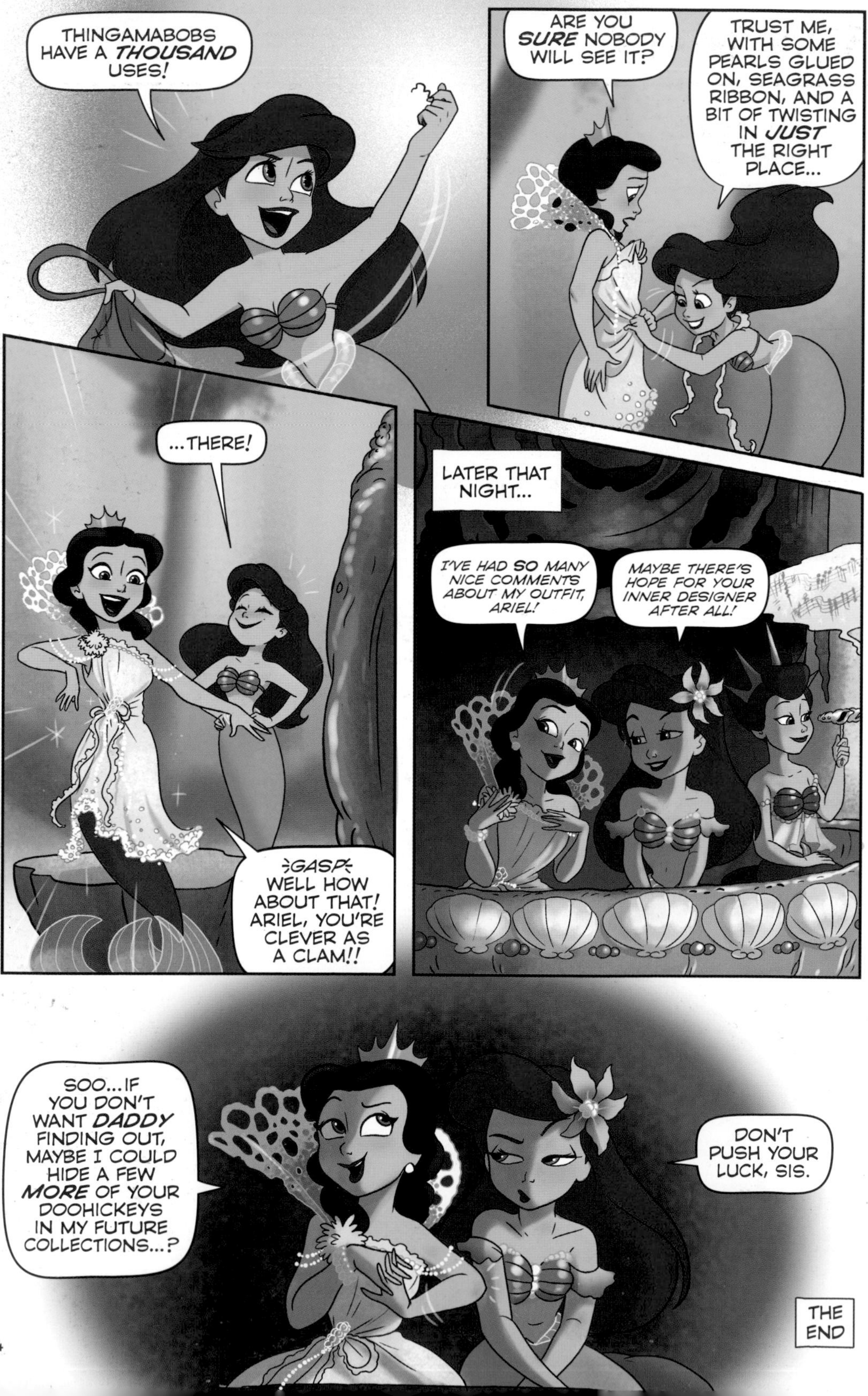
THINGAMABOBS HAVE A *THOUSAND* USES!
ARE YOU *SURE* NOBODY WILL SEE IT?
TRUST ME, WITH SOME PEARLS GLUED ON, SEAGRASS RIBBON, AND A BIT OF TWISTING IN *JUST* THE RIGHT PLACE...
...THERE!
GASP WELL HOW ABOUT THAT! ARIEL, YOU'RE CLEVER AS A CLAM!!
LATER THAT NIGHT...
*I'VE HAD **SO** MANY NICE COMMENTS ABOUT MY OUTFIT, ARIEL!*
MAYBE THERE'S HOPE FOR YOUR INNER DESIGNER AFTER ALL!
SOO...IF YOU DON'T WANT *DADDY* FINDING OUT, MAYBE I COULD HIDE A FEW *MORE* OF YOUR DOOHICKEYS IN MY FUTURE COLLECTIONS...?
DON'T PUSH YOUR LUCK, SIS.
THE END

"SNOW SPELLS"

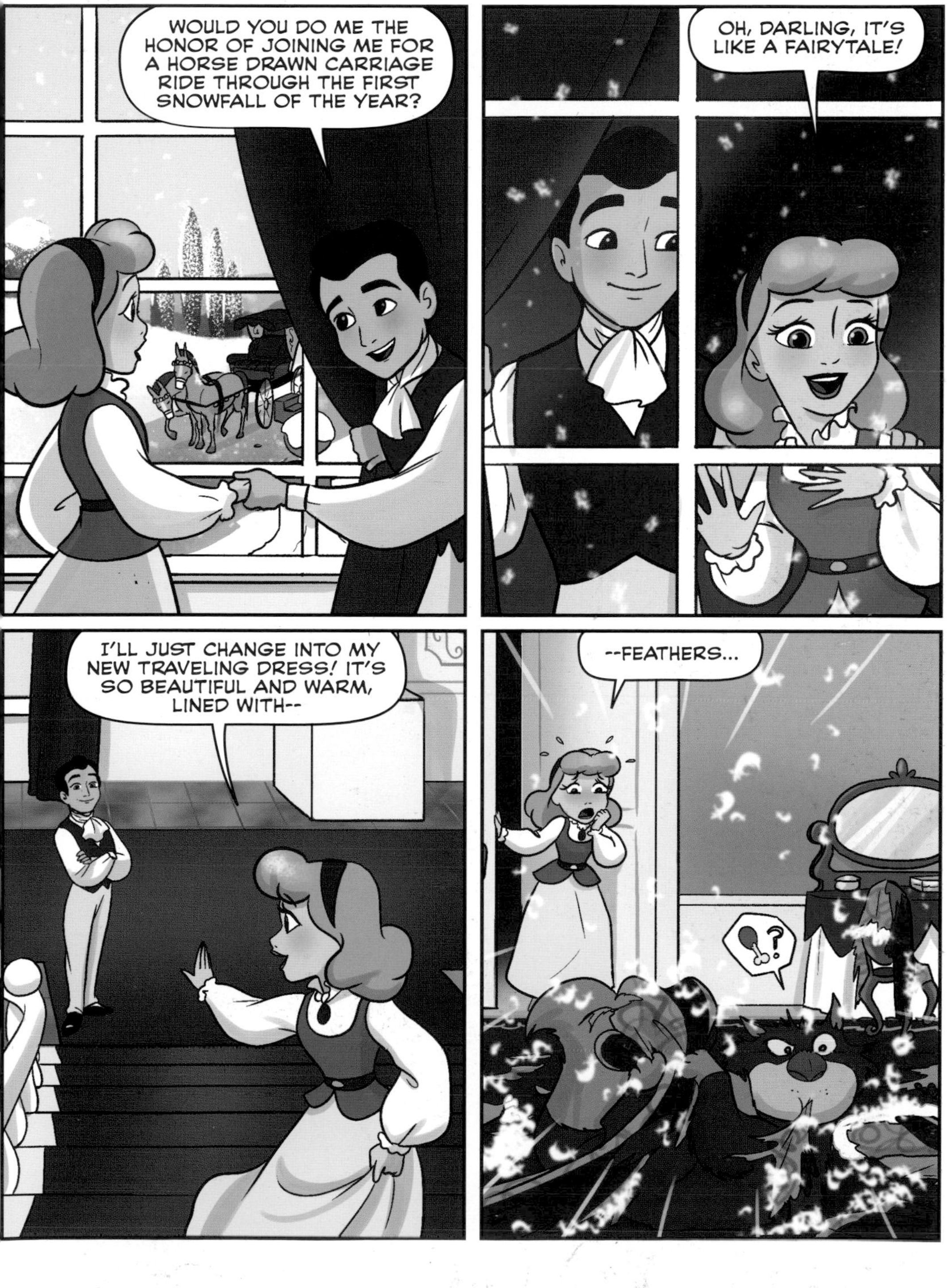
WOULD YOU DO ME THE HONOR OF JOINING ME FOR A HORSE DRAWN CARRIAGE RIDE THROUGH THE FIRST SNOWFALL OF THE YEAR?
OH, DARLING, IT'S LIKE A FAIRYTALE!
I'LL JUST CHANGE INTO MY NEW TRAVELING DRESS! IT'S SO BEAUTIFUL AND WARM, LINED WITH--
--FEATHERS...
?

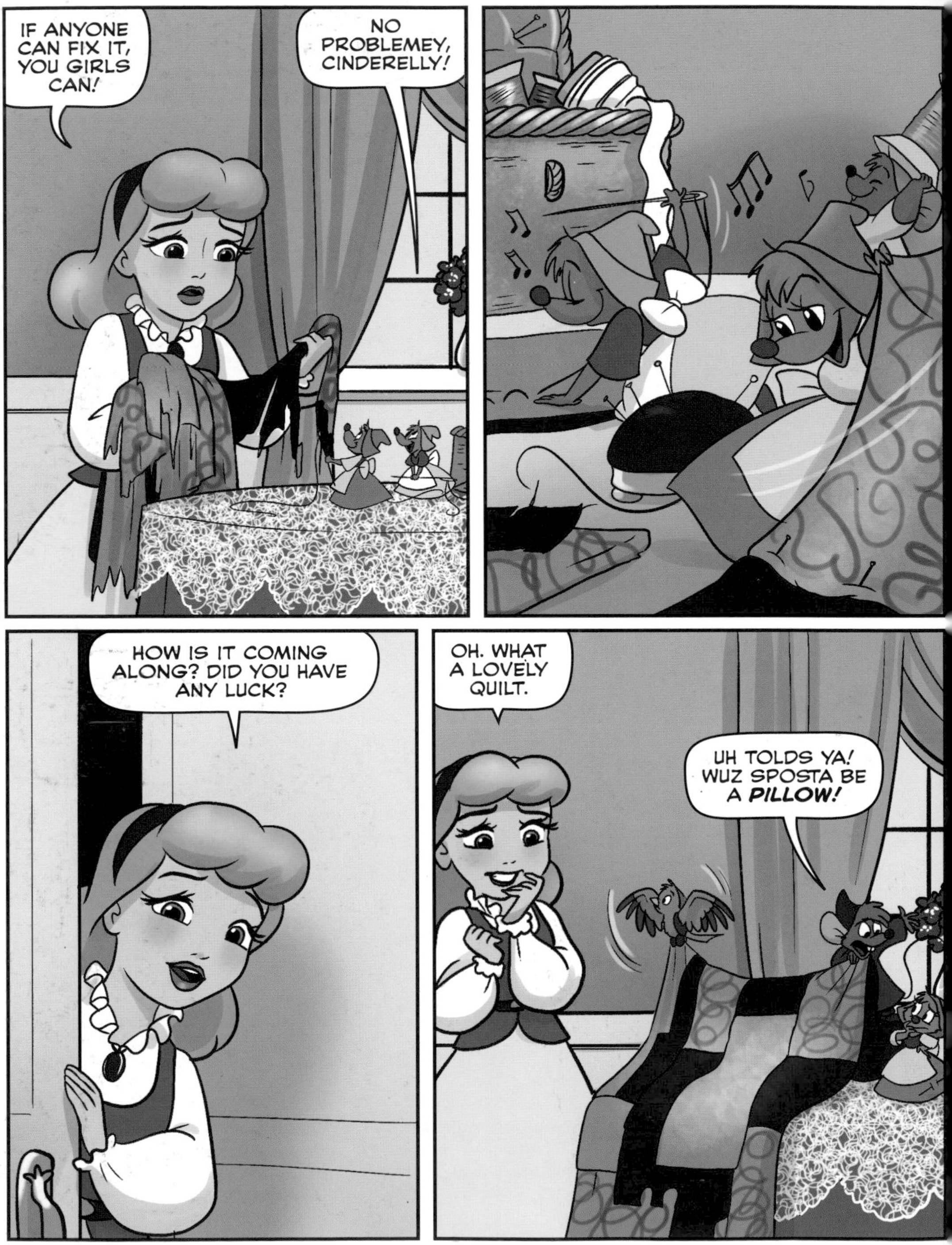
IF ANYONE CAN FIX IT, YOU GIRLS CAN!
NO PROBLEMEY, CINDERELLY!
HOW IS IT COMING ALONG? DID YOU HAVE ANY LUCK?
OH. WHAT A LOVELY QUILT.
UH TOLDS YA! WUZ SPOSTA BE A *PILLOW!*

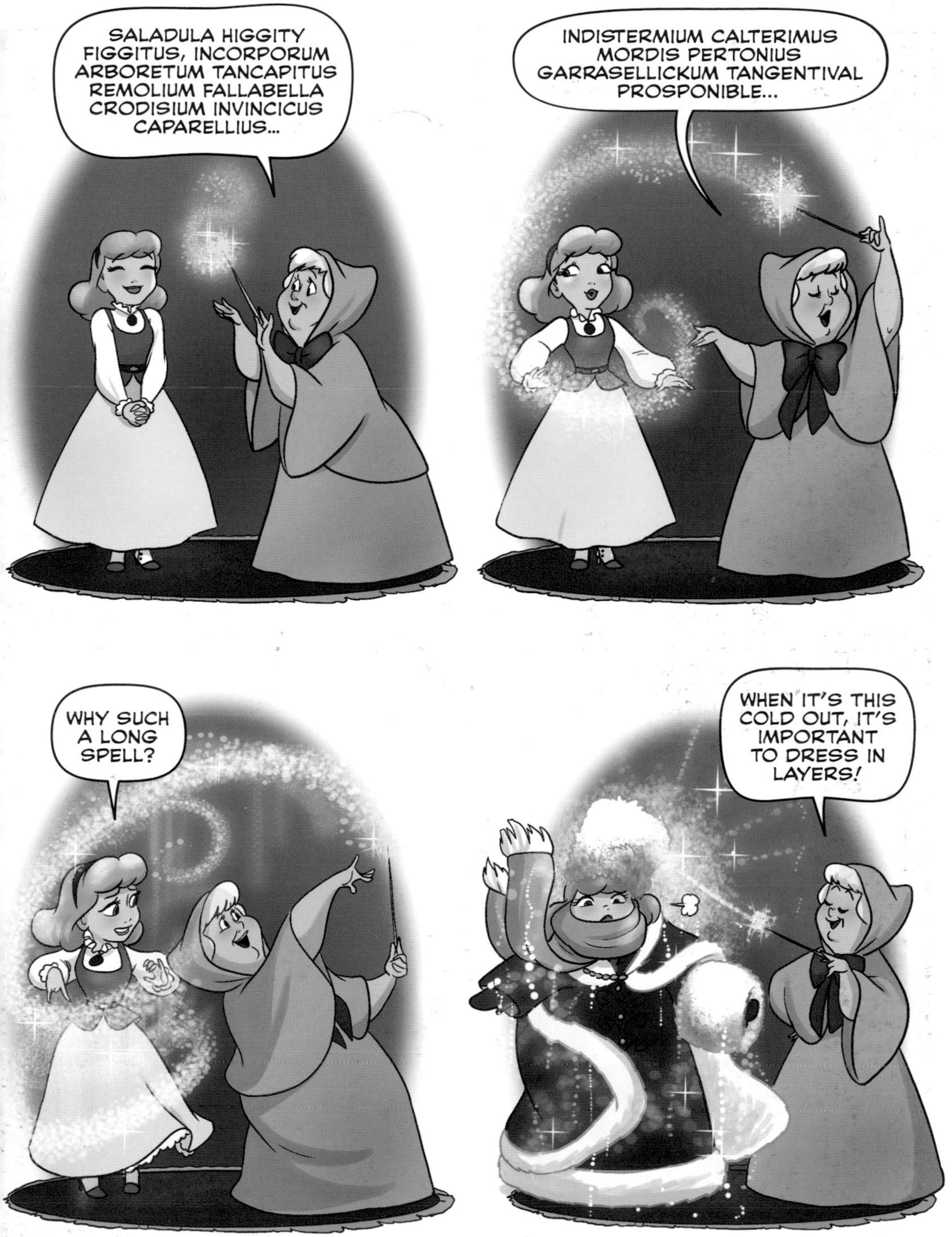
SALADULA HIGGITY FIGGITUS, INCORPORUM ARBORETUM TANCAPITUS REMOLIUM FALLABELLA CRODISIUM INVINCICUS CAPARELLIUS...
INDISTERMIUM CALTERIMUS MORDIS PERTONIUS GARRASELLICKUM TANGENTIVAL PROSPONIBLE...
WHY SUCH A LONG SPELL?
WHEN IT'S THIS COLD OUT, IT'S IMPORTANT TO DRESS IN LAYERS!

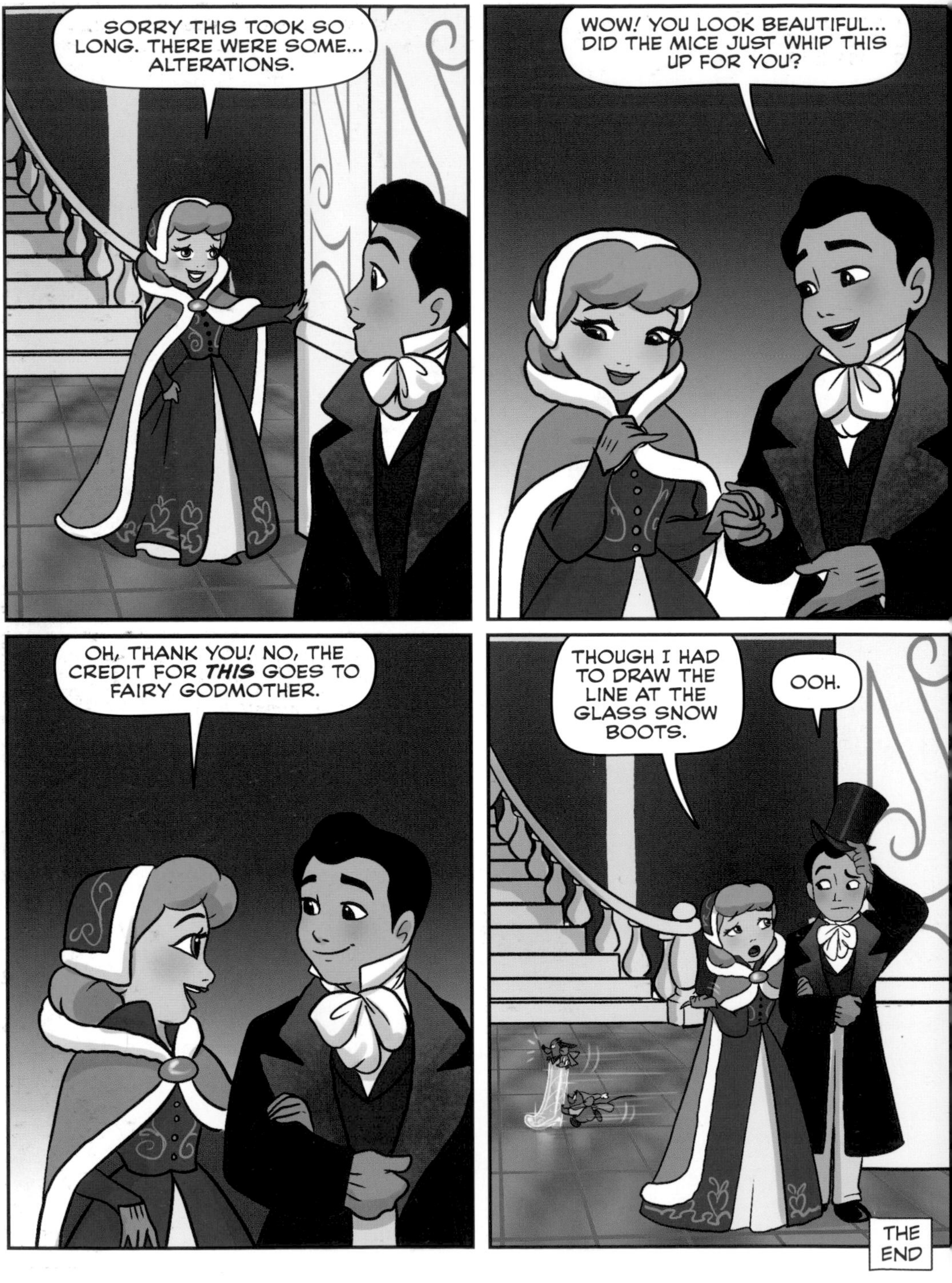
SORRY THIS TOOK SO LONG. THERE WERE SOME... ALTERATIONS.
WOW! YOU LOOK BEAUTIFUL... DID THE MICE JUST WHIP THIS UP FOR YOU?
OH, THANK YOU! NO, THE CREDIT FOR ***THIS*** GOES TO FAIRY GODMOTHER.
THOUGH I HAD TO DRAW THE LINE AT THE GLASS SNOW BOOTS.
OOH.
THE END

"GIFTS"

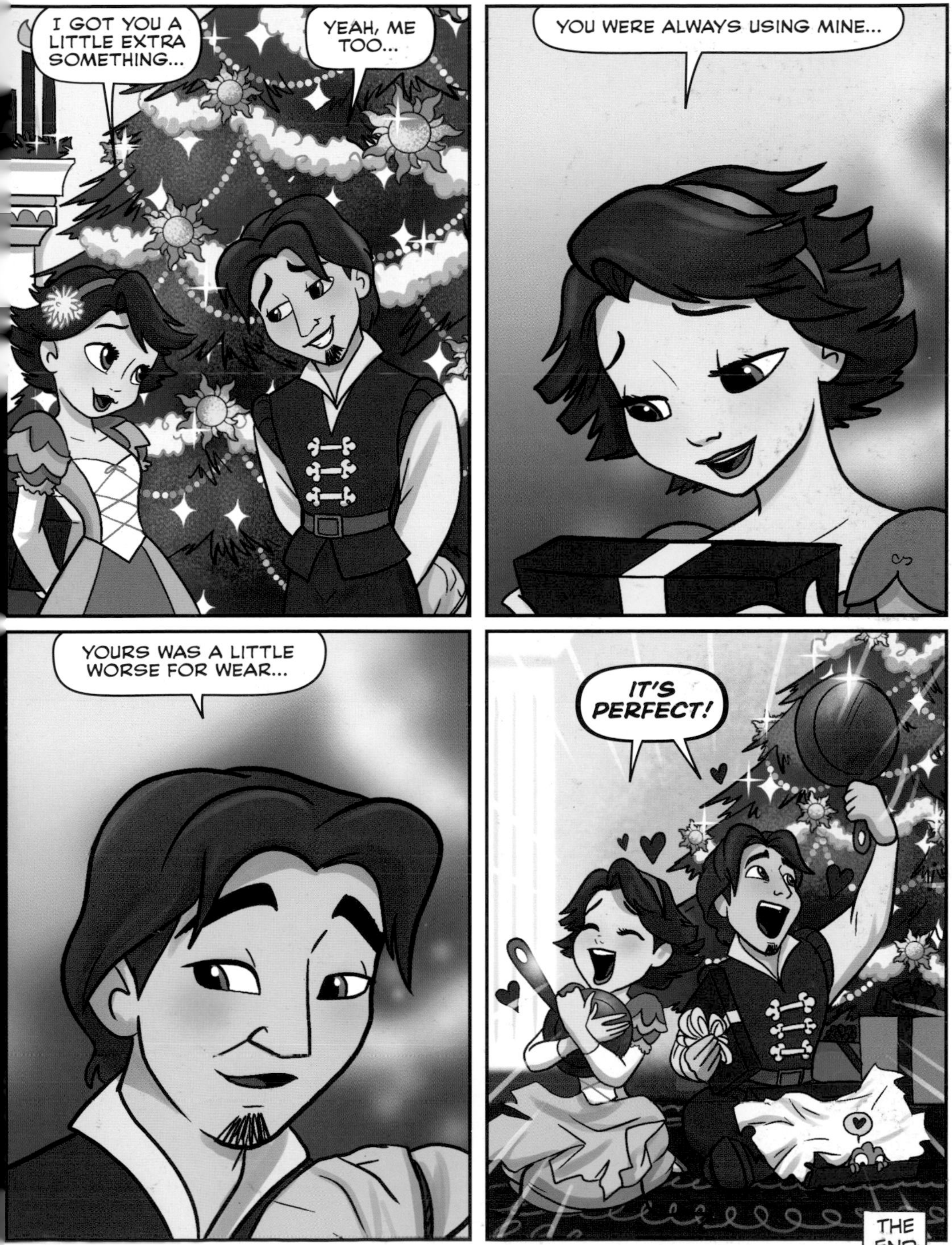

I GOT YOU A LITTLE EXTRA SOMETHING...
YEAH, ME TOO...
YOU WERE ALWAYS USING MINE...
YOURS WAS A LITTLE WORSE FOR WEAR...
IT'S PERFECT!
THE END

"HAIR MANAGEMENT"

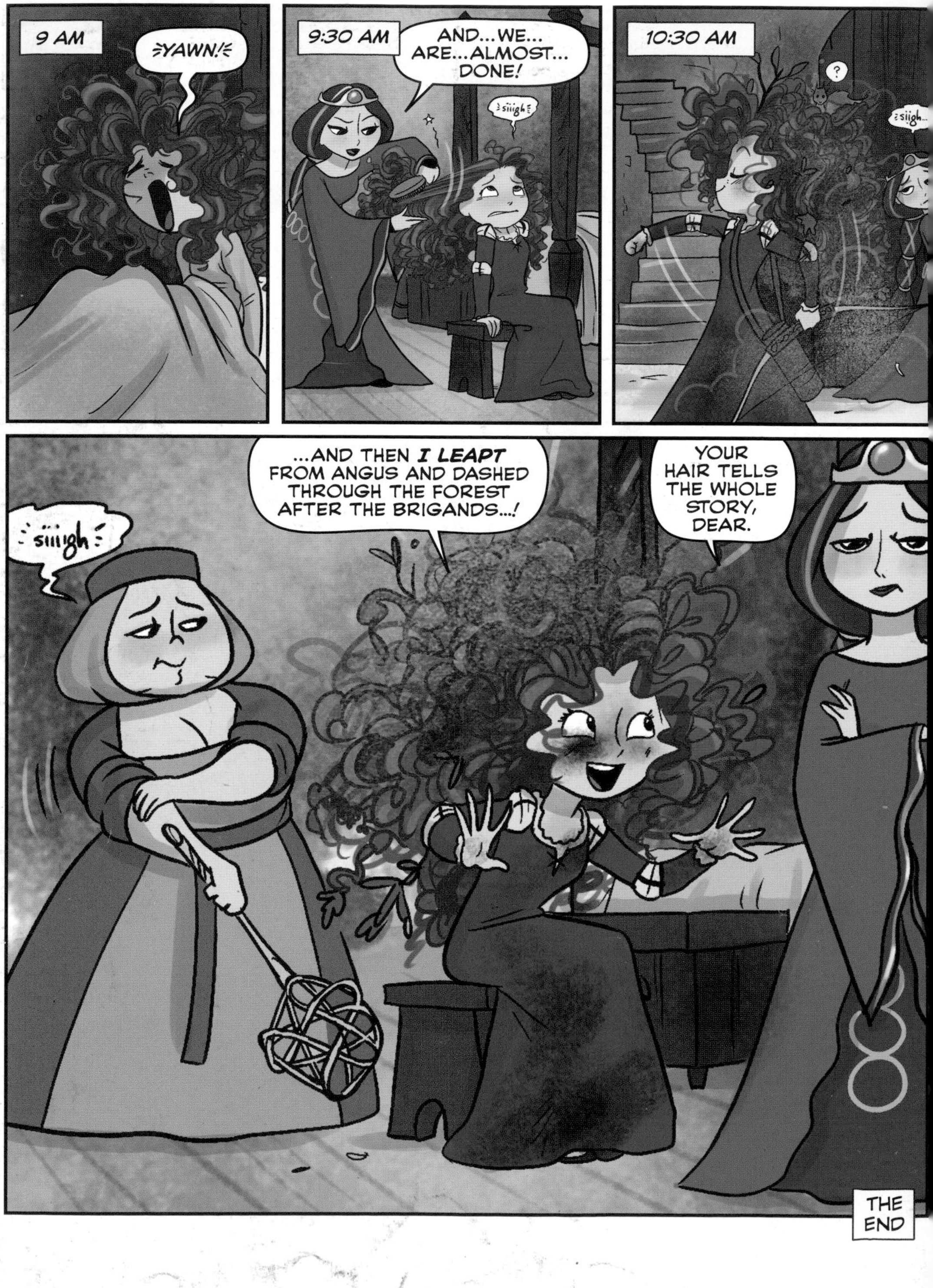

9 AM
YAWN!
9:30 AM
AND...WE... ARE...ALMOST... DONE!
siiigh
10:30 AM
?
siigh...
siiigh
...AND THEN I LEAPT FROM ANGUS AND DASHED THROUGH THE FOREST AFTER THE BRIGANDS...!
YOUR HAIR TELLS THE WHOLE STORY, DEAR.
THE END

"BEIGNET STAND"

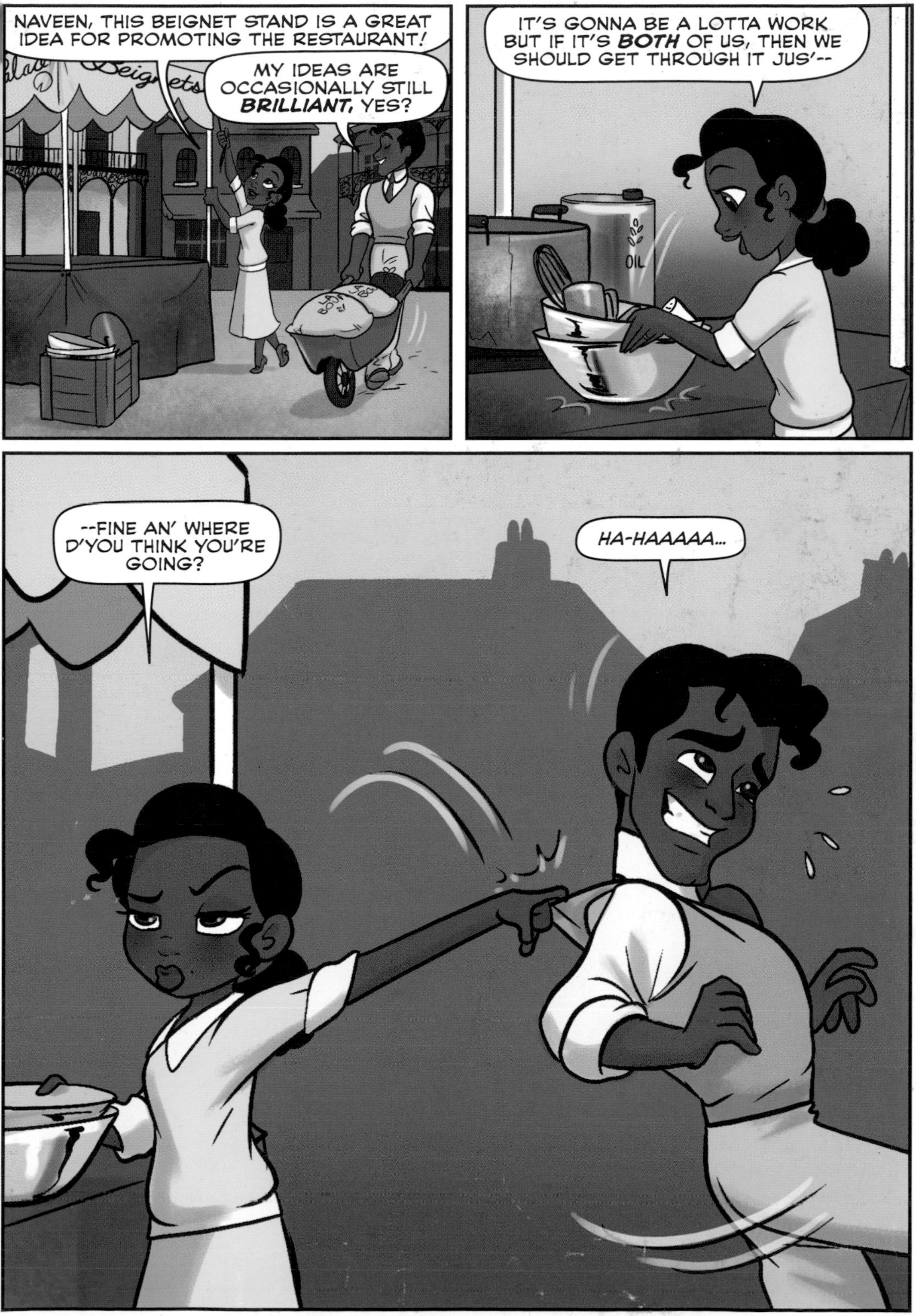
NAVEEN, THIS BEIGNET STAND IS A GREAT IDEA FOR PROMOTING THE RESTAURANT!
MY IDEAS ARE OCCASIONALLY STILL **BRILLIANT**, YES?
IT'S GONNA BE A LOTTA WORK BUT IF IT'S **BOTH** OF US, THEN WE SHOULD GET THROUGH IT JUS'--
OIL
--FINE AN' WHERE D'YOU THINK YOU'RE GOING?
HA-HAAAAA...

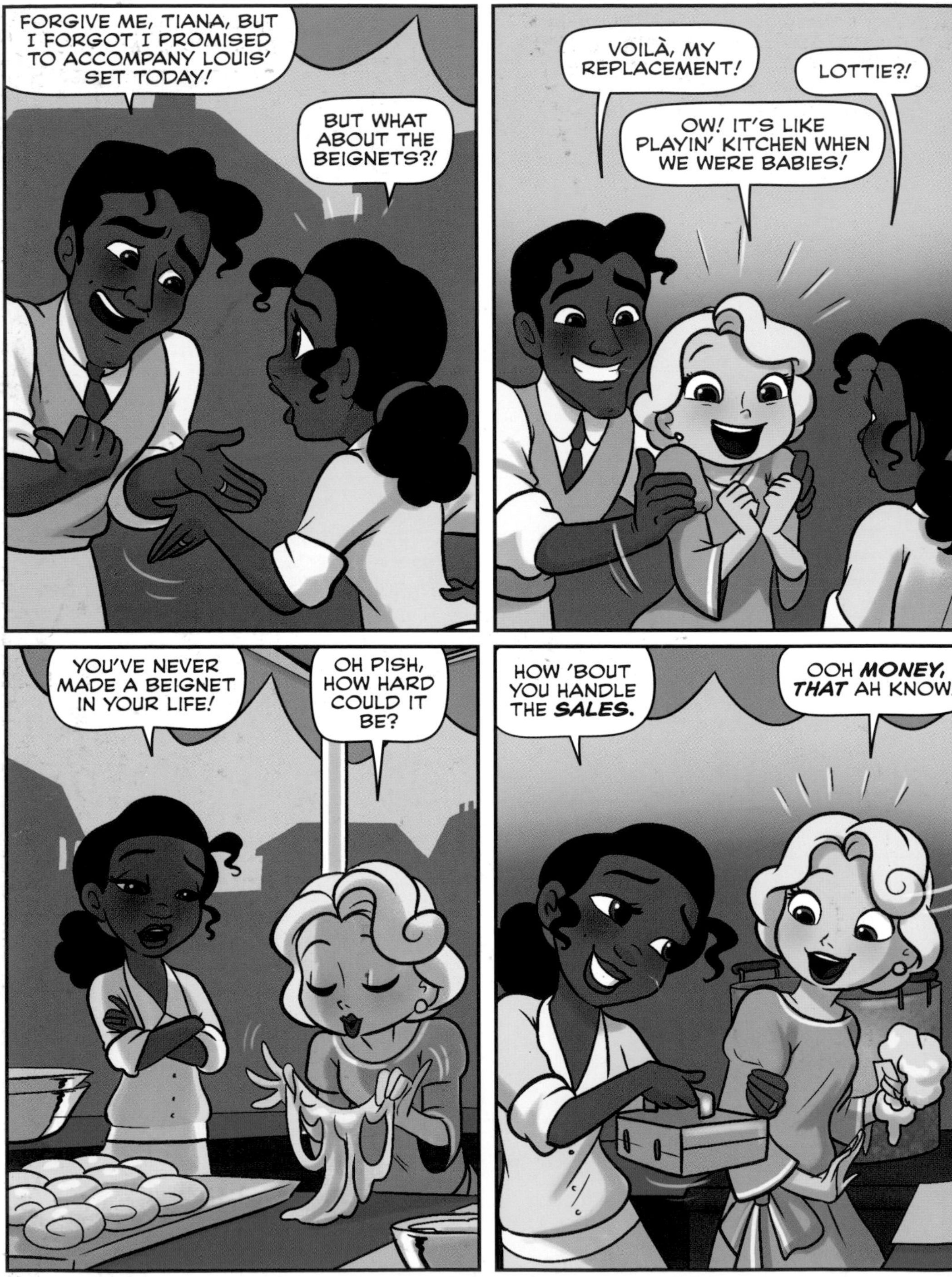
FORGIVE ME, TIANA, BUT I FORGOT I PROMISED TO ACCOMPANY LOUIS' SET TODAY!
BUT WHAT ABOUT THE BEIGNETS?!
VOILÀ, MY REPLACEMENT!
LOTTIE?!
OW! IT'S LIKE PLAYIN' KITCHEN WHEN WE WERE BABIES!
YOU'VE NEVER MADE A BEIGNET IN YOUR LIFE!
OH PISH, HOW HARD COULD IT BE?
HOW 'BOUT YOU HANDLE THE **SALES.**
OOH ***MONEY, THAT*** AH KNOW!

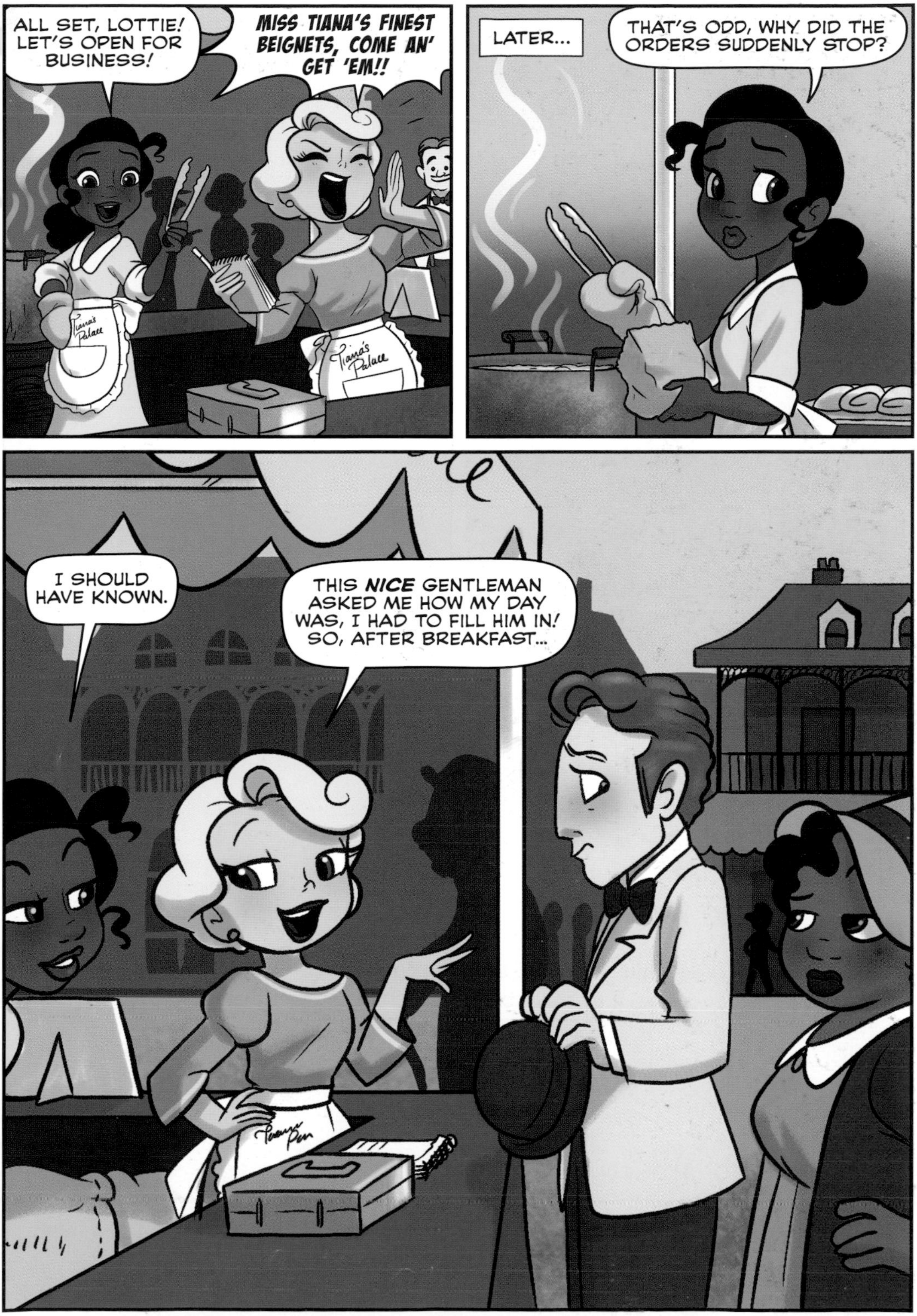
ALL SET, LOTTIE! LET'S OPEN FOR BUSINESS!
MISS TIANA'S FINEST BEIGNETS, COME AN' GET 'EM!!
LATER...
THAT'S ODD, WHY DID THE ORDERS SUDDENLY STOP?
I SHOULD HAVE KNOWN.
THIS NICE GENTLEMAN ASKED ME HOW MY DAY WAS, I HAD TO FILL HIM IN! SO, AFTER BREAKFAST...

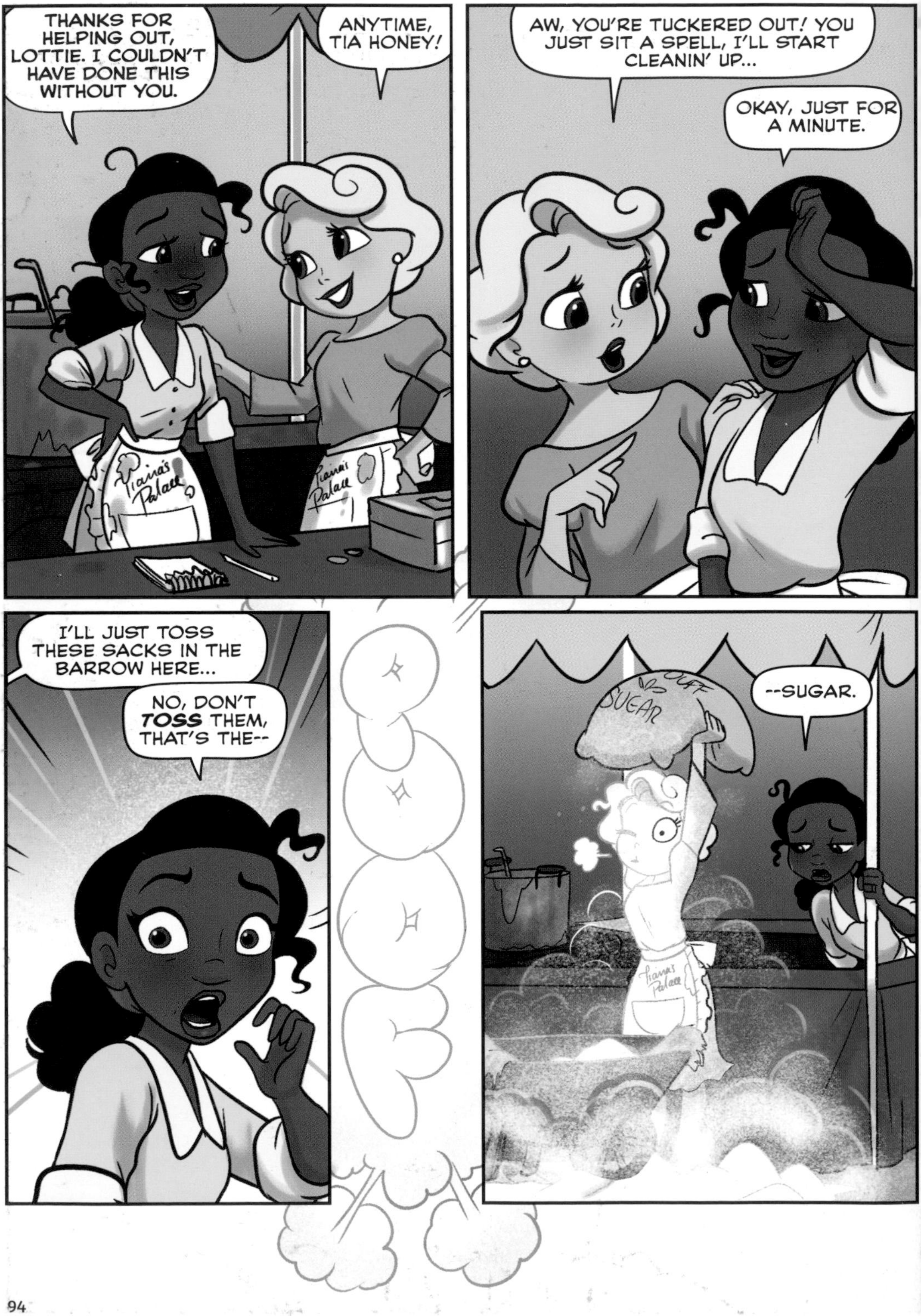
THANKS FOR HELPING OUT, LOTTIE. I COULDN'T HAVE DONE THIS WITHOUT YOU.
ANYTIME, TIA HONEY!
AW, YOU'RE TUCKERED OUT! YOU JUST SIT A SPELL, I'LL START CLEANIN' UP...
OKAY, JUST FOR A MINUTE.
I'LL JUST TOSS THESE SACKS IN THE BARROW HERE...
NO, DON'T *TOSS* THEM, THAT'S THE--
SUGAR
--SUGAR.

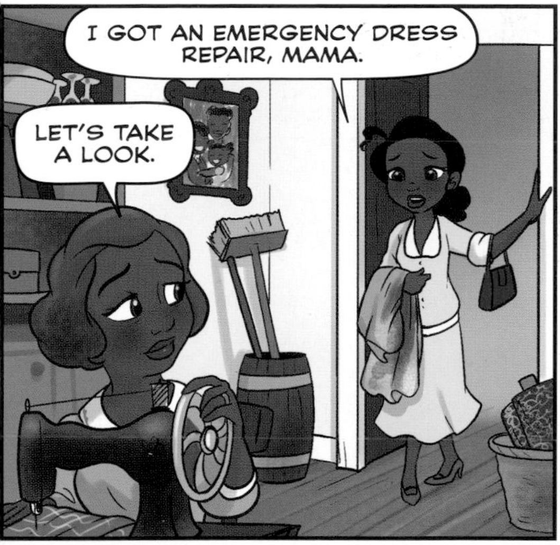
I GOT AN EMERGENCY DRESS REPAIR, MAMA.
LET'S TAKE A LOOK.
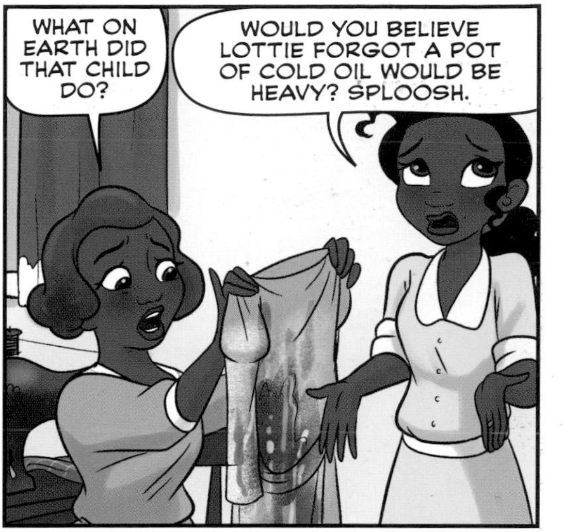
WHAT ON EARTH DID THAT CHILD DO?
WOULD YOU BELIEVE LOTTIE FORGOT A POT OF COLD OIL WOULD BE HEAVY? SPLOOSH.
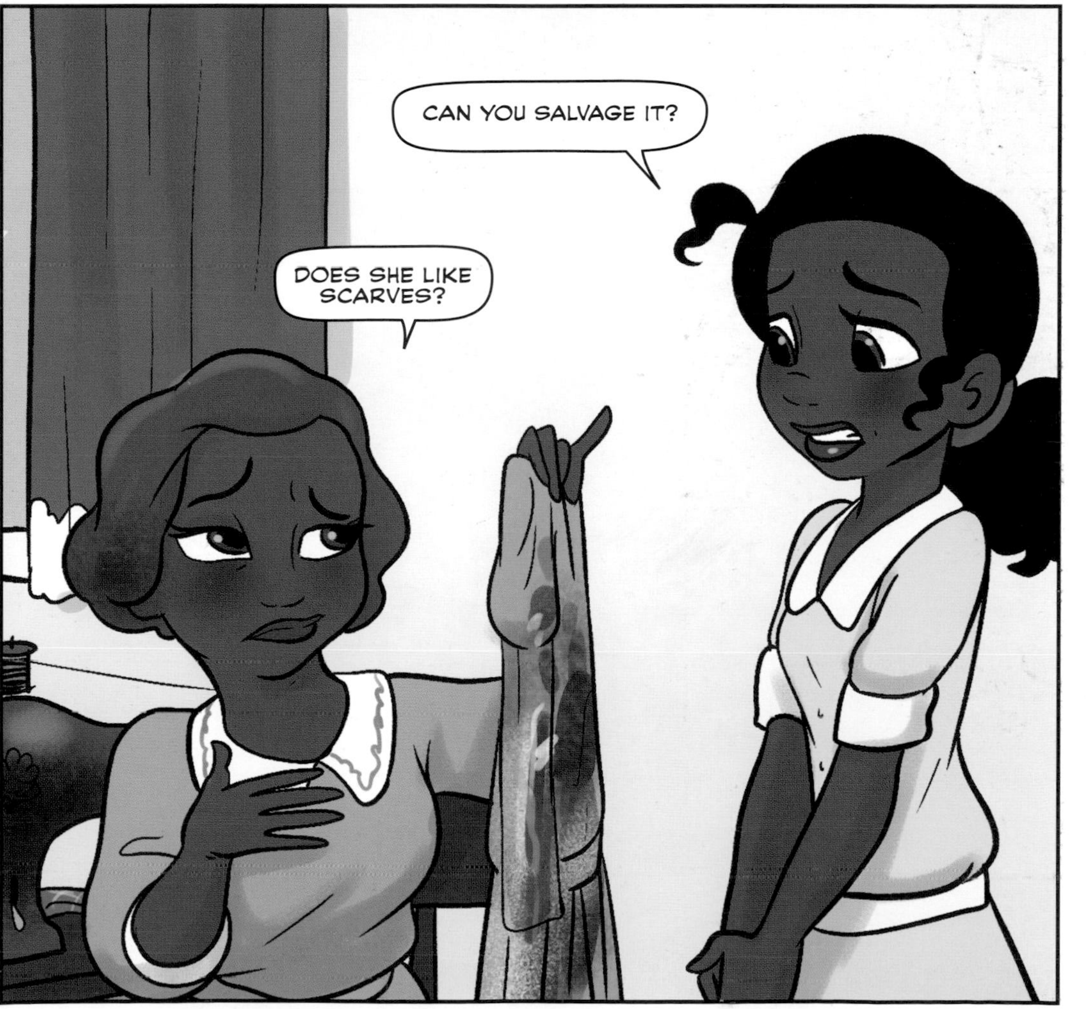
CAN YOU SALVAGE IT?
DOES SHE LIKE SCARVES?

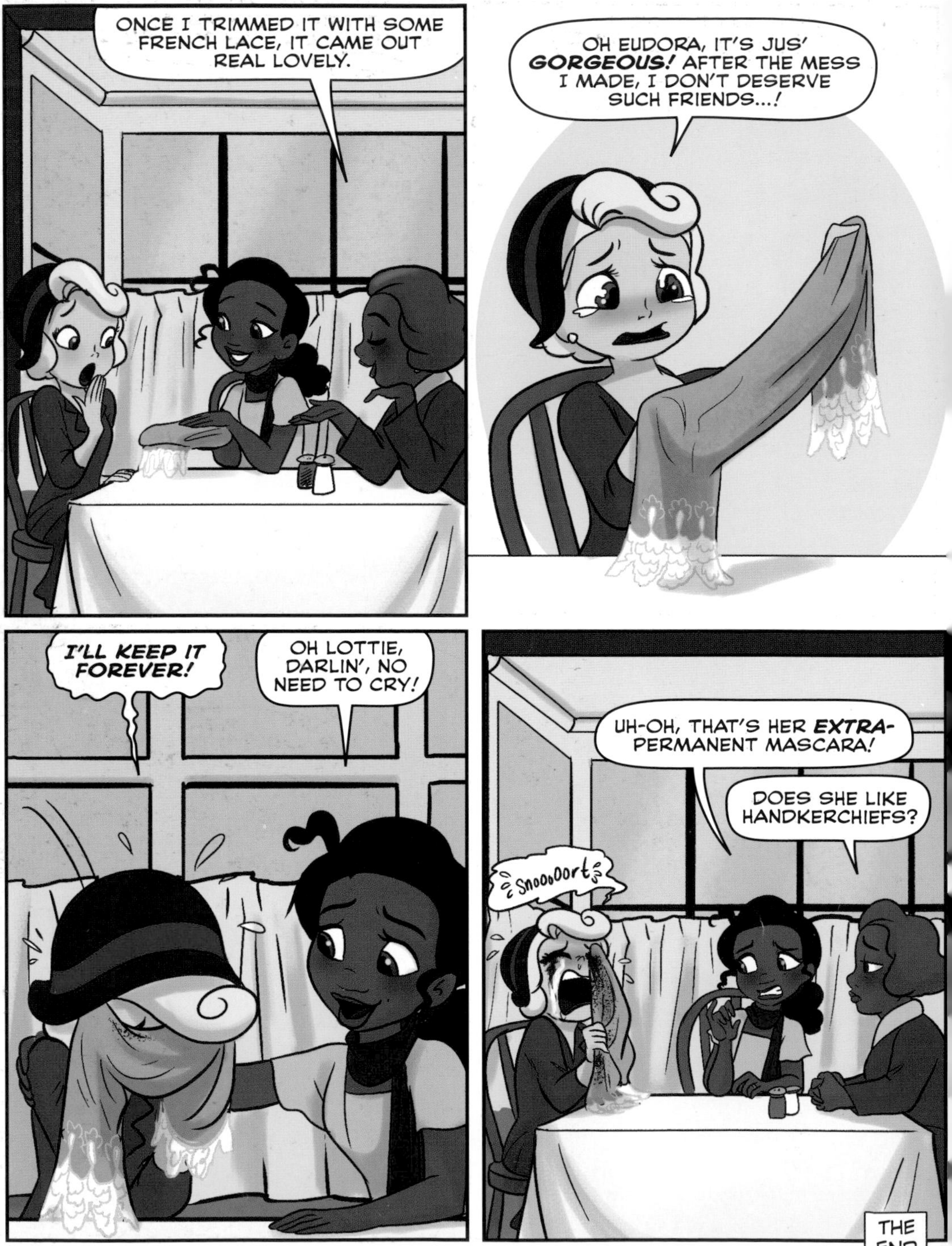
ONCE I TRIMMED IT WITH SOME FRENCH LACE, IT CAME OUT REAL LOVELY.
OH EUDORA, IT'S JUS' GORGEOUS! AFTER THE MESS I MADE, I DON'T DESERVE SUCH FRIENDS...!
I'LL KEEP IT FOREVER!
OH LOTTIE, DARLIN', NO NEED TO CRY!
UH-OH, THAT'S HER EXTRA-PERMANENT MASCARA!
DOES SHE LIKE HANDKERCHIEFS?
Snoooort
THE END

"BENT OUTTA SHAPE"

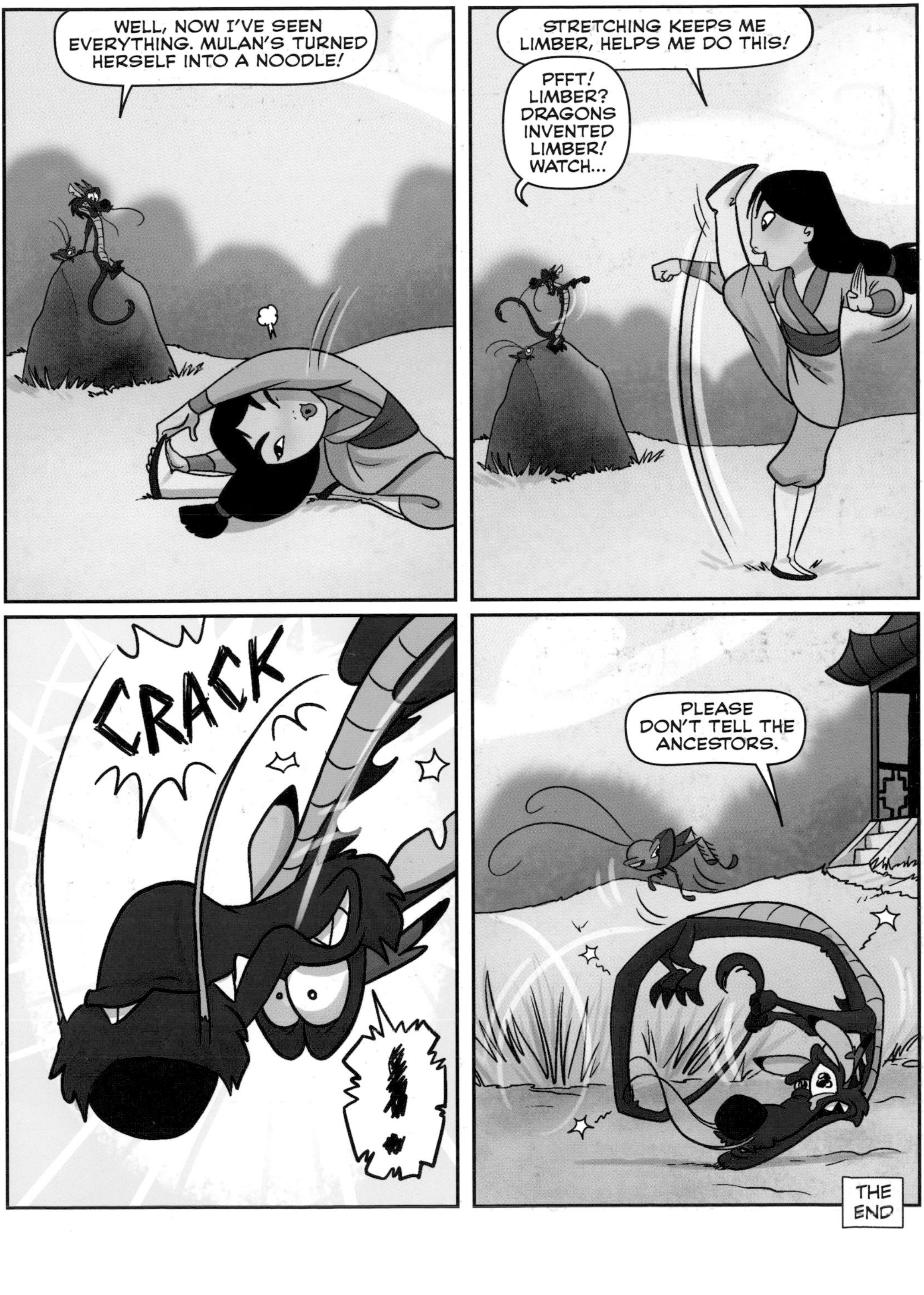
WELL, NOW I'VE SEEN EVERYTHING. MULAN'S TURNED HERSELF INTO A NOODLE!
STRETCHING KEEPS ME LIMBER, HELPS ME DO THIS!
PFFT! LIMBER? DRAGONS INVENTED LIMBER! WATCH...
CRACK
PLEASE DON'T TELL THE ANCESTORS.
THE END

"BUOY OH BUOY"

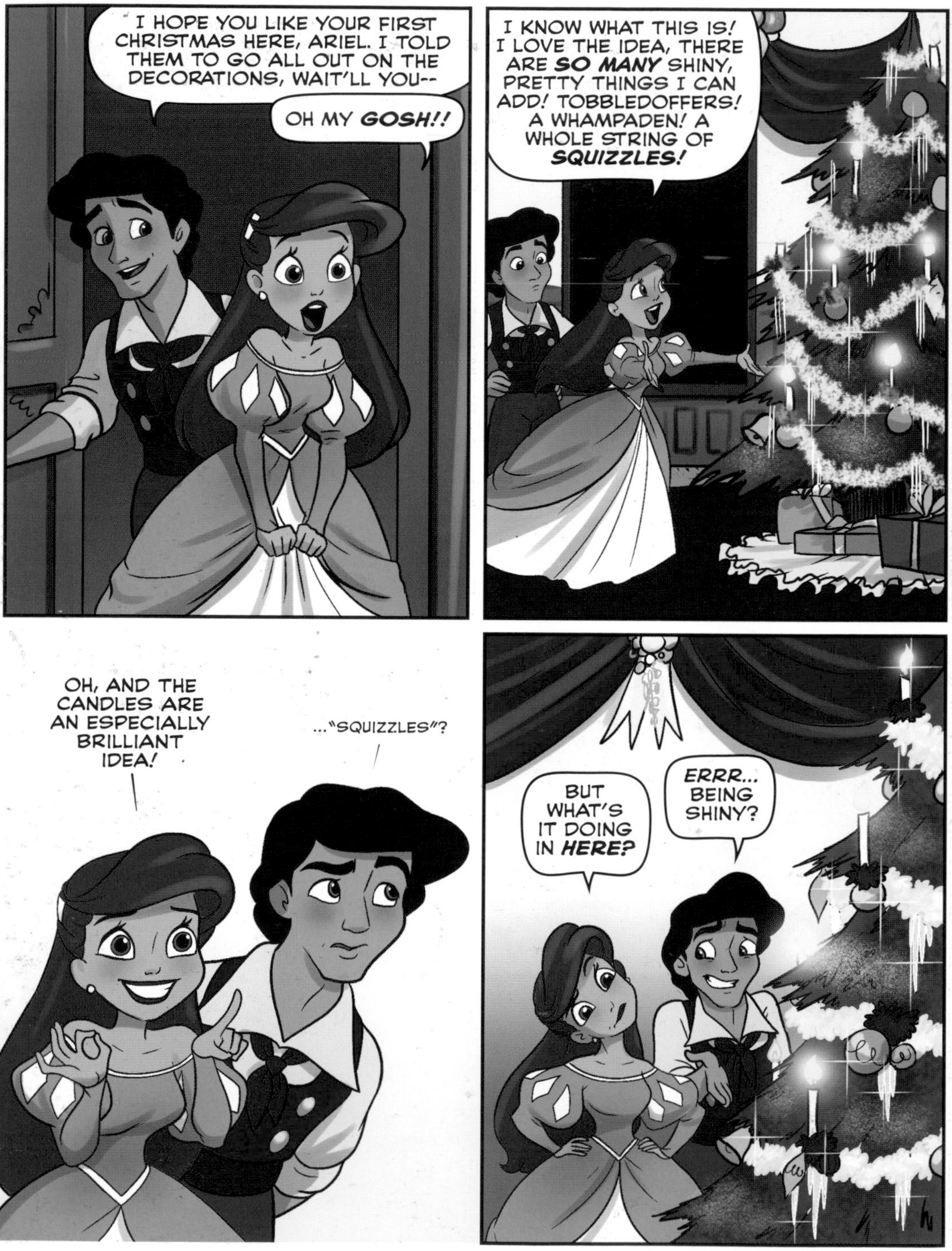
I HOPE YOU LIKE YOUR FIRST CHRISTMAS HERE, ARIEL. I TOLD THEM TO GO ALL OUT ON THE DECORATIONS, WAIT'LL YOU--
OH MY **GOSH!!**
I KNOW WHAT THIS IS! I LOVE THE IDEA, THERE ARE **SO MANY** SHINY, PRETTY THINGS I CAN ADD! TOBBLEDOFFERS! A WHAMPADEN! A WHOLE STRING OF **SQUIZZLES!**
OH, AND THE CANDLES ARE AN ESPECIALLY BRILLIANT IDEA!
..."SQUIZZLES"?
BUT WHAT'S IT DOING IN **HERE?**
ERRR... BEING SHINY?

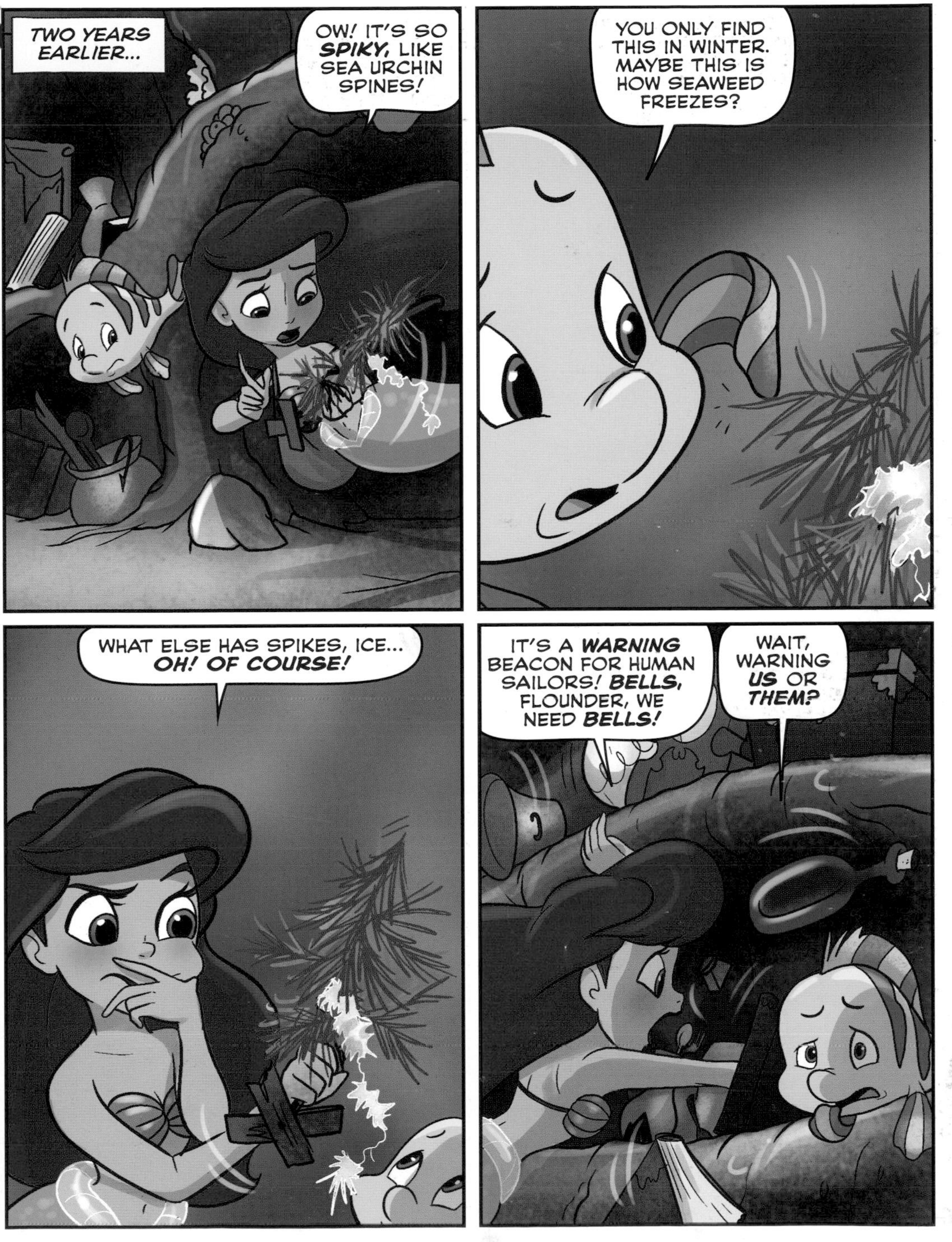
TWO YEARS EARLIER...
OW! IT'S SO SPIKY, LIKE SEA URCHIN SPINES!
YOU ONLY FIND THIS IN WINTER. MAYBE THIS IS HOW SEAWEED FREEZES?
WHAT ELSE HAS SPIKES, ICE... OH! OF COURSE!
IT'S A WARNING BEACON FOR HUMAN SAILORS! BELLS, FLOUNDER, WE NEED BELLS!
WAIT, WARNING US OR THEM?

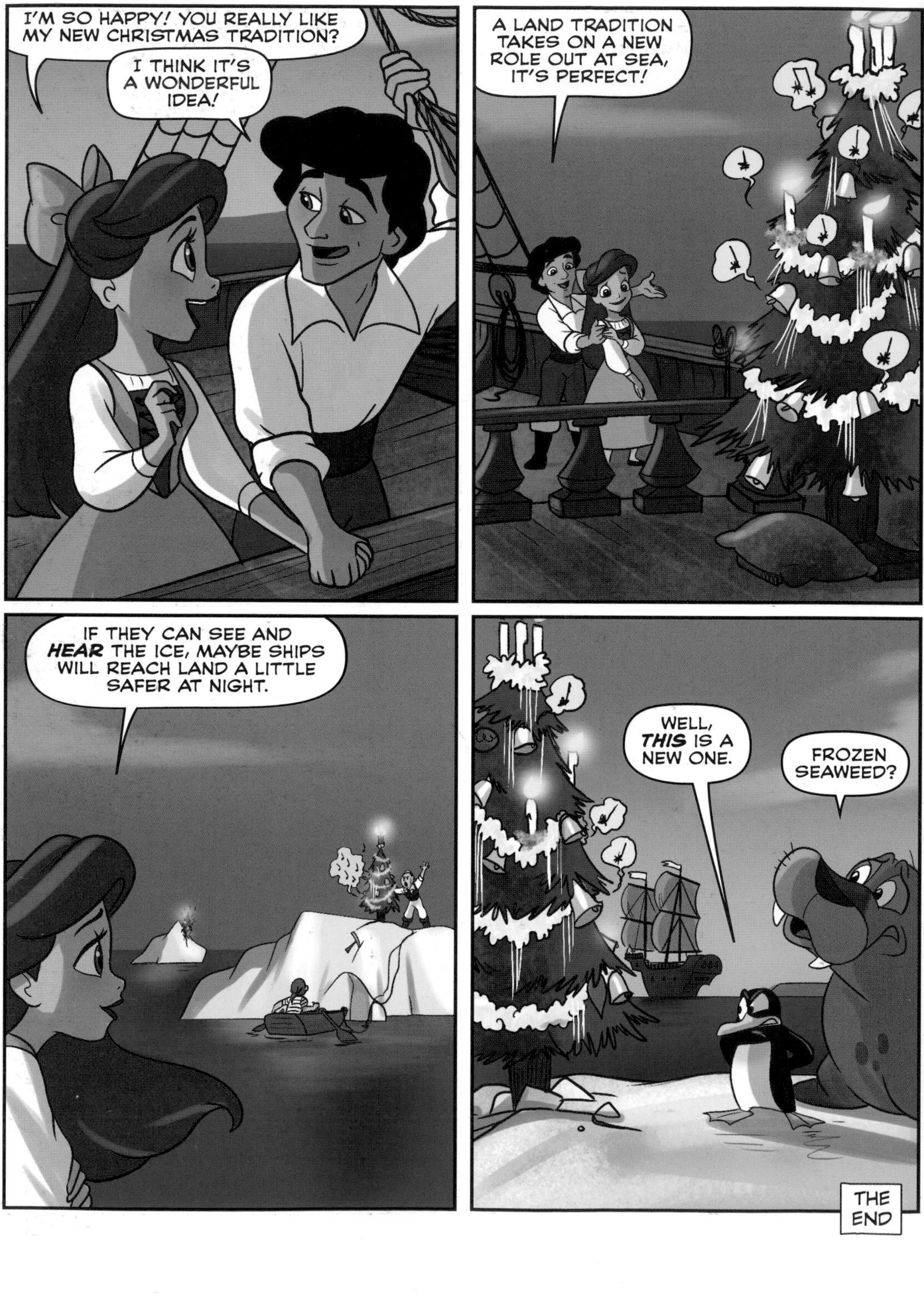
I'M SO HAPPY! YOU REALLY LIKE MY NEW CHRISTMAS TRADITION?
I THINK IT'S A WONDERFUL IDEA!
A LAND TRADITION TAKES ON A NEW ROLE OUT AT SEA, IT'S PERFECT!
IF THEY CAN SEE AND **HEAR** THE ICE, MAYBE SHIPS WILL REACH LAND A LITTLE SAFER AT NIGHT.
WELL, **THIS** IS A NEW ONE.
FROZEN SEAWEED?
THE END

"INSOMNIA"

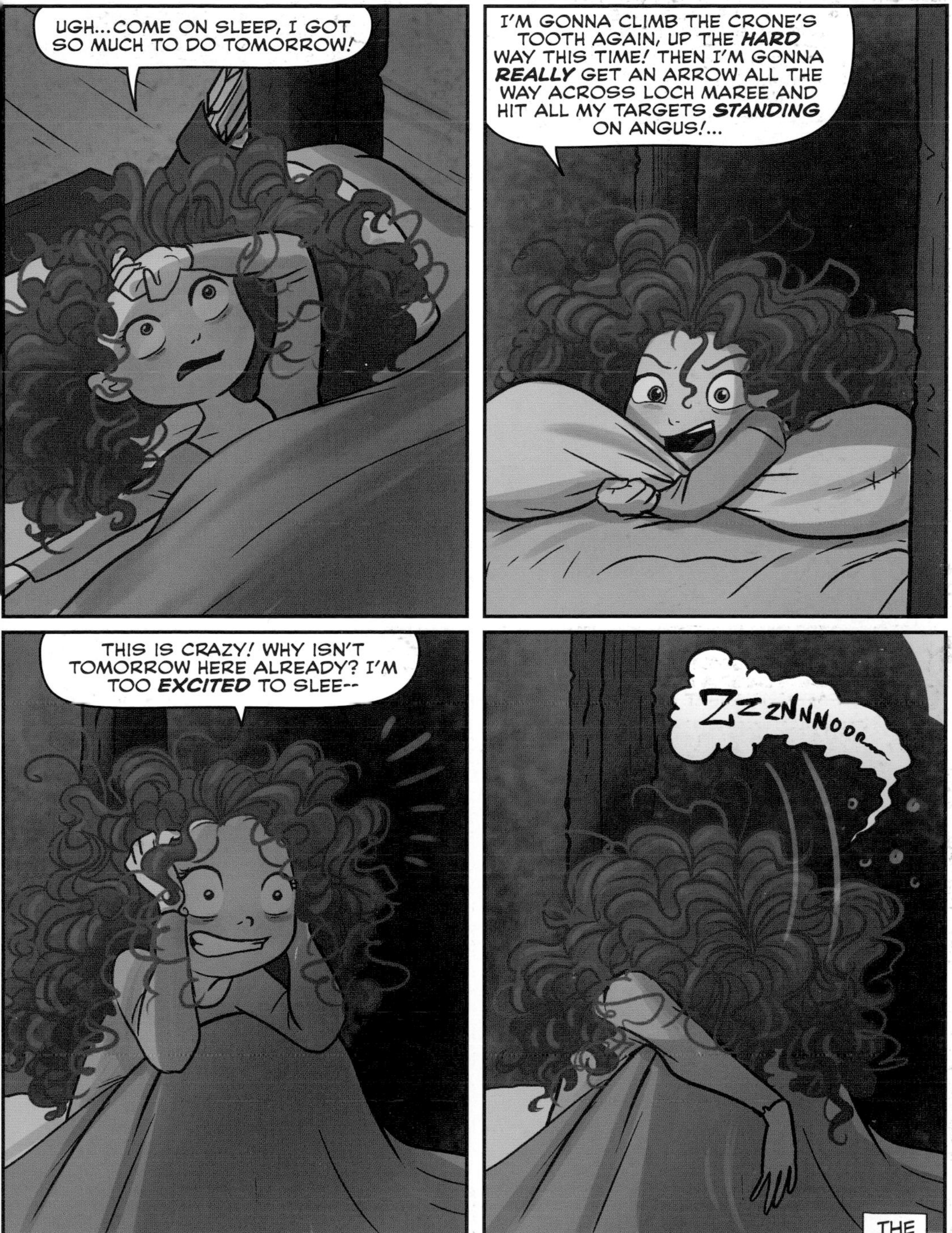

UGH...COME ON SLEEP, I GOT SO MUCH TO DO TOMORROW!
I'M GONNA CLIMB THE CRONE'S TOOTH AGAIN, UP THE **HARD** WAY THIS TIME! THEN I'M GONNA **REALLY** GET AN ARROW ALL THE WAY ACROSS LOCH MAREE AND HIT ALL MY TARGETS **STANDING** ON ANGUS!...
THIS IS CRAZY! WHY ISN'T TOMORROW HERE ALREADY? I'M TOO **EXCITED** TO SLEE--
ZZZNNNOOR~
THE END

DARK HORSE BOOKS

president and publisher
Mike Richardson

series editors
Steffie Davis, Judy Khuu, Deanna McFaden, Amy Mebberson, Freddye Miller, Jesse Post

collection editor
Freddye Miller

collection assistant editor
Judy Khuu

designer
Anita Magaña

digital art technicians
Christianne Gillenardo-Goudreau, Samantha Hummer

Neil Hankerson *Executive Vice President* ✦ **Tom Weddle** *Chief Financial Officer* ✦ **Randy Stradley** *Vice President of Publishing* ✦ **Nick McWhorter** *Chief Business Development Officer* ✦ **Dale LaFountain** *Chief Information Officer* ✦ **Matt Parkinson** *Vice President of Marketing* ✦ **Cara Niece** *Vice President of Production and Scheduling* ✦ **Mark Bernardi** *Vice President of Book Trade and Digital Sales* ✦ **Ken Lizzi** *General Counsel* ✦ **Dave Marshall** *Editor in Chief* ✦ **Davey Estrada** *Editorial Director* ✦ **Chris Warner** *Senior Books Editor* ✦ **Cary Grazzini** *Director of Specialty Projects* ✦ **Lia Ribacchi** *Art Director* ✦ **Vanessa Todd-Holmes** *Director of Print Purchasing* ✦ **Matt Dryer** *Director of Digital Art and Prepress* ✦ **Michael Gombos** *Senior Director of Licensed Publications* ✦ **Kari Yadro** *Director of Custom Programs* ✦ **Kari Torson** *Director of International Licensing* ✦ **Sean Brice** *Director of Trade Sales*

DISNEY PUBLISHING WORLDWIDE GLOBAL MAGAZINES, COMICS AND PARTWORKS
PUBLISHER Lynn Waggoner ✦ **EDITORIAL TEAM Bianca Coletti** *(Director, Magazines)*, **Guido Frazzini** *(Director, Comics)*, **Carlotta Quattrocolo** *(Executive Editor)*, **Stefano Ambrosio** *(Executive Editor, New IP)*, **Camilla Vedove** *(Senior Manager, Editorial Development)*, **Behnoosh Khalili** *(Senior Editor)*, **Julie Dorris** *(Senior Editor)*, **Mina Riazi** *(Assistant Editor)*, **Gabriela Capasso** *(Assistant Editor)* ✦ **DESIGN Enrico Soave** *(Senior Designer)* ✦ **ART Ken Shue** *(VP, Global Art)*, **Manny Mederos** *(Senior Illustration Manager, Comics and Magazines)*, **Roberto Santillo** *(Creative Director)*, **Marco Ghiglione** *(Creative Manager)*, **Stefano Attardi** *(Illustration Manager)* ✦ **PORTFOLIO MANAGEMENT Olivia Ciancarelli** *(Director)* ✦ **BUSINESS & MARKETING Mariantonietta Galla** *(Senior Manager, Franchise)*, **Virpi Korhonen** *(Editorial Manager)*

DISNEY PRINCESS: BEYOND THE EXTRAORDINARY

Published by Dark Horse Books
A division of Dark Horse Comics LLC
10956 SE Main Street
Milwaukie, OR 97222

DarkHorse.com
To find a comics shop in your area, visit comicshoplocator.com

First edition: April 2021
Ebook ISBN 978-1-50671-677-0
Trade Paperback ISBN 978-1-50671-672-5

1 3 5 7 9 10 8 6 4 2
Printed in China

Fun Disney Princess stories for all ages!

$10.99 each!

Collections of humorous and heart-filled comics short stories featuring all the Disney Princesses! Join them in a variety of amusing adventures and situations sure to make you laugh, smile, and jump for joy!

Disney
Princess
Friends, Family, Fantastic

Disney Princess: Friends, Family, Fantastic
978-1-50671-670-1

Disney
Princess
Follow Your Heart

Disney Princess: Follow Your Heart
978-1-50671-671-8

Disney
Princess
Gleam, Glow, and Laugh

Disney Princess: Gleam, Glow, and Laugh
978-1-50671-669-5

Disney
Princess
Make Way for Fun
by Amy Mebberson

Disney Princess: Make Way for Fun
978-1-50671-673-2

Disney
Princess
Beyond the Extraordinary
by Amy Mebberson

Disney Princess: Beyond the Extraordinary
978-1-50671-672-5
Available April 2021!

DARK HORSE BOOKS

Available at your local comics shop or bookstore!
To find a comics shop in your area, visit comicshoplocator.com
For more information or to order direct, visit DarkHorse.com

DISNEY COMICS

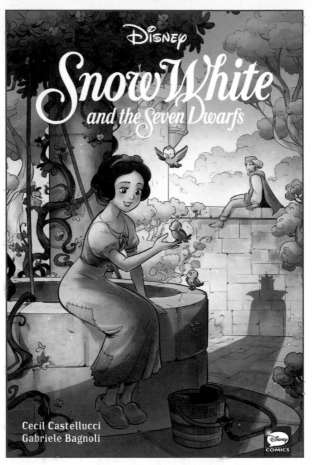